FILTER
HOUSE

FILTER
HOUSE

Short fiction
by
Nisi Shawl

Aqueduct Press

Seattle

Aqueduct Press, PO Box 95787
Seattle, WA 98145-2787
www.aqueductpress.com

Library of Congress Control Number: 2008924704
ISBN: 978-1-933500-19-5   ISBN: 1-933500-19-0
16 15 14 13 12 11 10 09 08   1 2 3 4 5

PUBLICATION ACKNOWLEDGMENTS

"At the Huts of Ajala" first appeared in *Dark Matter: A Century of
Speculative Fiction from the African Diaspora*, Sheree R. Thomas,
editor, New York, NY, July 2000, Warner Books.
"Wallamelon" first appeared on the website of *Aeon Speculative
Fiction*, http://www.aeonmagazine.com, in *Aeon* 3, May 2005.
"The Pragmatical Princess" first appeared in *Asimov's Science
Fiction Magazine*, New York, NY, January 1999.
"The Raineses'" first appeared in *Asimov's Science Fiction
Magazine*, New York, NY, April 1995.
"Maggies" first appeared in *Dark Matter: Reading the Bones*, Sheree
R. Thomas, editor, New York, NY, January 2004, Warner Books.
"Momi Watu" first appeared on the website of *Strange Horizons*,
http://strangehorizons.com, August 2003.
"Deep End" first appeared in *So Long Been Dreaming: Postcolonial
Science Fiction and Fantasy*, Nalo Hopkinson and Uppinder Mehan,
editors, Vancouver, BC, Canada, 2004, Arsenal Pulp Press.
"Little Horses" first appeared in *Detroit Noir*, New York, NY,
November 2007, Akashic Books.
"Shiomah's Land" first appeared in *Asimov's Science Fiction
Magazine*, New York, NY, March 2001.
"But She's Only a Dream" first appeared on the website of *Trabuco
Road*, http://www.trabucoroad.com, March 2007.
"The Beads of Ku" first appeared in *Rosebud Magazine*, Cambridge,
WI, Issue 23, April 2002, as Runner-Up in the Ursula K. Le Guin
Prize for Imaginative Fiction.

Front Cover Photo by Per R. Flood © Bathybiologica.no
Back Cover Photo (c) 2008 by Luke McGuff
Cover and Book Design by Kathryn Wilham

Printed in the USA by Thomson-Shore, Inc, Dexter, MI

For my sisters,
Julie Anne and Gina Mari

Cover photograph of a filter house is by Norwegian Research Scientist Per R. Flood of the Bathybiologica A/S. Dr. Flood first described the structural characteristics of appendicularian feeding filters in a 1973 publication. Since then, he has made significant contributions to the understanding of appendicularian feeding house architecture and function, mucus production and histochemistry, and bioluminescence.

Appendicularians (Larvaceans) are filter feeders that primarily occupy the euphotic zone (upper sunlit portion of the ocean), but some species can be found in deeper waters. The morphology of larvaceans superficially resembles that of the tadpole larvae of most urochordates; they possess a discrete trunk and tail throughout adult life.

Like most urochordates, appendicularians feed by drawing particulate food matter into their pharyngo-branchial region, where food particles are trapped on a mucus mesh produced by the pharynx and drawn into the digestive tract. However, appendicularians have greatly improved the efficiency of food intake by producing a "house" of glycoproteins that surrounds the animal like a bubble and that contains a complicated arrangement of filters that allow food in the surrounding water to be brought in and concentrated 400 to 800 times prior to feeding. These houses are discarded and replaced regularly as the animal grows in size and the filters become clogged. Discarded appendicularian houses account for a significant fraction of organic material descending to the ocean deeps.

Modified from text at
http://www.answers.com/topic/larvacea-1?cat=technology

Acknowledgments

I am grateful for the wonderful support given to me and my work by my mother, June Rose Jackson Rickman Cotton, my sisters Julie Anne Rickman and Gina Mari Rickman, and my father, Dennis Van de Leur Rickman. This book and the stories within it were made manifest by their help and the help of Ted Chiang, Octavia E. Butler, Elizabeth Finan, Andrew Scudder, Eileen Gunn, Cynthia Ward, Sara Ryan, Steve Lieber, Kate Schaefer, Glenn Hackney, Sabrina Chase, Victoria Elisabeth Garcia, John Aegard, Annette Taborn, Vonda McIntyre, Dave Linn, Sheree R. Thomas, Andrea Hairston, Luisah Teish, Nalo Hopkinson, L. Timmel Duchamp, Kathryn Wilham, Bob Brown, and Steve Barnes. Thank you all so much.

Filter House also came about in part with assistance from the following institutions: the Tiptree Fairy Godmother Award, the Untitled Writers Group, STEW, Clarion West, the Susan C. Petrey Scholarship, the Carl Brandon Society, Cottages at Hedgebrook, Ilé Orunmila Oshun, the Country Doctor Community Clinics, and the Starving Artist Fund.

Contents

Introduction: Where Everything
Is a Bit Different by Eileen Gunn   3

At the Huts of Ajala   7

Wallamelon   20

The Pragmatical Princess   48

The Raineses'   65

Bird Day   90

Maggies   93

Momi Watu   116

Deep End   127

Good Boy   143

Little Horses   181

Shiomah's Land   205

The Water Museum   238

But She's Only a Dream   256

The Beads of Ku   269

Introduction

Where Everything Is a Bit Different

by Eileen Gunn

One of the great delights of reading science fiction and fantasy stories is the feeling of being immersed in a world where everything is a bit different. Ordinary people—even children—have unusual abilities. The dangers are different, the power relationships are different, even "normal" is different, and the reader has to figure out this new world on the fly. Every word has potentially a different meaning than in the familiar work-a-day world. New words—made-up words, words you have never heard before—can indicate entirely new ways of thinking.

Samuel R. Delany, many years ago, mapped out the exhilaration of reading a sentence, word by word, that, because it is science fiction, can go anywhere and be anything. The door can dilate. The red sun can be high, and the blue one low. Delany's essays in *The Jewel-hinged Jaw* make the very act of reading a science-fiction adventure, an experience in which the reader intellectually and emotionally participates in creating the book.

The stories in this book offer that level of exhilaration. They are not all science fiction: some are fantasy, and some are really quite arguably neither—just life, with all its ambiguities and spiritual mysteries. In every story, remarkable words and thoughts and characters carry the reader from one sentence to the next, building a story so naturally that it's a surprise to realize that you're caught up in it like a child. Is there such a thing as an eaves trough? What's going to happen next?

The book is filled with voices, each one the voice of an individual in a particular place and time: someone of a particular age, a particular heritage and education. All are different: clamoring, wheedling, scolding, disagreeing, telling their stories, keeping their secrets. You can tell from their diction and vocabulary that the old lady's from the country, that the woman is in service, that the girl absorbs knowledge like a sponge.

The personal is political here: everything means something, and it is not always what you think at first. A candle is not necessarily just a candle: it might also be a message from the dead. Or maybe it *is* just a candle: will we find out? A character might use a divination technique and at the same time view it as a superstition. The stories embody a very science-fictional way of reading, actually: they require the reader to distinguish what is different and meaningful from what is just different. (An eaves trough, since you ask, is merely a gutter. Isn't it a wonderful phrase?) This shifting point of view, the experience of looking at the world from two perspectives at once, is a hallmark of reading science fiction.

Most of the stories examine the shifting of balances of power between men and women, adults and children, whites and blacks. Often the structure shifts internally without ever changing the balance: the poor get poorer and the rich get richer in a way that is all too similar to real life. In these stories, however, almost everyone has some sort of power, has control over something.

Which are my favorites? Maybe "Wallamelon," for the total pleasure it gives, making the reader once again a mature ten-year-old learning to understand the world. Maybe "The Raineses'," for all its remarkable characters, living and dead. (A bit of advice: Don't read "The Raineses'" late at night, all alone in the house.) Maybe "Good Boy," for its wacky verve, and simply because I've been trying to figure out a way to use *Programming and Metaprogramming in the Human Biocomputer* in a story for nigh onto forty years, and Nisi beat me to it. Really, every story in the book is a potential favorite. "But She's Only a Dream" is smokey and allusive. The folktale-like African story, "The Beads of Ku," is remarkably satisfying aesthetically.

Okay, they're all my favorites. Remarkably involving stories that pull you along a path of wonder, word by word, in worlds where everything is a bit different.

Eileen Gunn
Seattle
February 12, 2008

At The Huts of Ajala

They all keep calling her a "two-headed woman." Loanna wants to know why, so after the morning callers leave, she decides on asking her Iya. When she was little, the other kids used to call her "four-eyes." But this is different, said with respect by grown adults.

She finds the comb and hair-grease on the bureau in the room where she's been sleeping. When she left Cleveland three days ago, it was winter. Now she steps out onto the wrought-iron balcony, and it's spring. Her first visit, on her own, to the Crescent City, New Orleans, drowning home of her mother's kin.

Iya sits in her wicker chair, waiting. She is a tall woman, even seated, and she's dressed all in white: white headscarf, white blouse, white skirt with matching belt, white stockings and tennis shoes, and a white cardigan, too, which she removes now that the day has warmed. She shifts her feet apart, and Loanna drops to sit between them.

Certainly Loanna is old enough to do her own hair, but Iya knows different ways of braiding, French rolls and corn rows, special styles suitable for the special occasion of a visit to Mam'zelle La Veau's grave. Besides, it's nice to feel Iya's hands, her long brown fingers, gently nimble, swiftly touching, rising along the length of Loanna's wiry tresses and transforming them into neat, uniformly bumpy braids. Relaxed by the rhythm and intimacy, she asks, "Why all your friends call me that?"

"Call you what, baby?" Iya's voice is rough but soft, like a terrycloth towel. "Hand me up a bobby-pin."

"Two-headed," says Loanna. She lifts the whole card full of pins and feels the pressure as her Iya chooses one and pulls it free.

"Two-headed? It means like you got the second sight, sorta. Like Indian mystics be talkin about openin they third eye. Only more so."

"But why say it like that?" Loanna asks, persisting. Some odd things have gone on since she got here: folks dropping on one knee, saying prayers in African to the dry, exacting sound of rattling gourds. Tearful entrances and laughing exits, gifts of honey, candles, and coconuts. Not every question gets her an answer, but she's here to learn, so she always tries again. "Why call it two-headed, and why say that about me?"

"Oooh, now that's a story." Iya pauses for a moment, finishing off a row, and the murmur of a neighbor's voice rises through slow rustling trees and over the courtyard wall, light and indistinct. Iya sections off another braid and repeats herself. "That is *truly* a *story*, baby. You wanna hear it now?"

Loanna nods, then winces from the pain of pulling her own hair. "Ow! I mean, yeah," she says.

"*Try* to sit still, then, so I can concentrate. Lessee. This story started before you were born, Loanna, 'bout fifteen years ago. The night before you were born, actually, to be exact. You remember that night?"

"Naww," says Loanna, giggling.

"Your mama sure do. But she ain't the only one. I was *there*, and what I can't tell you ain't nobody can. Here, shift yourself this way so I can reach the back. You comfortable?"

Loanna scoots the pillow forward. "Mmm-hmm." She faces a peach stucco wall now, not so interesting as the view she had had of the garden. So Loanna closes her eyes, lets her Iya's words form pictures in her mind. This is what she sees—

She sees herself. She sees Loanna-that-was, Loanna-to-come, Loanna-she-who-will-always-be. She can tell by her feet, large like her mama's, by her strong, long legs. She can tell by her milk-and-honey skin. (How'd she get to be so fair? No white folks, counting back for five generations...but that's another story.) She recognizes her flat butt that reminds her daddy of Aunt Fiona, and there's the mark like two lips above it; Aunt Nono calls that an Angel's Kiss. Her back looks funny; maybe that's because she never really gets to see it. Her breasts look bigger. She can see them swaying in and out of sight as she walks away from her own disembodied point of view, down some sort of path.

But her breasts aren't the *main* difference. The *main* difference is her head. Actually the lack of it; her head is not there. In its place are rays of shimmering light that stream down from a luminous ball floating nearly a foot above the stem of her graceful neck. The ball of light itself is colorless, but as Loanna's viewpoint follows it she sees it sending flares of color in all directions. She understands from her Iya that this is her *ori*, which contains instructions and wisdom from the ancestors. With the guidance of her ori she has left the heavenly city, on her way to choose a head. It is a very important decision.

Coming too quickly around a turn in the path, she catches up with herself, suddenly merging with the ball of light. All at once, it is as if she has a thousand eyes. Each beam of light absorbs the significance of what it touches, in a depth and detail Loanna has difficulty handling. Images spin into her out of the formerly indistinguishable darkness: the stern trunks of trees stand in meaningful positions; their beckoning branches droop with leaves, each leaf a poem, waiting to fall with a sigh, reciting itself as it drifts free. But the piercing rays need not wait as they caress each layer of cellular structure, reading the secrets of greenness and sugar, tasting chlorophyll and acknowledging Loanna's part in its manufacture, her gaseous contribution to its growth. Then there is the throb and rustle of waves of wind, then the shift to shooting through the soil beneath her feet, which is alive: warm and changing with worms, and damp and seething with nameless hungers that are hers, it's all hers, all herself.

Somehow, she adjusts. She swims in the sea of the knowledge of everything around her. She wears an apron of fine cowrie shells ~*caressing tides of food; soft, sucking feet*~, a skirt of grass ~*dry whispers of a burning sun*~, a leather pouch—she tries to absorb it all. Directed by her ori, she even manages to move forward, toward her destiny. Wonders around her part and let her pass.

There is sand beneath her feet ~*silica, each grain a window in a castle on another world*~ and a curtain of vines before her ~*twisting, the eternal spiral up, and drinking from a hidden well~* when she reaches the place to which she has been led. She peers through the leaves and *sees* a firelit clearing *~the shape of a spicy scent in the wood burning, a curl of smoke—the eternal spiral up~.* Over the fire hangs a kettle *~the song of its making rings like a silent gong in the play of her vision~* filled with bubbling stew *~reluctant roots dug and diced apart, farewells from the nervous forager which gave its body, its blood~.*

Ajala, the maker of heads, enters the clearing. He is like a man. A drunken man, Loanna perceives. A mean drunk. He has lost, gambling. Lost to the King, a spirit of swords and justice. The cowries clicked and fell, clicked and fell, all day, till he was without a shell to pay. This is all Loanna can tell from a single "glance." Another ray streams out in his direction—and Ajala seizes it as it lands! He is no man, but a god! He pulls her forward by the ray of her perception.

She stands in front of Ajala. He is dark and crooked *~the better to become lost in~* and not at *all* in a happy mood *~a woman wrapped her goods in white cloth and walked away~.* He *speaks* to her, laying heavy slabs of speech upon her mind. He gives her anger, wet and cynically cold, which would mean this in words: "Ha, you come too late! You seek a head? I have ceased to make heads. What is the use, when they will all eventually belong to the King? Not even those already made will I sell to you, for with the rise of the sun all will belong to him, to Kabio Sile. And I am too drunk to bring you to them now. Besides, I want my stew. You are welcome to join me—except, of course, you have no mouth!"

Unkind laughter fills the clearing. Loanna turns to go, switching her hips angrily, which causes her cowrie shell apron to clatter. Ajala stops her with one hand on her shoulder and swings her back around.

"But what is this?" says Ajala. "You are *very rich*! With these beautiful shells I could cancel my debt! Very well, I will take you. But just to the F hut, no further."

The F hut...this is where he stores those heads barely worthy of the name. Loanna is sure the ancestors have provided her with enough goods for a C, the next grade up. But even an F is better than nothing, she figures. So she removes the apron, and he receives it, and they are off.

Stars have appeared above them. The ori touches their colors with its own and brings to Loanna their distance, their magnificently pure combustion, and their blazing bravery of the void. Then she is at the F hut, and it is time to choose.

These heads are made of mud, and they are really pretty bad. Some of them aren't even dry yet. The features are all rough and mostly irregular in size and shape. As she squats to turn the mud heads over and pick the best, the leather pouch swings out on its cord, then bangs against her belly. It sobs of lost herdmates, of running open-nosed, into the wind—but what's within?

Curious, she pulls it open, puts in her fingers and draws out a pinch of salt *~longing for the cresting waves, shh, the hissing of the sea, exposed before the sun now, but once, what is it that lies at the bottom of the ocean?~*. Ah, here is the rest of her fortune! Perhaps she can obtain a C head after all.

Ajala waits impatiently for her decision—too impatiently, it seems to Loanna. She picks an F at random, lifts it, makes as though to put it on. There is an angle, a hidden aspect to Ajala's waiting that is somehow wrong. His eyes are growing strangely larger as he watches her lower the head. They are almost all he has now for a face: huge eyes watching as she lowers the head over her ori. But what is this terrible blankness descending upon her mind? The telling colors cannot penetrate the thick mud of her head—it is a trap! Quickly she raises the F back up and sets it to the side. Ajala leans over her, silent yet threatening. She throws her hands up in defense, and two grains of salt fly from her fingers to his face. Of course they land in his enormous eyes. Tears spill from them and fall upon the ground. Ajala cries ~no love, alone, alone, no one, no love~. When he is finished he sighs wistfully. His sigh says, "It is too long since I've had the salt to spare for tears. Is there more?"

Loanna shows him the pouchful. Good. In exchange for the salt, he will take her to choose a C head. Through the songs of insects ~brief, brief, but sharp and fleet is our short leap, bright, sweet, the glittering of our span~ and the heavy dew they go, to come at last to the C hut.

These heads are made of woven wood. There is a certain uniformity of feature. They're better than the F heads, but there's nothing spectacularly exciting about any of them. Because she sees no real differences, Loanna chooses quickly. Before putting on her C head she checks out Ajala. He is withdrawn, brooding over his many ancient wrongs and sorrows. No trick this time, it seems. The head fits smoothly into place.

She can't see. It is dark. She can smell the soil, hear the crickets, but it is all filtered, lessened to the trickle of experience that she used to be used to. The rays of her ori tease her with flickering glimpses of the essence. She turns, blinks her eyelids, parts her lips experimentally. "I—" she says, a creaking in the night. The crickets silence themselves. "I want—" She wants an A head. An *A*. But she doubts this bitter god will grant her wish for the asking. And she has used up all the trade goods the ancestors gave her, just to reach the point where she realizes that what she wants is *more*.

She'll have to use what she's been given to get what must be gotten, then.

There. That darker darkness must be he. She addresses it. "I want—to thank you from the bottom of my heart. I mean like, this is so completely swollen! I thought you said you were only gonna give me a C head. But this A is—is—it's—"

The god appears clearly before her, shining with anger. It lights him as though it were a fire, and he glows like a maddened furnace. "IT IS A C! A C HEAD IS WHAT YOU HAVE AND NOTHING BUT A C!!"

Loanna fears the heat of Ajala's anger will ignite her poor wooden head. Also she feels something she's never felt before, a sort of…tugging…at the top. But she persists. "Oh, chill, it's all right," she says. "I'll let everybody know what a deal I got. Unless—" holding up a hand to forestall further wrath, "unless you don't want me to. No, okay, I won't tell. You made some kinda mistake, dincha?"

Ajala strives to control his anger. He succeeds in subduing himself to a dull red glow. "This is the C hut. It contains nothing but C heads!"

"Uhh, yeah. Sure. I understand. I won't tell anybody. Except if they notice and ask me how I got it, okay?"

"AARRGH!" bellows Ajala. "COME!" He grabs her with one hot hand and drags her into the forest.

There is no path; at least none that Loanna can detect. The way is a lot more difficult and a lot less interesting than the last two trips. Just stumbling through the dark, her hand sweating in the hot grip of the god's. She'd probably be a little steadier on her feet if it wasn't for the insistent tugging at her scalp, pulling her constantly off course.

After a while, the darkness lessens. This seems to increase Ajala's fury. Without warning he stops, picks Loanna up by the waist, and flings her over his shoulder. Then he's off again, at an uncomfortable trot.

"What's...the big...hurry?" she manages to whuff out between the god's jolting strides.

"Dawn," he explains. Between panting breaths he adds, "I must...return soon...to pay my debt...to the King...or lose my heads. But first...you will see...you are wrong. Not far now," he ends.

By the time they reach the A hut, Loanna's neck is sore from the odd tugging, which has for the most part been perpendicular to their path. The rest of her feels a little rough as well. And she feels even worse when she sees the A heads.

These heads are made of jewels.

Amethyst, rose quartz, aventurine, and other stones she cannot name, they glow with living light. Each is perfect, each unique. There is no way to pretend that what she wears is one of these. So much for deceit.

What else does she have? She has spent her inheritance. She has used her head, such as it is. She kneels before the luminous beauty of the As, but she's being pulled away by this unaccountable vacuum. What *is* it?

"Mama!" she screams in fear and frustration. "Maamaa!" And that's when she gets it: the answer to her question and the solution to her problem, too, all at once, all in one. Where she's going, where she'll soon be coming from. The door, the gate, the entranceway for everything that ever was in the world.

"Wait," she pleads to the unseen force. "Mama, wait just a minute. I got a idea." Her mother must hear her, or *some*body must, for the compelling pressure to be born lessens just a little.

"Ajala," she says. "You got the cowries. You got the salt. But you'd like more, right? Course you would. For an A head I—"

"You admit you have only a C head?"

"Yeah, well, I guess I did try to jack you around a little. Sorry. But now, if you let me choose an A head I can lead you to the source. Where I got the shells and cowries *from*. Take away as much as you can carry!"

"Is it far? I don't have much time...."

"No, no, it's really close. It'll only take a few minutes, okay? Can I pick one?"

Ajala nods. Breathlessly, she selects a large, round head of pale blue celestite. There is a moment of disorientation as she removes her C and is flooded by the universe ~*the turning, rising rightly, the eternal helix up*~. But then the celestite is over her ori, focusing and altering her perceptions, directing and filtering the rays of light that connect her to the world: her awareness of that connection. Plus she has her other senses: eyes, ears, nose; all working very well. Is that faint odor fish?

Ajala looks different through these eyes. Loanna decides that she now finds him cooler. She stands and beckons him to come and kneel before her. Parting her skirt, she brings him gently to the source.

The god is reverent. He prays to the source, mouthing soundless words. He speaks skillfully, with a silver tongue.

Loanna sags against him, pliable with pleasure. She is pulled taut again, stretched between these two irresistible forces: one between her legs, the other somewhere over her shoulders.

At last she can stand no more. "I like your approach," she says softly. "Now let's see your retreat." To her surprise he backs away without protest. He looks up at her, smiling happily. A huge pearl falls from his lips; his reward.

She has to go. She really must. But as she is drawn away from the A hut, out into her life, Ajala places the C head into her hands (long fingers like her grandfather's, but they don't look a bit artistic on top of Uncle Donald's square palms).

She is confused by the god's offering. "Put it on," he says in a receding shout. "Put it on, wear it over your A. You can always take it off again. And you may find it necessary, sometimes, to be less than you are capable of being. I know——" His last words are lost as she is born.

❧

Loanna opens her eyes. Shadows sway on the stucco wall, struck by the lowering sun. The lingering sweetness of the god's homage spreads like syrup through the afternoon air, mingling with the golden light. Her dream of the story is over, though Iya's voice continues, twisting its ends together, pulling them up and into the eternal spiral.

"Yeah, we finally got you to make up your mind to honor us with your presence, and you came all in a rush into this world," Iya finishes. "I was hot and dizzy from all that bendin up and down, all that runnin back and forth. Didn't nobody offer *me* no ice chips. But I got to see you first, and right away, I knew you were special. A caul, yeah, but that don't automatically mean that much." Iya pauses. Her swift fingers lie still in her lap, their task long done. "It was your eyes told me. Told me everything I just told you—and then some. I can't remember everything your eyes told me on the day that you was born."

"So then was when you decided you were gonna teach me?"

"When you was old enough, right," Iya says. "So let's get on off this balcony and go visit Mam'zelle La Veau. You got the coins? Your *gele's* on the bed, with the rest of your outfit. We'll pick us up some flowers for the gravesite on the way. Anything else your ori's tellin you to bring, baby?"

Loanna's eyes close again, enabling her to focus on the resonance within, the quiet bell of her consciousness. "A— a egg? A *blue* egg?! Iya, how we supposed to get that?"

Iya rolls her eyes. "Honey, I don know. But if the ancestors tellin you Mam'zelle need a blue egg, we gone get her a blue egg."

"But, Iya, don't you think it might—"

"Loanna!" Iya's voice is sharp and stern. "Here's the first thing you gotta learn: when your head tells you somethin, *listen*. Specially if you askin a question. You get an answer, accept that answer." She rises and holds out her hands to help her student stand.

"Today you prayin for the help and guidance of a woman who was famous for not takin nothin off nobody, the original Voodoo Queen. So you gotta be sincere, and you gotta stand firm for yourself. Like when we buy our flowers and you give the man a twenty-dollar bill, and if he only give you change back for a ten, what you gonna do?"

Loanna's fingers trace the braids curving above her ears. "Ask him where's the rest. Cause I know I'm not stupid. I can count."

"That's right. Same way with this. You know. You not stupid. That's what you gotta learn to believe, honey, you wanna live up to your potential. After all," Iya concludes as Loanna follows her inside, "what's the good of havin two heads unless you use em?"

Wallamelon

"Baby, baby, baby! Baby, baby, baby!" Cousin Alphonse must have thought he looked like James Brown. He looked like what he was, just a little boy with a big peanut head, squirming around, kicking up dust in the driveway.

Oneida thought about threatening to tell on him for messing his pants up. Even Alphonse ought to know better. He had worn holes in both his knees, begging "Please, please, please," into the broken microphone he'd found in Mr. Early's trash barrel. And she'd heard a loud rip the last time he did the splits, though nothing showed. Yet.

"'Neida! Alphonse! Come see what me an Mercy Sanchez foun!" Kevin Curtis ran along the sidewalk toward them, arms windmilling, shirt-tails flapping. He stopped several feet off, as soon as he saw he had their attention. "Come *on*!"

Oneida stood up from the pipe-rail fence slowly, with the full dignity of her ten years. One decade. She was the oldest kid on the block, not counting teenagers. She had certain responsibilities, like taking care of Alphonse.

The boys ran ahead of her as she walked, and circled back again like little dogs. Kevin urged her onto the path that cut across the vacant lot beside his house. Mercy was standing on a pile of rubble half the way through, her straight hair shining in the noonday sun like a long, black mirror. She was pointing down at something Oneida couldn't see from the path, something small, something so wonderful it made sad Mercy smile.

"Wallamelons," Kevin explained as they left the path. "Grown all by theyselves; ain't nobody coulda put em there."

"Watermelons," Oneida corrected him automatically.

The plant grew out from under a concrete slab. At first all she could see was its broad leaves, like green hearts with scalloped edges. Mercy pushed these aside to reveal the real treasure: four fat globes, dark and light stripes swelling in their middles and vanishing into one another at either end. They were watermelons, all right. Each one was a little larger than Oneida's fist.

"It's a sign," said Mercy, her voice soft as a baby's breath. "A sign from the Blue Lady."

Oneida would have expected the Blue Lady to send them roses instead, or something prettier, something you couldn't find in an ordinary supermarket. But Mercy knew more about the Blue Lady, because she and her half-brother Emilio had been the ones to tell Oneida about her in the first place.

"Four of them and four of us." Oneida looked up at Mercy to see if she understood the significance.

Mercy nodded. "We can't let no one else know about this."

"How come?" asked Alphonse. Because he was mildly retarded, he needed help understanding a lot of things.

Oneida explained it to him. "You tell anybody else, they'll mess up everything. Keep quiet, and you'll have a whole watermelon all to yourself."

"I get a wallamelon all my own?"

"*Wa-ter-mel-on*," Oneida enunciated.

"How long it take till they ready?"

They decided it would be at least a week before the fruit was ripe enough to eat. Every day they met at Mizz Nichols's.

Mercy's mother had left her here and gone back to Florida to be with her husband. It was better for Mercy to live at her grandmother's, away from so much crime. And Michigan had less discrimination.

Mizz Nichols didn't care what her granddaughter was up to as long as it didn't interrupt her tv watching or worse yet, get her called away from work.

Mercy seemed to know what the watermelon needed instinctively. She had them fill half-gallon milk bottles from the garden hose and set these to "cure" behind the garage. In the dusky hours after Aunt Elise had picked up Cousin Alphonse, after Kevin had to go inside, Mercy and Oneida smuggled the heavy glass containers to their secret spot. They only broke one.

When the boys complained at being left out of this chore, Mercy set them to picking dried grass. They stuffed this into old pillowcases and put these underneath the slowly fattening fruits to protect them from the gravelly ground.

The whole time, Mercy seemed so happy. She sang songs about the Blue Lady, how in far away dangerous places she saved children from evil spirits and grown-ups. Oneida tried to sing along with her, but the music kept changing, though the stories stayed pretty much the same.

There was the one about the girl who was standing on the street corner somewhere down South when a car full of men with guns went by, shooting everybody. But the Blue Lady saved her. Or there was a boy whose mom was so sick he had to stay with his crazy aunt because his dad was already dead in a robbery. When the aunt put poison in his food he ran away, and the Blue Lady showed him where to go and took care of him till he got to his grandparents house in Boston, all the way from Washington, DC.

All you had to do was call her name.

One week stretched, unbelievably, to two. The watermelons were as large as cereal bowls. As party balloons. But they seemed pitiful compared to the giant blimps in the bins in front of Farmer Jack's.

Obviously, their original estimate was off. Alphonse begged and whined so much, though, that Mercy finally let him pick and open his own melon. It was hard and pale inside, no pinker than a pack of Wrigley's gum. It tasted like scouring powder.

Oneida knew she'd wind up sharing part of her personal, private watermelon with Alphonse, if only to keep him from crying, or telling another kid, or a grown-up even. It was the kind of sacrifice a mature ten-year-old expected to make. It would be worth it, though. Half a watermelon was still a feast.

They tended the Blue Lady's vine with varying degrees of impatience and diligence. Three weeks, now. How much longer would it take till the remaining watermelons reached what Oneida called, "The absolute peak of perfection?"

They never found out.

❁

The Monday after the Fourth of July, Oneida awoke to the low grumble of heavy machinery. The noise was from far enough away that she could have ignored it if she had wanted to stay asleep. Instead, she leaned out till her fingers fit under the edge of her bunk's frame, curled down, and flipped herself so she sat on the empty bottom bunk.

She peeked into her parents' bedroom. Her father was still asleep; his holstered gun gleamed darkly in the light that crept in around the lowered shade. She closed the door quietly. Her dad worked hard. He was the first Negro on the police force.

Oneida ate a bowl of cereal, re-reading the book on the back of the box about the adventures of Twinkle-toes the Elephant. Baby stuff, but she was too lazy to get up and locate a real book.

When she was done, she checked the square dial of the alarm clock on the kitchen counter. Quarter to nine. In forty-five minutes her mother would be home from the phone company. She'd make a big breakfast. Even if Oneida wasn't hungry, it felt good to talk with Mom while she cooked it. Especially if Dad woke up; with Royal and Limoges off at Big Mama's, the three of them discussed important things like voting rights and integration.

But there was time for a quick visit to the vacant lot.

The sidewalk was still cool beneath the black locust trees. The noise that had wakened her sounded a lot louder out here. It grew and grew, the closer she got to the Curtis's. And then she saw the source: an ugly yellow monster machine roaring through the lot, riding up and down over the humps of rubble like a cowboy on a bucking bronco. And Kevin was just standing there on the sidewalk, watching.

There were stones all around. She picked up a whole fistful and threw them, but it was too far. She grabbed some more and Kevin did too. They started yelling and ran toward the monster, throwing stones. It had a big blade. It was a bulldozer, it was pushing the earth out of its way wherever it wanted to go. She couldn't even hear her own shouting over the awful sound it made. Rocks flew out of her hands. They hit it. They hit it again. The man on top, too.

Then someone was holding her arms down. She kept yelling and Kevin ran away. Suddenly she heard herself. The machine was off. The white man from on top of it was standing in front of her telling her to shut up, shut up or he'd have her arrested.

Where was the Blue Lady?

There was only Mizz Curtis, in her flowered house dress, with her hair up in pink curlers. No one was holding Oneida's arms anymore, but she was too busy crying to get away. Another white man asked what her name was.

"Oneida Brandy," Mizz Curtis said. "Lives down the street. Oneida, what on Earth did you think you were doing, child?"

"What seems to be the problem?"

Dad. She looked up to be sure. He had his police hat on and his gun belt, but regular pants and a tee-shirt instead of the rest of his uniform. He gazed at her without smiling while he talked to the two white men.

So she *was* in trouble.

After a while, though, the men stopped paying attention to Oneida. They were talking about the rich white people they worked for, and all the things they could do to anyone who got in their way. Kevin's mom gave her a crumpled up Kleenex to blow her nose on, and she realized all the kids in the neighborhood were there.

Including Mercy Sanchez. She looked like a statue of herself. Like she was made of wood. Of splinters.

Then the white men's voices got loud, and they were laughing. They got in a green pick-up parked on the easement and drove off, leaving their monster in the middle of the torn-up lot.

Her father's face was red; they must have said something to make him mad before they went away. But all Dad did was thank Mizz Curtis for sending Kevin over to wake him up.

They met Mom on the way home. She was still in her work clothes and high heels, walking fast. She stopped and stared at Dad's hat and gun. "Vinny?"

"Little brush with the law, Joanne. Our daughter here's gonna explain everything over breakfast."

Oneida tried. But Mercy had made her swear not to tell any grown-ups about the Blue Lady, which meant her story sounded not exactly stupid, but silly. "All that fuss about a watermelon!" Mom said. "As if we don't have the money to buy one, if that's what you want!"

Dad said the white men were going to get quite a surprise when they filed their complaint about him impersonating an officer. He said they were breaking the law themselves by not posting their building permit. He said off-duty policemen went around armed all the time.

Aunt Elise brought over Cousin Alphonse. They had to play in the basement even though it was such a nice day outside. And Kevin Curtis and Mercy Sanchez weren't allowed to come over. Or anybody.

After about eighty innings of "Ding-Dong, Delivery," Oneida felt like she was going crazy with boredom. She was sorry she'd ever made the game up; all you did was put a blanket over yourself and say "Ding-dong, delivery," and the other player was supposed to guess what you were. Of course Alphonse adored it.

Mom let them come upstairs and turn on the tv in time for the afternoon movie. It was an old one, a gangster story, which was good. Oneida hated gangster movies, but that was the only kind Cousin Alphonse would watch all the way through. She could relax and read her book.

Then Mom called her into the bedroom. Dad was there, too. He hadn't gone to his other job. They had figured out what they were going to do with her.

They were sending her to Detroit, to Big Mama. She should have known. The two times she spent the night there she'd had to share a bed with Limoges, and there hadn't been one book in the entire house.

"What about Cousin Alphonse?" she asked. "How am I supposed to take care of him if I'm in Detroit?"

"You just concentrate on learning to take better care of yourself, young lady."

Which wasn't a fair thing for Mom to say.

After dark, Oneida snuck out. She had stayed inside all day, exactly as she'd promised. Now it was night. No one would expect her to slip the screen out of her bedroom window and squirm out onto the fresh-mowed lawn. That wasn't the kind of thing Oneida ever did. She wouldn't get caught.

The big orange moon hung low over Lincoln Elementary. Away from the streetlights, in the middle of the ravaged vacant lot, it made its own shadows. They hid everything, the new hills and the old ones. It was probably going to be impossible to find the watermelon vine. If it had even survived the bulldozer's assault.

But Oneida walked to the lot's middle anyway. From there, she saw Mercy. She stood stock still, over on Oneida's left, looking down at something; it was the same way she'd stood the day they found the vine. Except then, the light had come from above, from the sun. Now something much brighter than the moon shone from below, up into her face. Something red and blue and green and white, something radiant, moving like water, like a dream.

Oneida ran toward whatever it was. She tripped on a stone block, stumbled through the dark. "Mercy!" she shouted as she topped a hill. Mercy nodded, but Oneida didn't think it was because she'd heard her. She ran on recklessly, arriving just as the light began to fade, as if, one by one, a bunch of birthday candles were being blown out.

Oneida bent forward to see better. The light came from a little cave of jewels about the size of a gym ball. A blue heart wavered at its center, surrounded by tiny wreaths of red flowers and flickering silver stars. As she watched, they dwindled and were gone. All that was left was a shattered watermelon, scooped out to the rind.

Magic! Oneida met Mercy's eyes. They had seen real magic! She smiled. But Mercy didn't.

"Blue Lady say she can't take care of Emilio no more. He too big." Emilio had been thirteen last New Year's, when he left with Mercy's mom. Mizz Sanchez hadn't been so worried about him; bad neighborhoods weren't so bad for bad boys. But now...

Mercy looked down again at the left-behind rind.

Oneida decided to tell Mercy her own news about going to Detroit Saturday and being on punishment till then. It was difficult to see her face; her beautiful hair kept hanging in the way. Was she even listening?

"You better not go an forget me, 'Neida."

What was she talking about? "I'll only be there until school starts! September!" As if she wouldn't remember Mercy for ever and ever, anyway.

Mercy turned and walked a few steps away. Oneida was going to follow her, but Mercy stopped on her own. Faced her friend again. Held out her hand. There was something dark in her pale palm. "Ima give you these now, in case—"

Oneida took what Mercy offered her, an almost weightless mass, cool and damp. "I can sneak out again," she said. Why not?

"Sure. The Blue Lady, though, she want you to have these, an this way I won't be worryin."

Watermelon seeds. That's what they were. Oneida put them in her pajama pocket. What she had been looking for when she came here.

She took a deep breath. It went into her all shaky and came out in one long whoosh. Till September wasn't her whole life. "Maybe Mom and Dad will change their minds and let you come over."

"Maybe." Mercy sounded as if she should clear her throat. As if she were crying, which was something she never did, no matter how sad she looked. She started walking away again.

"Hey, I'll send a card on your birthday," Oneida yelled after her, because she couldn't think of what else to say.

Wednesday the Chief of Police put Dad on suspension.

That meant they could drive to Detroit early, as soon as Dad woke up on Thursday. Oneida helped her mom with the last-minute packing. There was no time to do laundry.

Dad didn't care. "They got water and electricity in Detroit last time I checked, Joanne, and Big Mama must have at least one washing machine."

They drove and drove. It took two whole hours. Oneida knew they were getting close when they went by the giant tire, ten stories tall. There were more and more buildings, bigger and bigger ones. Then came the billboard with a huge stove sticking out of it, and they were there.

Detroit was the fifth largest city in the United States. Big Mama lived on a street called Davenport, like a couch, off Woodward. Her house was dark and cool inside, without much furniture. Royal answered the door and led them back to the kitchen, the only room that ever got any sunshine.

"Y'all made good time," said Big Mama. "Dinner's just gettin started." She squeezed Oneida's shoulders and gave her a cup of lime Kool-Aid.

"Can I go finish watching cartoons?" asked Royal.

"Your mama an daddy an sister jus drove all this way; you ain't got nothin to say to em?"

"Limoges over at the park with Luemma and Ivy Joe," she told Mom and Dad. They sent Royal to bring her home and sat down at the table, lighting cigarettes.

Oneida drank her Kool-Aid quickly and rinsed out her empty cup. She wandered back through the house to the front door. From a tv in another room, boingy sounds like bouncing springs announced the antics of some orange cat or indigo dog.

Mercy watched soap operas. Maybe Oneida would be able to convince the other children those were more fun. Secret, forbidden shows grown-ups didn't want you to see, about stuff they said you'd understand when you got older.

Limoges ran over the lawn shouting "'Neida! 'Neida!" At least *somebody* was glad to see her. Oneida opened the screen door. "I thought you wasn't comin till Saturday!"

"Weren't," she corrected her little sister. "I thought you weren't."

"What happened?"

"Dad got extra days off. They're in the kitchen." Royal and the other kids were nowhere in sight. Oneida followed Limoges back to find their parents.

It was hot; the oven was on. Big Mama was rolling out dough for biscuits and heating oil. She had Oneida and Limoges take turns shaking chicken legs in a bag of flour. Then they set the dining-room table and scrounged chairs from the back porch and when that wasn't enough, from Big Mama's bedroom upstairs. Only Oneida was allowed to go in.

It smelled different in there than the whole rest of the house. Better. Oneida closed the door behind her.

There were more things, too. Bunches of flowers with ribbons wrapped around them hung from the high ceiling. Two tables overflowed with indistinct objects, which pooled at their feet. The tables flanked a tall, black rectangle—something shiny, with a thin cloth flung over it, she saw, coming closer. A mirror? She reached to move aside the cloth, but a picture on the table to her right caught her eye.

It was of what she had seen that night in the vacant lot. A blue heart floated in a starry sky, with flowers around it. Only these flowers were pink and gold. And in the middle of the heart, a door had been cut.

The door's crystal knob seemed real. She touched it. It was. It turned between her thumb and forefinger. The door opened.

The Blue Lady. Oneida had never seen her before, but who else could this be a painting of? Her skin was pale blue, like the sky; her hair rippled down dark and smooth all the way to her ankles. Her long dress was blue and white, with pearls and diamonds sewn on it in swirling lines. She wore a cape with a hood, and her hands were holding themselves out as if she had just let go of something, a bird or a kiss.

The Blue Lady.

So some grown-ups did know.

Downstairs, the screen door banged. Oneida shut the heart. She shouldn't be snooping in Big Mama's bedroom. What if she were caught?

The chair she was supposed to be bringing was back by where she'd come in. She'd walked right past it.

The kitchen was crowded with noisy kids. Ivy Joe had hit a home run playing baseball with the boys. Luemma had learned a new dance called the Monkey. Oneida helped Limoges roll her pants legs down and made Royal wash his hands. No one asked what had taken her so long upstairs.

Mom and Dad left right after dinner. Oneida promised to behave herself. She did, too. She only went in Big Mama's bedroom with permission.

Five times that first Friday, Big Mama sent Oneida up to get something for her.

Oneida managed not to touch anything. She stood again and again, though, in front of the two tables, cataloguing their contents. On the right, alongside the portrait of the Blue Lady were several tall glass flasks filled with colored fluids; looping strands of pearls wound around their slender necks. A gold-rimmed saucer held a dark, mysterious liquid, with a pile of what seemed to be pollen at the center of its glossy surface.

A red-handled axe rested on the other table. It had two sharp, shiny edges. No wonder none of the other kids could come in here.

On every trip, Oneida spotted something else. She wondered how long it would take to see everything.

On the fifth trip, Oneida turned away from the huge white wing leaning against the table's front legs (how had she missed *that* the first four times?) to find Big Mama watching her from the doorway.

"I—I didn't—"

"You ain't messed with none a my stuff, or I'd a known it. S'all right; I spected you'd be checkin out my altars, chile. Why I sent you up here."

Altars? Like in a Catholic church like Aunt Elise went to? The two tables had no crucifixes, no tall lecterns for a priest to pray from, but evidently they were altars, because there was nothing else in the room that Big Mama could be talking about. It was all normal stuff, except for the flower bunches dangling down from the ceiling.

"Then I foun these." Big Mama held out one hand as she moved into the bedroom and shut the door behind herself. "Why you treat em so careless-like? Leavin em in your dirty pajamas pocket! What if I'd a had Luemma or Ivy Joe washin clothes?"

The seeds. Oneida accepted them again. They were dry, now, and slightly sticky.

"Them girls don't know no more about mojo than Albert Einstein. Less, maybe."

Was mojo magic? The seeds might be magic, but Oneida had no idea what they were for or how to use them. Maybe Big Mama did. Oneida peeped up at her face as if the answer would appear there.

"I see. You neither. That niece a mine taught you nothin. Ain't that a surprise." Her tone of voice indicated just the opposite.

Big Mama's niece was Oneida's mother.

"Go down on the back porch and make sure the rinse cycle startin all right. Get us somethin to drink. Then come up here again, and we do us a bit a discussin."

When Oneida returned she carried a pitcher of iced tea with lemon, a bowl of sugar, and two glasses on a tray. She balanced the tray on her hip so she could knock and almost dropped it. Almost.

It took Big Mama a moment to let her in. "Leave that on the chair seat," she said when she saw the tray. "Come over nex the bed."

A little round basket with a lid and no handles sat on the white chenille spread. A fresh scent rose from its tight coils. "Sea grass," said Big Mama in answer to Oneida's question. "Wove by my gramma. That ain't what I want you to pay attention to, though. What's inside—"

Was a necklace. Made of watermelon seeds.

"A'int everybody has this in they backgroun. Why I was sure your mama musta said somethin. She proud, though. Too proud, turn out, to even do a little thing like that, am I right?"

Oneida nodded. Mom hated her to talk about magic. Superstition, she called it. She didn't even like it when Oneida brought books of fairy tales home from the library.

"How you come up with these, then?"

"I—a friend."

"A friend."

"Mercy Sanchez."

"This Mercy, she blood? Kin?" she added, when Oneida's confusion showed.

"No."

"She tell you how to work em?"

"No." Should she break her promise?

"Somethin you hidin. Can't be keepin secrets from Big Mama."

Her picture was there, on the altar. "Mercy said they came from the Blue Lady."

"'Blue Lady.' That what you call her." Big Mama's broad forehead smoothed out, getting rid of wrinkles Oneida had assumed were always there. "Well, she certainly is. The Blue Lady."

Oneida realized why no one but Mizz Curtis and Dad had come to her rescue when the white men tried to arrest her: for the Blue Lady to appear in person, you were supposed to call her, using her real name. Which Mercy and Emilio had never known.

"What do you call her?"

"Yemaya."

Oneida practiced saying it to herself while she poured the iced tea and stirred in three spoons of sugar for each of them. Yeh-mah-yah. It was strange, yet easy. Easy to say. Easy to remember. Yeh-mah-yah.

She told Big Mama everything.

"Hmmph." Big Mama took a long drink of tea. "You think you able to do what I tell you to?"

Oneida nodded. Of course she could.

Big Mama closed the curtains and lit a white candle in a jar, putting a metal tube over its top. Holes in the sides let through spots of light the shape of six-pointed stars. She made Oneida fill a huge shell with water from the bathroom and sprinkled it on both their heads. Oneida brought the chair so Big Mama could sit in front of Yemaya's altar. She watched while Big Mama twirled the necklace of watermelon seeds around in the basket's lid and let it go.

"Awright. Look like Yemaya say I be teachin you."

"Can I—"

"Four questions a day. That's all Ima answer. Otherwise you jus haveta listen closer to what I say."

Oneida decided to ask anyway. "What were you doing?"

"Divinin. Special way a speakin, more important, a hearin what Yemaya an Shango wanna tell me."

"Will I learn that? Who's Shango?"

"Shango Yemaya's son. We start tomorrow. See how much you able to take in." Big Mama held up her hand, pink palm out. "One more question is all you got for today. Might wanna use it later."

They left the bedroom to hang the clean laundry from the clothesline, under trellises heavy with blooming vines. In the machine on the back porch behind them, a new load sloshed away. Royal was watching tv; the rest of the kids were over at the park. Oneida felt the way she often did after discussing adult topics with her parents. It was a combination of coziness and exhilaration, as if she were tucked safe and warm beneath the feathers of a high-soaring bird. A soft breeze lifted the legs of her pajama bottoms, made the top flap its arms as if it were flying.

❦

Mornings were for housework. Oneida wasted one whole question finding that out.

Sundays they went to the Detroit Institute of Arts. Not to church. "God ain't in there. Only reason to go to church is so people don't talk bad about you," Big Mama told them. "Anything they gone say about me they already said it." They got dressed up the same as everyone else in the neighborhood, nodded and waved at the families who had no feud with Big Mama, even exchanging remarks with those walking their direction, toward Cass. But then they headed north by themselves.

Big Mama ended each trip through the exhibits in the museum's tea room. She always ordered a chicken salad sandwich with the crusts cut off. Ivy Joe and Luemma sat beside her, drinking a black cow apiece. Royal drew on all their napkins, floppy-eared rabbits and mean-looking monsters.

Oneida's favorite part to go to was the gift shop. Mainly because they had so many beautiful books, but also because she could touch things in there. Own them, if she paid. Smaller versions of the paintings on the walls, of the huge weird statues that resembled nothing on Earth except themselves.

The second Sunday, she bought Mercy's birthday card there. It was a postcard, actually, but bigger than most. The French lady on the front had sad, soft eyes like Mercy's. On the back, Oneida told her how she was learning "lots of stuff." It would have been nice to say more; not on a postcard, though, where anyone would be able to read it.

In fact, in the hour a day Big Mama consented to teach her, Oneida couldn't begin to tackle half what she wanted to know. Mostly she memorized: prayers; songs; long, often incomprehensible stories.

Big Mama gave her a green scarf to wrap the seeds in. She said to leave them on Yemaya's altar since Oneida shared a room with the three other girls. After that, she seemed to forget all about them. They were right there, but she never seemed to notice them. Her own necklace had disappeared. Oneida asked where it was three days in a row.

"That's for me to know and you to find out," Big Mama answered every time.

Oneida saved up a week's worth of questions. She wrote them on a pad of paper, pale purple with irises along the edges, which she'd bought at the gift shop:

1. Is your necklace in the house?
2. Is it in this room?
3. Is it in your closet?
4. Under the bed?
5. In your dresser?

And so on, with lines drawn from one to another to show which to ask next, depending on whether the response was yes or no. On a separate page she put bonus questions in case Big Mama was so forthcoming some of the others became unnecessary. These included why her brother had hardly any chores, and what was the name of Yemaya's husband, who had never turned up in any story.

But when Big Mama called Oneida upstairs, she wound up not using any of them, because there on the bed was the basket again, open, with the necklace inside. "Seem like you learnt somethin about when to hole your peace," said Big Mama. "I know you been itchin to get your hands on my *eleke*." That was an African word for necklace. "Fact that you managed to keep quiet about it one entire week mean you ready for this."

It was only Oneida's seeds; she recognized the scarf they were wrapped in. Was she going to have to put them somewhere else, now? Reluctantly, she set her pad on the bed and took them out of Big Mama's hands, trying to hide her disappointment.

"Whynchou open it?"

Inside was another eleke, almost identical to Big Mama's. The threads that bound the black and brown seeds together were whiter, the necklace itself not quite as long.

Hers. Her eleke. Made out of Mercy's gift, the magic seeds from the Blue Lady.

"So. Ima teach you how to ask questions with one a two answers, yes or no. 'Bout what you *gotta* know. What you *gotta*. An another even more important lesson: why you better off not tryin to fine out every little thing you think you wanna."

Oneida remembered her manners. "Thank you, Big Mama."

"You welcome, baby." Big Mama stood and walked to the room's other end, to the mirror between her two altars. "Come on over here an get a good look." Stepping aside, she pulled the black cloth off the mirror.

The reflection seemed darker than it should be. Oneida barely saw herself. Then Big Mama edged in behind her, shining. By that light, Oneida's thick black braids stood out so clearly every single hair escaping them cast its own shadow on the glass.

"Mos mirrors don't show the difference that sharp." Big Mama pushed Oneida's bangs down against her forehead. "Folks will notice it anyhow."

Oneida glanced back over her shoulder. No glow. Regular daylight. Ahead again. A radiant woman and a ghostly little girl.

This was the second magic Oneida had ever seen. Mercy better believe me when I tell her, she thought. It was as if Big Mama was a vampire, or more accurately, its exact opposite. "How——" She stopped herself, not quite in time.

"S'all right. Some questions you need an answer." But she stayed silent for several seconds.

"More you learn, brighter you burn. You know, it's gonna show. People react all kinda ways to that. They shun you, or they forget how to leave you alone. Wanna ask you all kinda things, then complain about the cost.

"What you gotta remember, Oneida, is this: there is always a price. *Always* a price. Only things up in the air is who gonna pay it, an how much."

✤

No Mercy.

When Oneida got home from Detroit, her friend was gone. Had been the whole time. Not moved out, but run away. Mizz Nichols didn't know where. Florida, maybe, if she had left to take care of Emilio like she was saying.

Mizz Nichols gave Oneida back the birthday card. Which Mercy had never seen.

The white people's house next to Mizz Curtis's was almost finished being built. Everyone was supposed to keep away from it, especially Cousin Alphonse. While she'd been in Detroit, unable to watch him, he had jumped into the big basement hole and broken his collarbone. Even with his arm in a sling, Aunt Elise had barely been able to keep him away. Why? Was it the smell of fresh cut wood, or the way you could see through the walls and how everything inside them fit together? Or just the thought that it was somewhere he wasn't allowed to go?

No one wanted any trouble with white people. Whatever the cause of Cousin Alphonse's latest fascination, Oneida fought it hard. She took him along when she walked Limoges to Vacation Bible School and managed to keep him occupied on Lincoln's playground all morning. After school, they walked all the way to the river, stopping at Topoll's to buy sausage sandwiches for lunch.

So successful was this expedition that they were a little late getting home. Oneida had to carry Limoges eight blocks on her back. Aunt Elise was already parked in front and talking angrily to Dad in the tv room. It was all right, though. She was just mad about the house. She thought the people building it should put a big fence around it. She thought one of their kids would get killed there before long. She thanked Jesus, Mary, and Joseph Oneida had enough sense to keep the others away from it.

But after dark, Oneida went there without telling anyone. Alone.

Below the hole where the picture window would go, light from the street lamp made a lopsided square. She opened up her green scarf and lifted her eleke in both hands.

Would it tell her what she wanted to know? What would be the price?

Twirl it in the air. Let it fall. Count the seeds: so many with their pointed ends up, so many down. Compare the totals.

The answer was no. No running away for Oneida. She should stay here.

Her responsibility for Cousin Alphonse—that had to be the reason. The Blue Lady made sure kids got taken care of.

Would Mercy return, then?

Yes.

When? Before winter?

No.

Oneida asked and asked. With each response her heart and hands grew colder. Not at Christmas. Not next summer. Not next autumn.

When? And where was she? There were ways to ask other questions, with answers besides yes or no, but Big Mama said she was too young to use those.

Finally she gave up guessing and flung the necklace aside. No one should see her this way. Crying like a baby. She was a big girl, biggest on the block.

"Yemaya. Yemaya." Why was she saying that, the Blue Lady's name? Oneida had never had a chance to tell Mercy what it was. It wouldn't do any good to say it now, when no one was in danger. She hoped.

Eventually, she was able to stop. She wiped her eyes with the green scarf. On the floor, scattered around the necklace, were several loose watermelon seeds. But her eleke was unbroken.

Yemaya was trying to tell Oneida something. Eleven seeds. Eleven years? Age eleven? It was an answer. She clung to that idea. An answer, even if she couldn't understand it.

On the phone, Big Mama only instructed her to get good grades in school, do what her mama and daddy said, and bring the seeds with her, and they would see.

But the following summer was the riots. No visit to Big Mama's.

So it was two years later that Mom and Dad drove down Davenport. The immediate neighborhood, though isolated by the devastation surrounding it, had survived more or less intact.

Big Mama's block looked exactly the same. The vines surrounding her house hung thick with heavy golden blooms. Ivy Joe and Luemma reported that at the riot's height, the last week of July, streams of US Army tanks had turned aside at Woodward, splitting apart to grind along Stimson and Selden, joining up again on Second.

Fires and sirens had also flowed around them; screams and shots were audible, but just barely.

Thanks to Big Mama. Everyone knew that.

Oneida didn't understand why this made the people who lived there mad. Many of them wouldn't even walk on the same side of the street as Big Mama any more. It was weirder than the way the girls at Oneida's school acted.

Being almost always alone, that was the price she'd paid for having her questions answered. It didn't seem like much. Maybe there'd be worse costs, later, after she learned other, more important things. Besides, some day Mercy would come back.

The next afternoon, her lessons resumed. She had wrapped the eleven extra seeds in the same scarf as her eleke. When Big Mama saw them, she held out her hand and frowned.

"Yeah. Right." Big Mama brought out her own eleke. "Ima ask Yemaya why she wanna give you these, what they for. Watch me."

Big Mama had finally agreed to show her how to ask questions with answers other than yes or no.

Big Mama swirled her necklace around in the basket top. On the altar, the silver-covered candle burned steadily. But the room brightened and darkened quickly as the sun appeared and disappeared behind fast-moving clouds and wind-whipped leaves.

"It start out the same," Big Mama said, "lif it up an let it go." With a discreet rattle, the necklace fell. "Now we gotta figure out where the sharp ends pointin," she said. "But we dividin it in four directions: north, south, east, an west."

Oneida wrote the totals in her notebook: two, four, five, and five.

"An we do it four times for every question."

Below the first line of numbers came four, one, seven, and four; then six, zero, two, and eight; and three, three, seven, and three.

"Now add em up."

North was fifteen, south was eight, east was twenty-one, and west was twenty.

Big Mama shut her eyes a moment and nodded. "Soun good. That mean—" The brown eyes opened again, sparkling. "Yemaya say 'What you *think* you do with seeds? Plant em!'"

Oneida learned that the numbers referred to episodes in those long, incomprehensible stories she'd had to memorize. She practiced interpreting them. Where should she plant the seeds? All around the edges of her neighborhood. When? One year and a day from now. Who could she have help her? Only Alphonse. How much would it cost? Quite a bit, but it would be worth it. Within the Wallamelons' reach, no one she loved would be hurt, ever again.

Two more years. The house built on the vacant lot was once again empty. Its first and only tenants fled when the vines Oneida planted went wild, six months after they moved in. The house was hers, now, no matter what the mortgage said.

Oneida even had a key, stolen from the safebox that remained on the porch long after the real estate company lost all hope of selling a haunted house in a haunted neighborhood. She unlocked the side door, opening and shutting it on slightly reluctant hinges. The family that had briefly lived here had left their curtains. In the living room, sheer white fabric stirred gently when she opened a window for fresh air. And leaned out of it, waiting.

Like the lace of a giantess, leaves covered the house-front in a pattern of repeating hearts. Elsewhere in the neighborhood, sibling plants, self-sown from those she'd first planted around the perimeter, arched from phone pole to lamp post, encircling her home. Keeping it safe. So Mercy could return.

At first Mom had wanted to move out. But nowhere else Negroes could live in this town would be any better, Dad said. Besides, it wasn't all that bad. Even Aunt Elise admitted Cousin Alphonse was calmer, better off, here behind the vines. Mom eventually agreed to stay put and see if Dad's promotion ever came through.

That was taking a long time. Oneida was secretly glad. It would be so much harder to do what she had to do if her family moved. To come here night after night, as her eleke had shown her she must. To be patient. Till—

Then.

She saw her. Walking up the street. As Yemaya had promised. And this was the night, and Oneida was here for it, her one chance.

She waved. Mercy wasn't looking her way, though. She kept on, headed for Oneida's house, it looked like.

Oneida jerked at the handle of the front door. It smacked hard against the chain she'd forgotten to undo. She slammed it shut again, slid the chain free, and stumbled down the steps.

Mercy was halfway up the block. The noise must have startled her. No way Oneida'd be able to catch up. "Mercy! Mercy Sanchez!" She ran hopelessly, sobbing.

Mercy stopped. She turned. Suddenly uncertain, Oneida slowed. Would Mercy have cut her hair that way? Worn that black leather jacket?

But who else could it be?

"Please, please!" Oneida had no idea what she was saying, or who she was saying it to. She was running again and then she was there, hugging her, and it *was* her. Mercy. Home.

Mercy. Acting like it was no big deal to show up again after disappearing for four years.

"I tole you," she insisted, sitting cross-legged on the floorboards of the empty living room. One small white candle flickered between them, supplementing the streetlight. "Emilio axed me could I come help him. He was havin trouble...." She trailed off. "It was this one group of kids hasslin his friends...."

"All you said before you left was about how the Blue Lady—"

"'Neida, mean to say you ain't forgot *none* a them games we played?!" Scornfully.

The price had been paid.

It was as if Oneida were swimming, completely underwater, and putting out her hand and touching Mercy, who swore up and down she was not wet. Who refused to admit that the Blue Lady was real, that she, at least, had seen her. When Oneida tried to show her some of what she'd learned, Mercy nodded once, then interrupted, asking if she had a smoke.

Oneida got a cigarette from the cupboard where she kept her offerings.

"So how long are you here for?" It sounded awful, what Mom would say to some distant relative she'd never met before.

"Dunno. Emilio gonna be outta circulation—things in Miami different now. Here, too, hunh? Seem like we on the set a some monster movie."

Oneida would explain about that later. "What about your mom?" Even worse, the kind of question a parole officer might ask.

Mercy snorted. "She ain't wanna have nothin to do with him *or* me. For years."

"Mizz Nichols—" Oneida paused. Had Mercy heard?

"Yeah, I know. Couldn make the funeral." She stubbed out her cigarette on the bottom of her high-top, then rolled the butt between her right thumb and forefinger, straightening it. "Dunno why I even came here. Dumb. Probably the first place anybody look. If they wanna fine me." Mercy glanced up, and her eyes were exactly the same, deep and sad. As the ocean. As the sky.

"They won't." The shadow of a vine's stray tendril caressed Mercy's cheek. "They won't."

A disclaimer: the system of divination Big Mama teaches to Oneida is my own invention. It borrows heavily from West Africa's Ifa, and it also owes a bit to China's "I Ching." To the best of my knowledge, however, it is not part of any authentic tradition.

The Pragmatical Princess

(with apologies to Jay Williams)

Princess Ousmani had fallen asleep in her chains, from boredom. She woke to the weight of a dragon's head resting uncomfortably on her stomach. One rough, scaly paw kneaded her left shoulder, pricking at her skin.

Ousmani closed her eyes again. She did not believe in dragons, any more than she believed in the affrits and djinns of her father's homeland, or the water-demonesses of Mali, where her mother had been born. "It is a horse," she told herself. "A very large and very ugly horse." Peering out under her long, dark lashes, she considered the dragon's glittering snout, its gleaming, golden eyes. Its irises were formed like slits, as were the nostrils inches from her own, from which an occasional wisp of steam escaped.

"You have stopped sleeping," the dragon said. It spoke French, a mountain dialect of course. Ousmani understood, though at first with some difficulty. The beast continued. "Why do you pretend? To fool yourself, perhaps, for you can see it is impossible to convince me."

The princess shrugged, then winced as the tips of the dragon's claws insinuated themselves into her shoulder. "The illusion seemed a sensible one: if I slept, I dreamt. You have spoiled it, though, and must provide another."

"Must I?" Her ribs vibrated with its voice, which possessed an odd, dry timbre, seeming wide rather than deep.

"It seems only fair."

"Life is not fair," said the dragon. "Consider, for example, your plight." It drew back its head as if doing just that.

"I must admit, it does appear to be an unfortunate one." Princess Ousmani lay chained flat on her back, close to the edge of a precipice. She was not naked, but an unfriendly Northern chill pierced her scarlet silks. It had done so all day, except for a brief, sunny respite around noon. "My only comfort has been philosophy. But then, this has been true most of my life."

"A most unprey-like speech. I grow increasingly intrigued," the dragon said, consideringly. "Let us continue this conversation in an atmosphere more conducive."

The garish head moved from her field of vision. She heard a loud hissing, felt a sudden heat in first one, then the other of her shackled wrists.

"Rise." She tried, and found she was able to sit. The chains, which had run from wrist shackles to iron bolts fixed in granite, now ended in red-hot, half-melted links.

The chains that bound her feet were considerably shorter. The dragon paced closer and considered them dubiously. "I should like to melt these, too, but I fear to cause you unnecessary pain. Do you suggest another remedy?"

Unlike the others, these chains ended in a common terminus, an iron staple driven into the ground. Ousmani thought back to certain Greek texts she had recently acquired for translation; in particular a work by one Archimedes. "A stout stick, I think, will make the trick. And a stone of middling girth, flat on one side."

The dragon dove off the precipice, then circled overhead on oily-looking wings to shout one word: "Patience!"

The Princess Ousmani wondered when, if ever, some other virtue would be urged upon her, such as courage or resourcefulness. She shivered, and not entirely with the cold. Despite her show of stoicism, the Princess had never really resigned herself to death. Though rejecting as false the conclusion that because offerings made to a dragon disappeared, ergo there must *be* a dragon, she had made what hasty arrangements she could to be spared consumption by more prosaically horrible beasts. Barring treachery, she had expected rescue to come with the fall of night. But now it looked as though she might not be present to be rescued.

"I must just keep my wits about me," Ousmani admonished herself. "If my perceptions remain unclouded by expectations of any sort, the possibilities inherent in the moment will present themselves to me with much more readiness." So saying, she tucked her goose-bumped arms between her satin-trousered legs and amused herself with speculations as to the range of European wolves.

It was getting dark by the time the dragon returned, dropping to the ground with a rattling clatter. The source of this sound was soon revealed: a pike, a slim, straight Frankish sword, and a badly dented helm. "I hope you don't mind," the dragon said, depositing his acquisitions at her feet.

"Mind? Why should I mind? They are not exactly what I asked for, but they will do most admirably." She began scraping away the soil beneath the iron staple with the sword.

"Well, but what I meant was, the former owner of these implements is now completely incapacitated, and I thought you perhaps—"

"Might object? To the death of one of my father's enemies?" She dropped the sword and positioned the helm, dent-side down. "Or if not, of some turncoat who persuaded him to place me as I am now?" She picked up the pike, measured it against the helm and staple, moved the helm, and inserted the butt of the pike.

"We see. Perhaps you will do the favor of explaining recent political developments in greater detail."

"With pleasure, once we reach your conducive atmosphere, which I fervently hope will be a warm one." The princess gave a shiver. "And now if you will be so kind as to stand upon this pike-head, I will very soon be free." The dragon did, and it was as she had predicted. A little more scraping with the sword and the staple came up in the princess's hands.

"What now?"

"Now I will take you home."

"Is it far?" asked Ousmani, for she was hungry, cold, and despite her earlier nap, tired.

"Not far," the dragon reassured her. "But I'm afraid it will not be possible for you to walk."

The flight was a short one, and unspectacular. Evening mists obscured the view. Ousmani's only impressions were of rough, rushing winds and a bone-numbing chill, combined with the dull realization that the dragon failed to crash into any unseen obstacles. She discovered as she dismounted that the dragon's wings were quite as oily as they looked.

"You approve?" asked the dragon, as the princess gazed around its lair. A central fire revealed many-fissured walls hung with strands of jewels and a floor of glittering white sand.

"Oh, yes," answered Ousmani, hurrying to the fire. "Now if only—" She stopped suddenly. Perhaps it would be unwise to introduce the idea of eating. Reptiles, she remembered reading, could go for long periods without nourishment.

"If only what?"

The Princess made no answer.

"But, naturally, you do not wish to appear rude. I, by corollary, do not wish to epitomize the insufficient host. If you will examine the leather wallet directly opposite you, lying against that breastplate, I believe its contents will satisfy."

Ousmani seized the leather pouch and untied the drawstring. It held a crumbling lump of leavened bread, a withered onion, and four trapezoidal segments of some unrecognizable dried meat. Pork, probably, Ousmani thought, but she did not in the least care. It had been a day, more than twenty-four hours of the clock, since her last meal. She stuffed a brown slab into her mouth and chewed, suffusing her tongue with a delicious saltiness.

More than twenty years of training in the niceties of court conduct made themselves felt, and Ousmani spoke without thinking. "Sir, will you dine?"

"Not tonight," replied the dragon.

This ambiguous reply renewed Ousmani's uneasiness.

When the dragon saw that the princess had finished her meal, it directed her to a spring hidden in a recess of the cave. She returned refreshed and ready, as bid, to tell her tale.

"Kind Sir—" She faltered. "Or Madame, I know not which, and ought not to assume without scientific proofs—"

"Sir will do," interrupted the dragon.

"Kind Sir, then, know that I am Ousmani, oldest daughter of Musa the Magnificent, third cousin twice removed to the most merciful Caliph of Al-Andalus, Abd-er Raman. I was born of my father's third wife, Omiyinke, who also gave birth during that same night to a son, my brother Tikar. The best lawyers in Cordoba having spent several years arguing the question, they determined that as Tikar's birth preceded mine by some minutes of the clock, our mother's manumission took effect before I emerged into this world. Thus, at the age of ten, I was declared free."

A susurrus escaped from the dragon at this point, and Ousmani glanced suspiciously in his direction. "Most interesting, pray to go on," he assured her. "I was merely venting steam."

"Owing perhaps to these early legalistic associations," the princess continued, "my mind took an unusual turn for a woman. I immersed myself in scholarly pursuits, amassing a notable collection of scrolls, ancient and modern. My mother took no notice of this, being concerned with the advancement of my brother's career at court. She sent various suitors my way, but when they became discouraged by my unfeminine wit, did not press matters.

· "My father, however, is a different kettle of fish." The princess paused, perplexed as to how to elucidate the nature of this paternal bouillabaisse. "Although in almost all respects a worthy man, he has a——a mania. He wants to conquer France," she confessed.

"Languedoc?" inquired the dragon.

"No, *France*. *All* the land beyond these mountains. He says he will be the Hannibal of the Pyrenees." Both were silent a moment out of respect for this monumental folly.

"Hannibal, I believe, failed," said the dragon thoughtfully. "And then, if he must needs conquer, the sea would seem a less toilsome route, would it not?"

"I know. But he will not be dissuaded from his course by any counsel. The Caliph gives him leave, undoubtedly to prevent my father's ambitions from being directed toward the throne. Also, of course, any progress he does make enlarges the Caliphate."

"Of course."

"And I——I must admit I was happy in his misguided happiness, for he never seemed to care what I did. Until now." She rose and circled the fire, standing before the armor of the fallen Frankish knight.

"Upon testimony of some captives that a dragon dwelled among these peaks and that it demanded as sacrifice on each of four certain days of their calendar a virgin, live, and of noble blood, he decided that to secure his safe passage into France he would offer——me." Ousmani kicked a nail-studded gauntlet, nudged it closer to the fire, watched it curl, blackening. "What better use for an heterodox daughter, long past marrying age?"

"You are——?"

"Twenty-six," said the princess. "I never hesitate to tell anyone. The delights of matrimony are beyond me," she added, in a tone of voice that indicated that for their own good they had best maintain themselves in that position.

"I comprehend," said the dragon. "That is to say, your situation now seems clear. Mine, on the contrary, is enormously complicated by your advent, and by the news you bring." He stretched, let loose another audible burst of steam, half unfurled his wings, and folded them back again. "Let us see what wisdom sleep procures." Settling in the sand, he composed himself as if for the night. "Good rest, Ousmani."

Perforce, the princess laid herself down also. The sand was warm, she was weary, and soon she sunk in slumber, regardless of the threat of circumstance.

When she revived, she found herself alone and entirely uneaten. She refreshed herself at the spring and at a little crevice further in, where she hoped the smell would be unnoticeable.

Surely, she reflected, the most reasonable moment to have attacked her would have been during her incapacitation by sleep? Therefore it seemed probable that she should consider herself safe from consumption.

But as she explored the dragon's lair, her critical faculties sharpened, though not as quickly as they would have with her customary morning cup of koffi. The dying fire showed her no excreta, an absence unsurprising given the evidence of her nose. A cat could be just as cleanly, and there *was* all that sand.

More intriguing was the lack of bones. Ximonedes and all the more reliable bestiaries were emphatic in placing carnivorous middens within the confines of their constructor's quarters. There ought to be one here somewhere. Close inspection of former victims' remains might provide valuable information as to the dragon's method of attack. Did it lull its prey or exhale poisonous vapors? And if she found no bones, how might that be interpreted?

Abandoning for the moment speculations on archaic mid-flight feeding reflexes, Ousmani dropped to her knees to examine the dead knight's armor. She found no knives or other weapons, nor anything more useful than a delicate garter of green and purple ribands, attached to the front of a padded jacket. She had heard of this immodest habit of infidel knights, decking themselves with their paramour's linens. She donned the jacket for warmth, deciding that the stains were rust, not blood. As an afterthought she removed the garter and used it to secure her lustrous black curls.

The fire guttered low, almost all embers now. The jewelled walls barely glittered. Ousmani found the leather wallet and fortified herself with more unclean meat, also consuming half the onion. The last flame died, and she was left in a red twilight.

The princess was not afraid of darkness. But conditions made a scientific program of exploration impossible. She moved her inquiries out toward the cave's opening.

It was morning. Quite early; dawn, in fact. Thin, delicate clouds the color of apricots drifted jauntily above and on all sides. And as the Princess discovered by inching out to the edge on her silk-covered stomach, they drifted below as well. The dragon's lair was indeed completely unapproachable by foot. Unretreatable, too, or whatever the complementary verb might be. She was trapped.

Ousmani sat for some time contemplating the prospect of the new day, outwardly so bright and cheerful, yet in its essence bleak. She allowed herself some melancholy, for would not her situation upon escaping from the cave be almost as hopeless as it was now? Her rescuers, followers of the Imam, had been persuaded to deliver her to this holy man's hareem. There she would live, if breath alone meant life. But her mind would stifle, smothered in layers of doctrine like muslin, light but numberless swathes of it falling upon her till she was buried, though yet undead. And her body…she shuddered and drew back from the cave's opening. Best not to dwell on that. There would be a struggle, between the Imam and her father, between her father and the Caliph. Her loins would be the battlefield.

Resolutely, the Princess turned her back on these problems. If life looked to be so insupportable outside the cave, she would concentrate once more on what went on within it.

Her eyes adjusted, and gradually she saw what had escaped her notice on her way to the opening: dim recesses on either side. The one on the left proved to contain logs of wood, stacked in rough pyramids. If the dragon's absence continued long, she might be glad of such a ready supply of fuel. But from what she had observed on the journey into this cold and barbarous land, she would need some sort of kindling as well.

The recess opposite appeared to be smaller, containing only a pair of moldy boots and, further in, a large, open chest overflowing with pale, cylindrical objects. These might do, thought the Princess, if they were composed of some combustible material. Hastening to slip the boots over her saffron satin slippers, which were beginning to show a bit of wear, she shuffled eagerly toward the chest. She found to her delight that its contents were indeed of a highly combustible material, but that they would not do at all for starting up the fire. The chest was filled with books.

Reverently, Princess Ousmani knelt in the sand and began sorting through the dragon's library. She found a number of treatises on obscure points of infidel doctrine;

some extremely unexciting plays; that humorously inexact *History* by Paulus Orosius; *The Book of Ceremonies* from Porphyrogenitus; Dioscorides' *De Materia Medica*, untranslated, and sure to be authentic—alas that she had so little Greek—

She barely glanced up when, some time later, the dragon made its return. "Good day."

"Good day to you, Princess. I see you wasted no time in discovering my true treasure. Will you plunder me of my books, then?"

"Not I, but mice and insects have made a very good start. You should keep a cat," she said, forgetting to whom she spoke. "How came you by all these?"

"The legacy of a cleric, a plump young monk. He traveled here from Narbonne in hopes of converting me to the one true faith."

The words "plump" and "young" recalled to Ousmani that she was in the presence of an anthropophagic animal, an animal that had recently, perhaps only yesterday, slain the paladin whose weskit she now wore. She looked at him closely, searching for signs of hostility or hunger. "Of which one true faith do you speak?"

"Surely there can be only one," said the dragon, bringing his head closer in what she hoped was an inquisitive gesture.

"By definition, yes. But in my experience of religious claims they are all 'true,' and all similarly singular in this truth."

"You have a pragmatic turn of mind."

"Yes," said the princess, rolling up the scroll she held and reaching automatically for another. "And pragmatically speaking I have been throughout my life a follower of the Prophet, Mohammed. But now that I am here with you, I should no doubt subscribe to some more dragonish creed—unless, of course, the monk from Narbonne met with success?"

"Sad to relate, he did not."

"Then you must teach me all of your beliefs."

"I am afraid there will be insufficient time for that exercise."

So it would be soon. "I am not nearly so dull as I look," Ousmani asserted in a voice that quavered slightly. "You might at least attempt..." Words failed her.

"I have assessed the situation," said the dragon, "and find it to be worse than your words led me to fear. It is more than conquest your father desires; it is colonization." A gentle hiss of escaping vapors, a fitful flick of one glistening wing betrayed its agitation. "His train contains not only siege machines but seeds, not just warriors, but women. He has recruited his retainers from the inhabitants of some far Southern mountains; the Atlas range, I gather they are called."

"You discovered all this...how?"

"An outrider was careless, and when I captured him, rather rude. It took much restraint to— But these explanations are unnecessary." He turned his golden gaze full on her face. "I regret to inform you that your stay must end all too abruptly for my tastes."

"Really?" asked Ousmani, fascinated with dread. "It will be quite, quite quick, then?"

"No more than the time it takes to sing a rondelay," the dragon promised. "But first I must turn myself around the right way. I have never really mastered the reverse ascent." With this puzzling assertion the dragon moved into the depths of its lair. Ousmani had only a moment's wonder before it reappeared, this time with its head foremost.

"Be seated, Princess, and we will be off."

Ousmani remained where she was, cross-legged before the chest, arms full of books. She shook her head. "No. I have concluded that it would be unreasonable for me to cooperate with you in my destruction. If you must slay me, it shall be here, no matter what your custom or instincts."

"*Slay* you? You—my dear Princess, how did you manage to arrive at this deduction? Slay you? I am merely attempting to return you to your father's camp."

"I thought you were going to eat me. Like the monk."

"At first, I admit, the thought did enter my head. But soon enough, I had already supped to a sufficiency. Again, you proved so charming that the notion of you as no more than a source of nourishment became offensive. Finally, at my age, consuming large quantities of humans is a luxury I simply can no longer afford."

"Why?"

"Salt. You all have an abominably high salt content. It makes you difficult to resist, but I am convinced that the retention of fluids which inevitably results when I succumb is damaging to my delicate constitution."

While Ousmani digested this novel concept, the dragon slithered to the cave's entrance and peered out, wings flickering nervously. "This will proceed the better," it suggested, "the sooner we depart. You wish to arrive before the evening, do you not?"

The Princess gathered her wits. "On the contrary," she asserted, "I see no necessity for me to arrive there ever. At any time. If you explained this before, I am afraid I missed your arguments, which I hope you will not object to repeat in all their doubtless elegance."

"Why, I—" The dragon's glittering head drew back, and a hiss of steam came from its suddenly dilated nostrils. "It appears obvious. These mountains will soon be filled with your people, who at best will be far more punctilious than the present scattered peasants in offering me a food that I know to be too rich for my health. This while removing my accustomed dietary sources through their husbandry.

"At the worst, they will hunt me down and slaughter me. Their greater concentrations betoken a greater likelihood of success."

Ousmani opened her hands and held them up as if to protect herself from this eventuality. The opportunity for research, the wasted knowledge, the sheer, strange *beauty* of the beast, lost to her father's madness. Not to mention access to a marvelous and altogether unappreciated library. "This must not happen."

The dragon smiled. "I am glad to see you agree. Princess, I must leave, and while it desolates me to deprive myself of your discourse, I cannot take you with me, for I know not where I go. I have some distant relatives in Sind. Also, in Hyperborea..."

"Stay!" said Ousmani. "There is another solution, one that has just now occurred to me. The more I think upon it, the more good I see. But wait—your cleric from Narbonne, had he upon him any implements for writing, or tools with which one might illuminate a book?"

"He did, Princess, though I fail to see what use such scholarly activities will prove in the face of my persecution."

"You will see, though, for I shall show you. First, the tools. Or, no, stay—we must prepare a suitable place in which to work. A desk—I suppose a log will do, if you will roll it near the fire. And speaking of the fire, I must ask you to build it up—"

The dragon proved most pliable when apprised of the details of the Princess's plan. It kept the flames burning brightly through the entire night, sleeping but fitfully. The Princess slept not at all, but toiled without ceasing, for penmanship was not one of her areas of greatest expertise.

"Your name," said Ousmani, when the dragon put its head over her shoulder during one of its wakeful spells. "We ought to include your name, and I don't know what it is."

"My mother called me Bumpsy.... I suppose that will not do."

"No." The princess retied the dead knight's garter, from which tendrils of black hair were escaping to daub themselves with gold and cochineal. "What of your victims? Did they construct any memorable epithets?"

"Their remarks were always decidedly insipid, dear Princess, unlike yours. 'Gaaah,' I believe, was one of the more cogent exclamations."

"Have you no preference as to how you will be styled?"

"I never gave the matter any thought. I am that which I am."

"You are the very seat of reason. I will name you Aegyptus," decided the princess. "Aegyptus was the ancient ruler of a kind and learned land called Egypt. Many defenders of the faith call this place their home. Also, it is warm there."

The proclamation of Aegyptus's conversion to Islam and renunciation of his former dragonish ways was complete by mid-morning. After a lengthy nap, the Princess declared herself much refreshed and not at all hungry. So they set off at once in order to be able to deliver the proclamation during the call for evening prayer.

Unlike her previous ride, this trip afforded the Princess a splendid prospect. Partially obscured by her mount, marguerite-embroidered valleys and dazzling waterfalls fell behind her. The wide-winged shadow of the dragon's passage stained white snows with purple, scattered flocks of sheep and dark-winged birds, rippled over grey fogbanks, growing larger and more distorted with the lowering of the sun.

All too soon, the last straggling slaves and pack animals of her father's train slid into view, plodding wearily through the dust of their superiors. Next she saw a broad, marshy looking meadow full of half-erected tents. Above the noisy wind of their passage, Ousmani asked Aegyptus to circle higher, that they might wait for the most opportune moment unobserved.

It seemed forever coming. The horses, understandably nervous due to the hovering draconic presence, took forever to settle, and the tents were pitched and re-pitched in a futile search for dry ground. In fact, the camp was still in total disarray when the piercing cry of the muezzin floated up to Ousmani's ears. But those with prayer rugs procured them and rolled them out aside those less fortunate, all prostrating themselves on the damp, green ground. All aligned with the hope of the faithful, the source of enlightenment on Earth, with Mecca and the East. "Now," shouted Ousmani in her dragon's ear, and they soared out of the West, swooping over the backs of the astonished congregation.

Circling back, Aegyptus held his huge golden wings fully unfurled, gilding them again with the light of sunset. Impossibly, they seemed to pause, and Ousmani held her breath, expecting to drop helplessly from the sky.

"There is no God but Allah," intoned the dragon into this unnatural silence. "And Mohammed is his prophet." With that he lowered his tail almost to the ground, and uncurling it, deposited the parchment scroll detailing his conversion exactly at the head of the alarmed and immobile Imam. Glancing back as they flew away, Ousmani saw him rise to stand, still reading.

"Success!" she screamed into the wind.

"Perhaps," Aegyptus equivocated. "I have my doubts." Suddenly veering, the dragon flew in an unfamiliar direction. Presently they came to the base of a steep cliff. Aegyptus climbed the updraft, circling like a hawk. Again, it was startlingly quiet.

"You are as much a Muslim as I," she tried to reassure her mount. No, her friend. "More, for you have never consumed alcohol, nor rebelled against the wearing of the veil. The scroll we left for my father tells nothing but the truth. You decided to convert because of my example."

"But even if they believe you, will they not abominate me as an—an abomination?"

Ousmani had considered this carefully, from the instant in which she formulated her plan. "Some might," she replied. "But my third cousin thrice removed, the most merciful Caliph of Al-Andalus, Abd-er Raman III, is of a liberal turn of mind. If I were you, I should prepare myself for guests. Interesting and illustrious ones."

"Of a certainty?"

"Of a complete and utterly ravishing certainty."

"It is necessary, then, that we make adjustments in the economy of our household, do you not think?"

And the dragon and the princess turned homeward to do just that.

The Raineses'

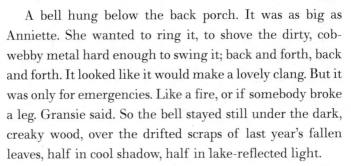

A bell hung below the back porch. It was as big as Anniette. She wanted to ring it, to shove the dirty, cobwebby metal hard enough to swing it; back and forth, back and forth. It looked like it would make a lovely clang. But it was only for emergencies. Like a fire, or if somebody broke a leg. Gransie said. So the bell stayed still under the dark, creaky wood, over the drifted scraps of last year's fallen leaves, half in cool shadow, half in lake-reflected light.

Walking over the bell, you could go lots of ways. The porch went all around the house, though it changed in nature several times during its journey. To the left it widened into a verandah furnished with dusty, deserted deck chairs. To the far right was a door into a long glass passage, which, as Anniette realized one rainy and intuitive afternoon, was really the porch with windows on. It led to the front hall and the archery range.

But usually she went in the doorway that was right, but not so very far right as that. This led to steps that she had promised never to go down, and to another choice: left or right? Right was a tiny yellow room, crowded with narrow wooden chairs, a lace-covered table, and lots of cupboards with glass behind glass doors. So most of the time she went left, into the big broad kitchen.

The kitchen sparkled blue and white. Painted cupboards gleamed, floor to ceiling. The linoleum was skating smooth. On a little platform two tall-backed benches curled up together over a pale blue table-top. That's where Gransie was, with her breakfast.

Gransie had made Anniette her Maypo. Steam rose up from the solid, green-rimmed bowl on the table. Gransie always made her hot cereal for breakfast, even in summertime.

"Your hands clean?"

Anniette nodded. They had to be; she hadn't done anything yet. Just run out into the morning to make sure that it was there.

"Let's see, then."

She held her hands out for inspection, pink palms up.

"The other side. All right. You be sure and wash em, though, after you're through eatin. Specially if you're plannin on playin inside again. I don't want you messin up with none of Miz Raines's things."

Butter melted in her mouth, mixed with cream and sugar. "I want to go swim. In the lake. Can I?"

Gransie frowned. "You better wait. After an hour you can go in. I'll let you know. Stay where I can see you until then."

"Yes, Gransie." Anniette finished her cereal and washed her bowl and hands in the low kitchen sink, then headed back outside. This time she went through the "morning" room, out onto the verandah. Cement steps swept down to the lawn, cradled by fieldstone arms. Anniette walked along the curving stones. The sun struck through distant trees, making pretty patterns on the big white house and the empty, weedy lawn. At the end of the steps she looked around, deciding what to do. The rose arbor beckoned. She jumped to the ground and ran obediently toward it.

The rose arbor was an arching trellis of soft grey and white wood. The roses were just beginning. Later in the summer they smelled so sweet and sent spent petals drifting down, covering the seats. But now they were secret, dark green and closed.

Anniette picked one. She sat down and tried to peel back the first layer with her nails.

"It won't work. What you're trying to find isn't in there, yet."

Anniette looked up. It was a tall, grey-clad woman with straight brown hair pulled back in a bun. She had a white scarf around her shoulders. She was one of them from next door.

"I'm not trying to find the flower," Anniette explained. "I'm trying to find what makes the flower."

"A budding botanist."

"What's that, a botanist?"

"A botanist is someone who studies plants." The lady took the other seat. She did it without brushing aside the twigs and leaves lying there. "Someone who dedicates their whole life to the study of plants."

"Unh-unh," said Anniette. "That's different than what I want."

"Really?" said the lady, sounding like grown-ups always did when they thought that she was cute. "What exactly is it that you want, then? Do you know?"

Anniette thought how to say it. "I want to know what makes things. What makes everything happen."

The lady laughed. Not in a mean way, but she laughed. "A little colored philosopher-girl. How fine. Things have truly changed. And we actually are related?"

There were layers of pink, packed tight under the green. They were thin, pressed way down from what they were going to be. She pulled one petal off, held it up to look through at the sun. The lady was gone.

She had on her swimsuit. Gransie said it was okay. As she walked, tiny wrinkles of blue and green stretched and bunched together in a way that pleased her. This was the favorite swimsuit she'd ever had, with seahorses like in Daddy's aquarium.

Dirt steps boxed with big boards led down to the lake. It was called Maple Lake. Most of the trees were on the other end. This side had reeds and lily pads and that strange, hollow grass that squeaked when you pulled it apart.

She went out to the end of the dock and waved up at the house. Gransie waved back from the kitchen window. She was not supposed to go in past the bleach bottle buoy. Maybe later Uncle Troy would come by and take her out to fish.

She sat down, careful of splinters in the weathered wood. She slipped her bare feet into the dark green water. It was cold. Maybe she would just sit there with her feet in for a while. An enormous lavender dragonfly streaked past her head to land glittering on the tip of a nearby reed. The reed, bent under the insect's weight, arched and quivered in the breeze.

The sound of a car engine swooped up the driveway and shut off. A car door slammed. She looked up. Uncle Troy was taking a suitcase out of the trunk of his car. It must be some of the Raineses. She couldn't see who. She waited, swirling the water with her toes. They would be down here soon, if it was anybody nice. She wasn't supposed to get in their way.

Footsteps on the dock. "Anniette, is that really you?" Miss Margaret came up and sat down beside her.

"'Course it is," Anniette said. Grown-ups.

"I didn't recognize you; you've grown so big since the last time I saw you."

"Thanks," Anniette said. Trying to be polite she added, "You look like you've grown too." That wasn't quite right; it sounded like she was calling Miss Margaret fat. She didn't know what to say to make things better, so she shut up.

Miss Margaret was quiet too, for a while, then went on. "Well, I *have*. I've been at college for a whole year, now. But Mama still fussed about me staying in Chicago all alone while she and Daddy went to meet Bruce in New York. So we compromised. Do you know what that means, Anniette?" Anniette shook her head no. "It means we neither of us got what we really wanted. She didn't get to drag me to New York and dangle me in front of all her phoney-baloney friends, and I didn't get to stay in Chicago with Roger."

"Who's Roger?"

"Oh, he's someone *very* special! He's a painter, Anniette." Miss Margaret moved her round, serious face closer to show how important this information was.

"Pictures?"

"Yes. Wonderful pictures. Oh, Anniette, maybe he'll come here, maybe you'll get to meet him. Mama didn't say he couldn't. She and Daddy and Bruce won't be up till the end of next week, at the earliest."

Good. She still had time to explore the house. She looked up at the sky. Hazy clouds melted imperceptibly into the blue. Maybe tomorrow it would rain, and she wouldn't feel so bad for staying inside.

Uncle Troy came down the stairs. His white T-shirt had little dark spots of sweat around the collar and big ones under his arms. "Your bags all up in the Rose Room, Miss Margaret. If there's anything else?"

"Not at the moment, Troy. I might ask you to go into town to pick some things up at the drugstore; I packed in kind of a hurry, and I'm not sure what I missed."

"If it's all right with you, then, I'll just use the boat and take Anniette out on the lake."

"Fishing? Wrong time of day for that, isn't it?"

"Well…"

"Tell you what, save the fishing for evening. See if Aunt Nancy's got anything for you to do. I'm sure she can find something. This place is getting to be a wreck."

"Yes, ma'am. But Anniette…"

"Oh. Well, Anniette, you're going swimming, aren't you?"

Anniette nodded. There was nothing more to say. She slipped into the water and dog-paddled away.

The gentle mutter of rain through the eaves troughs woke her. Her room was high up, a turquoise-colored place full of bunks and cots. Lots of people used to stay there and help out around the place. But now there was only Gransie, and sometimes Uncle Troy drove over from Paw Paw.

Gransie stayed downstairs as much as she could because of her rheumatism. So during her visits Anniette had the whole room to herself. She slept in the top bunk, opposite the window.

Scorning the knotty pine ladder, she jumped down onto the sea-grey carpet, then crossed to the window seat. The sash was already up. All she had to do was rest her forearms on the white enameled sill, press her forehead against the dark, rusty screen, and breathe.

Cool. The scent of grass, of wet clover. The exhalations of worms, writhing in the earth. And closer, sad, pungent mildew rose into the air, remembering itself from other rainy days.

Clouds hung low over the lake, almost seemed as though they would touch the trees. The rain would be here for a while, for all day probably.

She put on her clothes: red corduroys and her black-and-yellow-checked cowboy shirt. There were stars sewn over the pockets and pearl snaps instead of buttons. A shirt to have adventures in.

She went down to the back porch and stood over the bell. The rain was louder here, falling in fine streams from the porch roof, splashing on the sidewalk. Breakfast smelled good. She washed her hands and considered how to approach the day's project: top to bottom, or bottom to top? Miss Margaret wasn't up yet, so downstairs first, she decided.

After they ate Gransie headed to the little yellow room, so she went into the "morning" one. Bare boards stretched before her. There used to be a big pretty rug here, with so many colors she didn't know all their names.

There was still a dark spot on the floor where it used to keep off the sun.

The wall to her left was made up of glass doors with sparkly handles, so that one was not worth checking. But to her right square panels of wood promised great things. She pressed along the trim with patient, sensitive fingers. There would be a whir, a click. Something would give way, and a new aspect of the house would be revealed, mysterious facet of a familiar stone.

She came to the end of the wall without discovering anything. Maybe higher up...but she couldn't reach all the way unless she had a stool. She would have to see about that later.

The bathroom next. Black and yellow, like her shirt. The tile gleamed royally. The shiny black toilet was just a little bit scary.

"Did you find it yet?" The boy leaned against the sink's butter-yellow pedestal.

"No," she answered. "I just started. Is it in here?"

"I'm going to teach you a song."

"Okay." She had learned from past experience, it was best to let them take the lead. Some questions they just ignored.

"It's a very bad song. Promise you won't tell anybody that I taught it to you, or I'll get in trouble."

She felt a thrill of guilt as she hunkered down next to him, shoes scuffing damp echoes from the floor. "Promise."

"It goes like this:

Well, it's wine, wine, wine
that makes you feel so fine
in the corps (in the corps), in the corps (in the corps);
Well, it's wine, wine, wine
that makes you feel so fine
in the good old actor's co-o-orps!"

Anniette loved it. The boy's voice went down real low when he sang in the core, in the core. Then it swooped all around like a circus band on the last word. Very satisfying. Too bad it was bad. It would be a wonderful song to sing real loud while marching around. She learned all the verses.

In the library she pulled all the books from the shelves one by one, then put them back. Nothing moved or turned or revolved. Nothing lurked behind the red leather couch except dust and old chew toys left from Turk's last sojourn. The Raineses didn't bring him up much anymore. She asked Gransie why as she ate her bologna sandwich in the kitchen.

"Gettin old," Gransie said. "Same as me, he just doesn't want to move around much anymore. Eat your salad; it's good for you."

Anniette pulled a pickled bean from the crystal bowl next to her plate. One was enough, she decided, as the vinegar bit its way up through her sinuses, bringing tears to her eyes. A sip of Kool-Aid, a bite of bologna and mayonnaise, and she was all better.

"Gransie, can I have a stool?"

"A stool? What you want a stool for?"

How much to explain? "I want to reach up on the walls, in the morning room. Up where that pledge sticks out."

"The pledge? You mean the *ledge*, don't you? Where they keep the keys?" She nodded. "What on earth do you want up there?"

Anniette paused. Should she tell? There was no other way to get what she wanted. "I want to find a secret passageway," she said.

Gransie snorted, pushed herself away from the table, and rose ponderously. "Child, however do you manage to fill your head with such nonsense? Must be all those books you read."

Anniette lowered her eyes in shame. It was a silly idea. She was a silly girl to have had it.

Metal legs scraped lightly on the linoleum. She looked up. Gransie was pulling the white enameled step-stool from its place next to the fridge. "That room could use some dustin anyway, I guess." She reached into a drawer for an apron. "Now don't you go touchin any Miz Raines's things, Anniette. She forgave you over that leopard, but if you ever break a real expensive piece, I don't know what'll happen. Some of those things are real nice. Worth more than I make in a month." She tied the apron on Anniette, folding it up at the middle so it wasn't too long.

"Now." Anniette stood still for inspection. "Go get me a head-scarf," said Gransie.

She shot up the stairs and almost collided with Miss Margaret, talking and laughing on the telephone. "Sorry," said Anniette. Miss Margaret patted her on the head to show that it was all right and went on talking.

"Honestly, Roger," she said to the receiver. "You really should come up. What does it take to convince you? It's the most frightful old place—you'd love it. It was actually a stop on the Underground Railroad. Just a moment, dear. Anniette, is there something you wanted?"

Anniette realized she had no reason to be standing there besides her utter amazement. She shook her head and continued slowly down the hall to her room.

"Oh, that was just our maid's little granddaughter. The cutest thing. Yes, Nancy's been with us practically forever, like family really…." Anniette heard Margaret's voice trailing off behind her as she walked away. But there was nothing more about the Underground Railroad. She tried to remember all about it, what she knew from school. It was how they got colored people out of the South, away from Slavery. White people helped the colored. They had to; it must have been a lot of work to build so many tunnels and lay all that track.

She rummaged in her drawer for several minutes before she remembered what she was supposed to be looking for. A scarf. Here was one, white with yellow flowers. She carried it downstairs, deep in thought.

Gransie tied the scarf over her pigtails to keep off the dust. She grumbled that the scarf was so light and would surely show the dirt, but she didn't send Anniette back for another. She gave her two cloths and a bottle of lemon oil and showed her what to do.

The panels did look much nicer after they'd been polished. She liked the candy shop smell she spread around herself. And best of all she had a perfect excuse to press and finger every inch of wood on the walls. Only, there was no response.

She had to leave the stool behind when she went into the yellow room. It just wouldn't fit. All that glass. It made Anniette nervous, since the leopard broke. She was very careful, really she was, but still she dropped the goblet.

Not because she got startled. Nothing was sudden like that; first there was a dry, sweet, scent, like burning flowers, and then a golden flame. The dark lady showed up slowly, like a shadow growing from the light of the candle that she held. There was nothing sudden or scary about the way she came or how she looked. But looking, Anniette forgot to hold onto the glass. It fell and rolled along the white lace table cloth, turning over and over till it came to the other end, to where the lady stood.

The candle wavered and sank, so Anniette could see the lady's smooth, dark face. Not one that she had ever seen before. Her chin was sharp and pointy, like Anniette's.

"You the maid?" Her voice was sharp and pointy, too.

"No."

"You live here, though, don't you?"

"No, I'm on a visit.

"How long?"

"All summer, if I want. Mommy says—"

The lady interrupted. "How long?"

"The end of August, when school's gonna—"

"How *long*? *How long*? *HOW*—" The lady stopped herself from shouting and looked down at the table. "Rufus gave his word. It ain't broke. It ain't. Yet." She raised her candle and looked at Anniette again. "You come on along. I can show you."

When Anniette got to that end of the table, the lady and the light were gone. But she could still see by the windows. Like the lady said, it was all right. The only marks on the goblet were ones that were supposed to be there: flowers, carved twisting up the curving sides.

Gransie grumbled, but Anniette was able to go over the kitchen without getting too much in the way of dinner. Miss Margaret had a tray in her room. After they ate, Anniette had to bring it down.

Then she tried the archery range. There weren't many possibilities there, so she finished quickly and went to bed. As she knelt to pray she remembered what Gransie was saying as she left Anniette to her task that afternoon. Grown-ups always said strange things, especially as they got older and closer to being one of them. Like Grandfather. But this stuck in her head and went along with the prayers. She had said something like in church: "Not mine, but Thine, oh Lord." Then: "But still, it's such a shame. For the sake of the child alone, it's a sin, and a cryin shame."

A cryin shame. Not mine, but thine. Oh, lord.

It rained again next morning. Miss Margaret ate in the kitchen with Anniette and Gransie. She had cornflakes. She was up early so Uncle Troy could take her to the station to meet her friend.

So Anniette could explore upstairs.

The Red Room. It was so pretty. She always wanted to sleep in here. Once, she did. It was in winter, and this room had a fireplace that still worked. She checked there first, running her hands over the cool, rough stone. No. And the closet was nothing but a closet. Disappointed, she solaced herself with the feel of the silky red curtains hanging down over the bed. They rustled, whispering of beauty. She rubbed her face in them, wished she could wear them, nothing but red silk, like a lady, a queen.

"So. This is what comes of recklessness."

It was a man. One of them? Another new one? Or was Uncle Troy back already with Miss Margaret and her friend? Couldn't be.

The man smiled under his curly moustache. He walked away from her, toward the fireplace, then turned and looked back. He wore funny old clothes, like an ad for an ice-cream parlor. Them. "Well," he said, "at least you are a fairly good-looking pickaninny. If I do say so myself. Rachel was true unto me, and I was true unto my word."

"What's a pickaninny?"

"That you can see me at all is proof, I suppose." The man frowned. "You haven't seen *her*, have you? Rachel? Rachel?" His voice faded and he was gone.

How come they were around so much right now? She searched the other rooms listlessly, strangely disturbed. The one with the green wallpaper, called the Nursery. The Rose Room, where Miss Margaret's bags still waited to be unpacked. The Study. The Master Bedroom, white and untouchable. All were void of mystery. She gave up and retreated to her room. As she put her hand on the doorknob she suddenly thought, "It might be in here."

She went straight to the window seat. With growing sureness she searched along the woodwork, pressing, pressing.... Ah. A small section of trim moved under her touch. She looked around the room. No dim, dusty openings, no magically appearing stairways. The change was much smaller and closer. Below the seat's blue-green cushion a wide crack showed in the enameled wood. Anniette put the cushion on the floor and jammed her fingers into the crack. She pulled. A board flipped up. Two boards.

She was looking in someone's hidey-hole. Nice, though not as exciting as a secret passage. She reached into the darkness and pulled out a wooden box, tied around with pale blue ribbon. Underneath the box was a fan like ladies used in church. Only this fan was made of cloth. Silk, deep red silk, like the curtains in the Red Room.

She untied and opened the box. Papers. She could read print. But these were mostly letters. The writing was sharp and difficult looking, not the round, loose script she had sneaked a look at in a third-grader's book. Regretfully, she set the letters aside.

Underneath was something mostly printed, with words and numbers written in. The printing was fancy, like on the cover of Gransie's bible. She decided the short word at the top was d-e-e-d, deed.

A deed was what you did, if you were a boy scout or a shining knight. Maybe it would be exciting to read, but the alphabets were all twiney and hooked together, and anyway, what about those numbers? What would they have to do with an adventure?

"Lot 392...16 circle East...by 90 circle South...3 chains..." It didn't make sense. She scanned the page for what did. "I, Ruff-us Raines, do grant, war-rant and con-" con-something.

The word Rachel appeared several times. Like the man had said. She knew how that name looked, print or cursive. It was her own. Anniette Rachel Hawkes.

The rain stopped around noon.

Miss Margaret was back for lunch. She ate on the verandah with her friend, Roger. He had big yellow teeth. Anniette didn't like him, but that didn't count. He was going to stay in the Red Room.

Uncle Troy and Gransie and Anniette ate in the kitchen, after Miss Margaret and her friend. While they were still having their dessert Miss Margaret stuck her head in and asked Uncle Troy if he would mind terribly getting the boat ready to go out. He said no, of course.

Anniette went with him, for lack of anything better to do. The papers were still up in her room, in their box. Later, when Gransie wasn't so busy, she would ask her to look at them. They were probably even important. They just weren't a train station.

The boathouse was spooky in a nice way. The boat made big booming sounds as Uncle Troy lowered it to the water. The sun came out while they were still inside, shining in little star-shapes through holes in the ramshackle walls. They sagged so much that Uncle Troy had to duck as he rowed out under the lake side.

Miss Margaret had changed into a pretty white dress. She was smiling and said that Anniette could come along. Anniette ran back to the boathouse for a life jacket. They smelled bad, but Gransie wouldn't let her on the lake without one, even though she could swim.

The sun was all the way out to stay. Anniette relaxed in the warmth, watched the water lilies unfolding in light that the rain had newly purified. She was happy. So she sang.

"Well, it's wine, wine, wine
that makes you feel so fine
in the corps (in the corps), in the—"

"Anniette!" Miss Margaret snapped. "What's that you're singing? Where did you learn that song?"

She had promised. She couldn't tell her. She felt really bad, since Miss Margaret had let her come in the boat.

"Speak up, child."

"What's wrong?" asked Roger. "Insubordination in the ranks?"

Margaret laughed. It didn't sound like she thought anything was funny. "Not that it matters, only it seemed sort of...creepy."

"What seemed creepy?"

"That song she was singing. I suppose she could have learned it anywhere. It's just that I associate it so strongly with Cousin Freddy; I guess because he taught it to me when we were kids here."

"So what?" said Roger. "So he taught it to the help, too."

"Hardly," said Miss Margaret. "He died three years before Anniette was born."

"Oh."

"As I said, it's not important. I just…wondered."

"I taught her," said Uncle Troy suddenly from where he sat rowing. "Mr. Fred taught it to me and I taught it to her."

Everybody in the boat stared at him. Miss Margaret and her friend looked like they had forgotten he was even there. Anniette stared too, because Uncle Troy hardly ever talked unless you asked him something. And he never told lies.

Without another word from anyone the boat returned to shore.

After supper Anniette sat at the top of the stairs, looking down. Down. How could she have been so stupid? The train station was *underground*. That's why they called it the *Underground Railroad*. And here she'd been looking for the entrance on the second floor.

The problem was, she wasn't allowed to go into the cellar.

She always tried to be good.

Gransie was with some ladies from church. They were writing invitations to the ice-cream social. They wouldn't let her help, even though she colored real good. And she couldn't show the papers to Gransie while she was having company.

There was nothing else to do.

There was no place else to look.

She could hear Roger and Miss Margaret talking on the landing. He said, "Parrish is a fine illustrator. But that's all he is." She said, "I suppose you're right. Still, it's so pretty."

They must be talking about the girl on the swing, Anniette decided. Anniette didn't know who the girl was. Not one of them, like a lot of pictures in the house.

"Pretty. A pointless, stupid word. A shallow compliment. I, I must confess, *I* am drawn to—the depths." There was a heavy silence, then the sound of clothes rubbing together. Kissing noises. "Tonight?"

"Roger, I—"

"You can't mean to make me wait. Maggie, I came here on trust. I came all the way from Chicago, tourist class. Maggie, my dear, you…you gave me your *word*."

Maggie was Miss Margaret. Had to be. No one else was there.

"I…Roger, I know, and my word means so much to me—"

More kissing noises.

"Nothing has changed, has it, darling? No, I can feel it. You are still the same true, dear, loyal, trustworthy soul. Oh, Maggie—"

"All right, Roger."

"You *will* come?"

"Yes. It's sure to be safe. Nancy never comes upstairs any more, and Anniette will be on the other side of the house, in the old servant's quarters. I'll come."

The next day was disappointingly sunny. Neither Miss Margaret nor Roger seemed to want to do much with their breakfast. They came down, long after Anniette had enjoyed her Maypo, and moped around the morning room. Gransie suggested a game of croquet, but Roger thought the lawn needed cutting, and Uncle Troy wasn't going to be around till later.

After a while Anniette saw them heading for the rose arbor. She wondered if the lady from next door would be there. She seemed to show up there mostly, maybe because her house burned down so long ago there were trees growing up inside the place where the basement used to be.

It was Thursday. Time to change the beds. Anniette offered to do it and save Gransie's rheumatism from the stairs. Gransie took her to the linen closet off the cellar steps.

"Gransie," she asked. "What's more important? To keep a promise or to do what you really think is right?"

"Well, chicken, you sure do ask some tough questions. Where'd you get this one?"

"I was just thinking..."

"Thinkin, hunh?" Gransie picked up a stack of sheets and placed it over Anniette's arms. "Well, when it comes to questions like that, time to stop thinkin and start prayin. God will let you know. He answers every prayer."

Anniette reflected on God as she carried the piles of linen up the stairs. It took her two trips. Basically, she decided, God was one of them, only really old and related to all the people on the earth. So everybody could see him and talk to him if they tried. But you had to try hard, because he was so old. Was it something she was capable of? She didn't know.

The boy came in while she changed Miss Margaret's bed.

"Did you find it?"

"No, but I think I've got it figured out where to look."

"Pretty keen, huh?"

Sometimes she wondered if they heard a word she said. "Is your name Fred?" she asked.

"You might say that, yes."

"I almost got in trouble over that song myself."

"Nifty, isn't it? *Well it's gin, gin, gin—*"

"Don't worry, I didn't tell." She had never said anything about them to grown-ups. She didn't know exactly why. She tried to imagine explaining to Gransie. It came out like a conversation with one of them: frustrating.

Freddy followed her to the Red Room. A note was taped to the door. It was in cursive, and she couldn't read it. She opened the door. The Red Room was a mess. Blankets and clothes were tossed all over. It looked like somebody had had a fight. One of them got a nose bleed. A red-brown stain showed where they'd slept.

She thought maybe she should still just change the sheets. But when she pulled them off she saw how a little blood had soaked through to the mattress pad. So she went downstairs. Freddy was gone; she hadn't seen him since opening the door.

Gransie was in her room. It was really part of the kitchen, where they used to keep some food. The bed was small and dipped down in the middle, even though Gransie wasn't sleeping there right now.

She was sleeping in her chair. Soft zuzzing sounds came from where she sat. They mixed with the static and singing voices from the radio:

Just a closer walk with thee;

Grant it Jesus, if you please...

Gransie's feet were out of their shoes, resting on a pillow. They were a funny shape, with bumps. Bunyumps, they were called. Anniette decided she could find another mattress pad herself. She closed the door quietly. Not to be sneaky, but so Gransie could stay asleep.

The part of the linen closet she needed to get into was right over the cellar stairs. Maybe she could reach it if she took the stool down and stood on it on the landing. She was careful dragging it across the floor. No marks on the linoleum, and no noise.

It was harder taking it down the three steps to the landing. And when she got up on it, the shelf where Gransie kept the mattress pads was still out of reach. She could see them, but....

She could also see the shadows at the bottom of the stairs.

She sat on the landing, to rest and think. Her feet were on the next step down. Then one slipped and wound up on the one right after that.

She stood up. Six more steps to go.

But it was bad. Uncle Troy had made her cross her heart not to go there. It was dangerous, with bare electrics.

But how else was she going to find what she was looking for? The iron rails pulled her down.

Five more steps. Four more.

She stopped. A bitter smell came to her now: the captive earth. Wet, but never growing anything. A grey, unpromising weight upon the air. Maybe there was nothing. Nothing to be found. She would be breaking her word. For nothing.

She was ready to take the next step anyway. But suddenly there was a light. She had to turn around and see what from.

The lady with the candle was standing on the landing. "Don't tell me you ain't found it yet," she said. "Guess I better show you, then. Come on up."

"Oh," said Anniette. "I thought it was down here." She climbed the shallow stairs, happy she wasn't going to do anything wrong.

"I kep it," the lady said. "Hid it away." She shrugged. "Didn' know what good it was when he give it to me, but I kep it anyway. Long as Hawkeses was livin here, it appeared to be some hope." Outside, a car door slammed. Footsteps drummed on the porch. "Now I guess we'll see."

Uncle Troy opened the door and stared at her. At the lady, not at Anniette. They didn't like that, so the lady wasn't there anymore. Then Uncle Troy picked Anniette up in a big hug and asked if she was okay.

He didn't even listen to her explanation about the stool. He got her a glass of Kool-Aid and made her sit down at the kitchen table to drink it. Grape.

She heard some of their talking in Gransie's room. "Oh, no," said Gransie's voice. "Not the whole family."

"They were all three on the passenger list."

"Poor Margaret. Last to carry the family name…"

Nobody said anything for a while. Then Uncle Troy started again. "Mom. I—I saw Rachel. She was talkin to Anniette."

"Troy, you know she's been at rest in the arms of her savior these fifty years."

"But maybe she wanted to tell us where she put—"

"If it is meant to be, it will come to pass, through the grace of our Lord."

"But—"

"Anniette!" It was Gransie, calling her. She ran to the doorway. Gransie was putting on her shoes. When she looked up, Anniette saw that she was crying. "Fingers off the woodwork. Go find Miss Margaret. Tell her the Sheriff's comin round, there's been a bad accident."

Anniette stood on the verandah outside the morning room. The rose arbor was empty. Roger was on the beach. She saw him from the steps, throwing pebbles at the bleach-bottle buoy and missing. He was by himself.

She found Miss Margaret at the place next door. The lady from there was talking and talking. "...and so that's the connection. My half-sister married your great-great uncle, Chester Raines." Miss Margaret didn't seem to hear what she was saying.

She didn't give much sign of hearing what Anniette said, either, except to drift away through the trees in the direction of the house.

Anniette apologized. Just because they didn't always tell you what you wanted was no reason to be rude.

"Oh, don't concern yourself," the lady said. "Not every-one is as equanimous as you are. That means," she went on before Anniette could ask, "that not everyone is able to take the situation in stride. In fact, most are not able to take it in at all."

Like Uncle Troy, she thought. He got scared when he saw the lady with the candlestick. Which reminded her to wonder why he lied, why he told Miss Margaret that about the song.

"The truth," said the lady, "can sometimes lead to unpleasant conclusions. As a potential philosopher, you should learn to understand this.

"I detest this spot," she added. "I always have." And Anniette was left alone.

❦

Vacation had just barely begun, but already it was time to leave. Gransie was riding the train down to Chicago with Miss Margaret for the funerals. Roger had already

gone; he left the same day the Sheriff came. Miss Margaret didn't seem to miss him. The last time Anniette saw
her she was standing on the verandah, staring out across
the lawn. She was all dressed in black, stiff and quiet.

Mommy came and picked her up at lunch, so Gransie
and Miss Margaret could leave with Uncle Troy in time to
catch the 2:45. Anniette hated cars; usually she got sick in
them. But she was so glad to be with Mommy again she
forgot about that. Mommy let her lie with her head on
her lap, on the soft beige skirt she wore. Just before she
drifted off to sleep, Anniette remembered that she'd left
the box behind.

Most of the rest of that summer she spent at the library, downtown. It was cool in there, like the lake, and she
found plenty to explore. Between columns covered with
rose and olive tiles, she entered books on butterflies, books
on boogie-woogie, books on Buddha, books on books.

Later, other libraries led her further on her search to
understand "what makes the flower." The seed it comes
from, or the light toward which it grows? By the time she
was ready to leave the University it seemed to Anniette
these were the two most likely choices. Trying to decide,
she examined her past, her seed. She came to no conclusion. But she learned many things.

For instance, she found out that for her forty years of
service to the Raineses, Gransie received a lump sum of
$500. She lived with Uncle Troy in Paw Paw on this and
her Social Security, helping out at church till she came to
rest in the arms of her savior.

The deed in the hidey-hole had probably been valid—
at the time it was drawn up. And the law student Anniette
talked to thought that because Rachel's descendants continued to live there, they might have had "visible, notori-

ous, and open possession" of the place. If the deed had ever been registered at court, if it could be proved that the Raineses conspired to prevent their claim, if....

But Miss Margaret had sold the place as soon after the funerals as was humanly possible. The buyer paid an extremely low price, since it was rumored to be haunted. The price was low, but the buyer didn't exactly get a bargain, for the house burned down before he could set foot on the property.

The bell never rang.

Bird Day

We sat in a circle on the side of the street. Some of us had lawn chairs, or folding chairs we'd brought out from our houses. Stepstools, even. We had a bunch of different kinds of seats we were sitting in.

This was the day to commune with birds. It was a beautiful, cool, early spring morning. The pavement smelled clean and damp.

I was wearing a warm, comfortable caftan, embroidered with silver and dark colors. There were a lot of interesting-looking birds flying around low and purposefully, looking for the person they had a message for. It wouldn't do any good to get someone else's message, or to worry too much whether or not one was ever coming. We relaxed and watched the birds, and talked with neighbors who stopped by our circle. There were a few empty chairs. Eventually, someone might sit in them.

Suddenly, a bird approached me. It was a sort of bird I'd never seen before, a large duck with a sheeny, blue back, the blue of a clear sky just before dawn. I'd never seen a bird like this before, but I knew it was mine. It hovered awkwardly in front of me and gripped my index fingers with its webbed feet, pulling me. My heart lifted and I stood up.

The duck flew backwards, its feet still wrapped around my fingers. I went with it. It let go and turned to fly forward, and I followed it out of the city.

I wasn't about to let it get away from me. This was definitely my bird.

I saw a Great Auk from the corner of my eye, huge, black-and-white, with a broad, brightly-colored bill. It flew down a side road, but I stayed focused on my bird.

The paved road had turned into well-graded brown dirt, dark and wet. I saw houses that people were building: open, pleasing structures. I lost sight of my bird, but went on in the direction it had taken, out of the city. I stayed focused on it, even when I couldn't see it anymore.

I heard the soft beating of its wings and knew it flew on before me.

A stream joined me, running alongside the road. Daffodils joined the stream. Together, we left the houses behind.

I kept walking. I couldn't see my bird anywhere. I closed my eyes. The stream murmured to itself. The only beating I heard was my heart.

How could I catch up? Without wings, how could I fly?

I opened my eyes again and looked around. Where was I? Maybe this was where my bird had been bringing me. Maybe it had left me where I was supposed to be.

Tall trees with their leaves just beginning arched over the road. It was really more a wide path than a road, now. It moved among the tall trees slowly, one way, then another, quite casually. As if it knew where it was going, but felt no rush to get there.

Filter House

This didn't seem like a place to stop at, an end.

Maybe my bird had left me because I would be able to figure out everything on my own from here.

I saw sky through the trees. I went at the path's pace till I came to their edge.

It was quite an edge. Only clouds beyond. Very beautiful clouds, with popcorn-colored crests and sunken rifts full of shadows like grey milk.

It was evening already. I could tell by the light. I had been following my bird all day. How had that happened? I had lost track of the time.

That didn't matter, though.

My bird did matter. And its message for me.

It had to be around here somewhere.

The clouds' lighter parts changed and became the color of the insides of unripe peaches. Against them rose black flecks, the flocks of birds flying away from us. Away once more, until next year.

Silence stirred the hairs on the nape of my neck. Silence and a small wind fanned them so they extended upward. And outward. Up and out. Above my head, my bird flew forward, over the edge.

I went with it.

Maggies

~ ⟳ ~

Tata's skin was golden. Sometimes she let me help her feed and brush it. She showed me how my first worlday on New Bahama.

I was way off schedule. After a couple of hours I couldn't stand to stay in my room, let alone in bed, pretending to sleep. I had masturbated all I wanted. My desk was on, but empty. No matter what my father said, I had to get up, run the small circuit of the station's corridors.

Some were smoothly familiar, plasteen walls like any ship or tube. Others, where the station's prefab had burrowed into New Bahama's unpolished bedrock, seemed sullen in their unreflectiveness.

I wasn't going to think about things, about my mother, whether my father really wanted me to come here and live with him, would she ever get better, if I could have done anything to help. I just wanted to walk. One flight down, generators, locks, stores, vats. Big, smelly objects I'd already been warned to keep away from. The opposite flight of steps back up, kitchen lab, private rooms, all with curtains closed.

On my third go-round, though, Tata's curtain hung to one side, offering a glimpse of her tiny living space. Her skin gleamed in its frame. She stood behind it, fussing with one of the securing ties. When she saw me, she signed a welcome. I hesitated, and she signed again. I was pretty sure she was the same one who'd helped me with my luggage, so I went in.

She showed me the port where the nutrient bulb fitted into the skin, and the way to squeeze it—slowly, steadily.

Her skin's thick, retracted facemask repulsed me— maybe because I'd seen pictures of how the things flattened and brutalized their wearer's features. And of course I knew not to touch the skin's underside. Even though I hadn't been taught all the history of its abuse, I understood that I could hurt Tata there. I didn't want to do that.

But I fell in love with the alveolocks, her skin's fur. They rippled so softly beneath my brush. Later, I learned that these rhythmic contractions aided a skin's oxy uptake and diffusion. That night, and for a long time after, all I cared about was their beauty.

I had a heavy hand with the protective oil. When you're young, you don't realize how precious things are; you think there will always be plenty, at no cost. And that's how it should be—when you're young.

So Tata never corrected me when I oiled her skin so lavishly that clear droplets splashed down upon the metal frame where it was strung. She only guided my hand gently, so that my over-enthusiastic brushing wouldn't pull the golden fur out by its roots. I felt proud of my handiwork.

Tata didn't really need my help, though. Her skin had plenty of time to reoxygenate without the brush's added stimulation; she didn't wear it much.

She was supposed to go out into the Nassea every Day, supervising my father's other maggies as they planted coral buds on the submerged mountaintops of New Bahama.

But the others didn't need her watching them, telling them what to do. Terraforming work is simple, though hard; repetitive, dangerous, but nothing that requires any initiative. They were used to it; it's the sort of thing they had been engineered to do in the first place, before the rebellion.

My father plotted the maps, which the hull window displayed. The maggies had no trouble reading them. They filled their quotas, mostly. Dad's team was a little ways behind all but two of the other stations. I don't know if there would have been fewer problems if Tata had gone out there as often as her contract said she was supposed to. Dad didn't think so.

Tata wore her skin once a worldday, swimming in it through the Nassea to Quarters. I went with her, once, fifteen Days after I arrived. That is, I followed her in Dad's scooter. Squirming to keep from slipping down its couch's gentle curves, I wondered what sort of passenger its designers had had in mind. Not me; I was so short I could barely keep my face in the navigation display's headsup field. But not Dad either. I have great spatial-relational skills for a girl, and I could see he'd have a hard time fitting in here. Which was probably why he never used the thing.

Not that that would keep him from punishing me for borrowing it.

I struggled back to the headsup. Tata's skin lost its golden color in the infrared, but it gained a luminescent trail, a filigree of warmth flowing from her skin's alveolets as they dissipated her waste gases. Fizzing like a juice-tab in the murky silence of the Nassea, my father's chief maggie dropped down towards Quarters.

Or so I assumed. All I saw in the headsup were a few patches of heat, hardly more than a supercolony of microbes could produce.

I settled into the sediment and switched on the visibles. The headsup compensated quickly, and I saw an opening in the silver egg-shape of Quarters, cycling shut on shadows. The scooter's lights shone steadily into the diminishing hatch. Tata had to know I was out here, now, if she hadn't sensed me earlier. I'd been hanging back, more shy than afraid of being shooed back home.

So what exactly did I expect to happen, now that I'd gotten this far?

Quarters were detachable modules, little self-contained living units sent out from the maggies' huge Habs. Maybe the rule against us entering their protected areas was relaxed here. Or maybe they'd make an exception for a child.... But that hatch was obviously too small for the scooter. I knew there was an inflatable suit somewhere under the cushions. After I put it on, though, I'd have to flood the scooter to get outside, and I was probably in enough trouble already. The headsup's clock warped and disappeared as I slid lower and lower, disappointed with the limits of my success.

I jerked up like an electrified water-flea. The phone! I let it ring a few more times before cutting it on with one wavering hand.

"Kayley?" It was Tata, voice only. Among themselves, especially, maggies mostly signed. But of course since the rebellion, they'd maintained a strict embargo on visual broadcasts from their Habs. And from Quarters, too, it seemed. "Your father knows that you're here?" she asked.

"Well, not really." He might, if he'd noticed that I was gone.

"Your presence equals a desire for what?"

I had no answer to that but an honest one. "I want—to—I want to way with you."

Tata had adopted that bit of solar slang almost as soon as she heard it from me. Using one word to denote a deliberate interdependency of time and space and attention was apparently a very maggie concept. But a short silence followed my statement, as if she hadn't understood me. "Here? This would not be in alignment with the highest good of all involved."

In other words, no.

"Okay." I didn't know what else to say. I reached out to close down the connection. Maybe I could get home before Dad noticed the scooter missing.

"Wait."

My hand hovered. My arm began aching.

"My task here is to be rapidly accomplished. Then I can return with you. Would this carry adequate compensation?"

I wasn't exactly sure what she meant. Compensation for what? For being unable to enter a space forbidden to non-engineered humans for the last one hundred and fifty Years?

"Not complete compensation, of course, I understand. But in adequate amount?"

"Okay," I repeated. "Yeah. All right."

Waying with Tata through the Nassea was much more than all right. The background itself was boring, dead, a waste of water populated only by muddy motes. But Tata's presence charmed the empty scene to life. And the face-mask gave her a faintly silly sadness, instead of the menacing air I'd expected.

I wished I was able to hear her singing, the sonar she used to navigate. I couldn't hear the music, but I watched her, and I saw the dance.

Switching between infrared and a cone of visible, I followed her homeward, entranced by the strength and delicacy of her movements. For a while I tried to get the scooter to imitate them, swooping and halting clumsily. But sliding back and forth on the cushions interfered with my view.

Even though I knew practically nothing of the language at that point, I understood some of what she signed: big, small, honor of your trust, straight to the heart. These things sound so abstract, but they seemed extremely solid when she showed them to me. Her long limbs stretched, swept, gathered softly together.

I wish now I'd saved a recording of at least part of her performance. Maggies have wonderfully expressive faces, but the fine muscles of the alveolocks are, we're told, even more minutely controlled. Within their skins, maggies are able to communicate multiple messages simultaneously, with ironic, historical, and critical commentaries layered in over several levels. So the scholars say.

I couldn't swear to the truth of that. There was only one other time Tata wore her skin while speaking to me.

Because of course my father knew I'd taken his scooter. No more trips out into the Nassea for Kayley. Not for at least a Year. I wasn't even allowed to poke around in my lousy little inflatable.

I told my father this was an overly repressive reaction typical of reformed criminals. He smiled. "Good. I wouldn't want to do anything abnormal. Think of the psychic scars you'd have to bear."

Tata's infrequent trips to Quarters continued after this, naturally. I begrudged them; I didn't see why she couldn't just stay and way with me. Didn't she know how much I missed her, how the loneliness curdled up in my throat as she swam out of sight, out of the misty particulate light shining such a short way into the water?

I think she did.

Tata always made it a point, on her return, to give me some treasure found on her excursions. Something interesting, something different, with a story behind it. This must have been hard for her. Far off, over invisible horizons, maggies spread corals around other stations as ours did here. Aside from this the Nassea was empty of life, void of history. There were the sludges, various excretory masses of bacteria that accumulated in the presence of certain chemicals. There were fossilized sludges and other mineral formations. That was it.

I let the third sulphur sword she gave me fall to the floor. It shattered on the napless carpet, dull yellow shards of petulant guilt. It had been a pretty good sword, maybe half a meter long. But I had two almost as good in my room; the first from a hundred and fifty-five Days ago.

I tried to lie. "I'm sorry," I told Tata. "It slipped." I looked up, ready to elaborate, and saw it wouldn't work. It never did, with her.

"That's all right, Kayley," she said aloud. "I don't have to bring you presents. You don't have to like them." Her soft, round face looked embarrassed for us both.

"I'm sorry," I said again, using my hands the way Tata had taught me. And this time I meant it. She nodded, then walked down the tunnel to her room.

I didn't know what to do with the sword's pieces. I picked them up and took them to my dad. He was in the kitchen lab, putting a coral bud in the micro-slicer. "Tata's back?" he asked. "Poor specimen you've got there."

"It's broke," I explained. "I don't want it."

"Maybe your mom will be able to use it somehow." Penny was planning the cities that were going to be built on the land masses the coral was going to produce. Mostly she used cad, but sometimes she liked to work directly on models, making physical changes before she molded them into the program. Touching stuff with her real hands gave her different ideas for how to use things, she said.

I walked past Tata's room on the way to Penny's. Tata was singing. Her curtain was on one side of the doorway; that's how I could hear her. Through the arched rock I caught a glimpse of her skin, half-stretched upon its frame. I decided I would help her on my way back.

Penny was Dad's latest wife. She wasn't really my mom, though sometimes I called her that to make her feel good. She had the biggest room, a natural cave. The ceiling and some parts of the walls had been left exposed: raw basalt, rough and black. White, blue, and green spots hung suspended from the roof.

On the floor a display rose: a pink nest of concentric rings, like the crests of ripples spreading out, higher and higher. The highest came to my waist.

I walked to the center where Penny crouched down like she was the stone that had made the splash-of-pink city. "Hi, Mom."

"Hi. Gardens in here," she said without looking up. "Protected from storms and high seas."

"Clean. So then these low rings are where people live?"

"That's right. And the next out are trade and culture, then storage, processing...." She looked up, pulling down her smock's sleeves and putting her hands on her hips. "Trouble is this coral foundation we're building on is so sickin fragile. Can't let it get exposed, but what else are people going to walk on?"

"Dirt?"

"That's what I'm thinkin, Kayley, but I hate to have to make it from scratch. Sludges from the bottom," she said, as if I had suggested it. "That's a possibility, but..." She continued the conversation without me, silently. I left the sword shards on her workbench and walked out.

Tata's curtain was now in place. Its reddish tresses still stirred, settling themselves in their optimal array, fluffing up over their insulating air pockets. Not long since she'd shut herself in, then.

Dad was gone from the kitchen. I figured he was probably in his room, behind his curtain, too. I had learned on the ship coming out here to join him that in cramped off-Earth accommodations the right to privacy deserved and got the utmost respect. In other words, I could have gone to him. He would have interrupted whatever he was doing. But then he'd want to know what was wrong. It would turn out to be a very big deal. I didn't like very big deals.

I punched myself a pbj on white and went off to my room to do some school. I was way ahead for the semester.

Only another worldday's worth of program left. Maybe Tata could do something about that.

After I finished a section on Latter Day Lacanians, ortho and heretic, I switched to a book I'd pirated from Penny. It was about strong-limbed athletes, a man and a woman. The woman wanted to squeeze the man. The man wanted to be squeezed, but he didn't like the *way* he wanted it. He spent a lot of time trying to determine if the problem was with him, or the woman, or if it was the result of well-meaning interference from his coach. In between his bouts of reflection there was some pretty hot sex. I stayed up reading and masturbating till midnight.

Usually, Tata got me up. But not this Morning. I woke up because I was hungry. The swimming clock-faces on my desk's default read nine-thirty-three. I had to hurry if I wanted breakfast.

The kitchen program was pretty strict. The idea was to keep the scattered reef-builders on the same planet-wide circadians, disregarding New Bahama's five-Day rotation. Less mental isolation. More likelihood of a healthy global culture developing later on. So meals were on a schedule. Snacks I could always have, but I really didn't feel like another pbj. And I hated gorp, which was the only other thing there would be till lunch if I didn't make it in time.

I showered quickly, with only the most cursory of examinations. Still no pubic hair, breast development, enlarged or parted labia. Any year now, they'd be showing up.

I made it to the kitchen before ten and was rewarded with a choice of grits and kippers or yogurt and granola (gorp without even the saving grace of chocolate). "Who programmed this thing?" I muttered, punching for the gruel and fish-bacon as the lesser of two evils. I made the grits into a sort of white, starchy pudding by entering Dad's sugar codes along with my own. He wouldn't mind; he never used up his share anyway. I forced down the kippers by closing my eyes and visualizing the charts from med class: in North American historical studies, early onset of puberty correlated directly with increased protein consumption. I chewed as quickly as I could and swallowed, determined not to hold back my sexual maturity by one unnecessary moment.

I dumped my dishes in the tub for Tata to deal with. It was empty, nothing from Penny or Dad, so she had to be up. I wondered where. I wondered if she was still mad at me. Why else hadn't she got me up?

She was in her room, curtain back. She smiled as I came in. No, she wasn't mad. But she wasn't happy, either. She sat half-foetal on her bed, black, hairless curves rich with captive light. Delicate indentations, the wells for her skin's funiculi, formed swirling, tattoo-like patterns, subtly shining with deeply embedded drops of protective fluids. Her smooth head rested sideways on one knee.

On their Habs and in Quarters, maggies supposedly went naked, or maybe they wore jewelry or a hat. The extra layer of fat made them uncomfortable in clothes. Their nudity made us equally uncomfortable. In our place, Tata wore a sort of super-loin-cloth, which came up over the front of her long breasts and was held in place by a knotted strip of elastic. This one was red.

I signed. Signs are better than words for expressing all sorts of concepts, and I'd gotten pretty good by this time. I told her something like, "Tata's sadness equals/creates the sadness of Kayley. Is Tata's sadness also equivalent to/ the result of Kayley's imbalanced behavior? This would lead to even further loss of Kayley's balance and cool, but

knowledge is the first step towards the retrieval of alignment." Only it didn't take that long or sound that pomp-
ous and detached.

She raised her head and pointed at me with her chin
(the only polite way to point at some*one*, as opposed to
some*thing*), then twisted it to show that I should sit next
to her, on the bed.

I only knew how to make words with my hands. Tata
signed with her whole, huge, wonderful body. She spoke
like water, flowing from one phrase to the next by the
path of least resistance. She uncurled, and that meant her
sadness was not so heavy she couldn't leave it behind to be
fully present with a friend. Her right hand swept aside the
chopping, stabbing motion of her left—the sword. She
barely bent to notice the imaginary sword fall to the floor,
then casually rubbed it out with one eloquent toe. It was
not worth the bother of classifying it as unworthy.

"What's wrong?" I asked her, slowly. Sometimes I felt
too awkward to use anything except maggie "phonemes,"
laboriously spelling out English words. "What can I do
to help?" She sat still and silent for so long I tried again.
"Can Kayley aid Tata in any way to receive the gifts of her
highest heavenly head?"

"Stay close," signed Tata. "Don't leave me. Don't leave
me alone with—anyone else." She pulled me closer to her,
and I nestled against the soft, warm folds of flesh exposed
by her loin-cloth.

We were like that when my Dad came in. He spoke. He
had never learned to sign. He said, "We have to talk." He
looked at me. "About my plan for the next worldday."

"Yes," said Tata.

"In my office."

"Okay. Come on, Kayley." She stood, still holding me close to her side.

"Kayley can stay here."

"No. She needs to be with me."

Silence. Even Dad must have heard the lie. "I see," he said. "All right." He turned and left the room. We followed.

Dad grew up on an old tube, in orbit around Saturn. He was always shouldering his way through imaginary crowds, eyes and ears open for the first signs of a fight or a panic. Even in middle age, even flight years from any-one else's turf, he walked like a bangboy on patrol. He stopped in front of his door and automatically looked both ways down the dim corridor. The glow from the glamp showed his short, blond hair swinging around his head, his round, blue eyes narrowing to sweep the air for trouble spots. Then he pulled the curtain, which parted for him, and we went in.

Dad's room wasn't quite as big as Penny's. It could have been twice the size and still it would have seemed too small, because of all the stuff. Three walls full of ho-loscreens, with crates of 2-D transparencies ready for the hull display, stacked alongside them. His glass kiln against the outer wall. And the rows and rows of shelves filled with bottles, bowls, balls, and figurines. In the midst of this maze of fragility was his desk. Somewhere, too, he had a bed, though I think he almost always slept with Penny.

He took Tata to one wall and showed her the latest maps, which looked nothing like the Nassea I saw outside the port. These were bright, abstract topos, with clouds of yellow, golden-orange, and crimson to show where dif-ferent varieties of coral buds had been sown. Projected plantings for Dad's station were turquoise, green, and aquamarine. All these colors dappled the highest peaks, warm ones at the center, cooling as they reached the upper edges of the display. Tata placed one black finger in a valley near the map's bottom. "Quarters."

Dad nodded.

"It will be far to the new sites. Too far for skins."

My father shook his head impatiently. "That's not what my figures say. You're capable of two Days work and travel in a skin."

"Oh, no. I don't think so…or, perhaps. But capable means only that it can be done. Not that it should. We are capable of many things which nevertheless it is better to refrain from doing."

"Fine. You look at the topos. Come up with a more efficient array and I'll use it, Tata. Over here." Dad led her off through the shelves to his desktop. She invited me along with her eyes, but I stayed near the wall, sure I would be bored by the rest of the discussion. Why would she need me to stay *that* close?

A familiar configuration caught the corner of my eye. It was a face—mine. I moved toward it. Not all the holos were maps, charts, graphs, and grids. There I was, in all my pre-adolescent splendor. And there were images of Mom, my real mom. She looked pretty, not crazy at all. The way she used to be. Next to her were pictures of other women. Probably more former wives. Nobody I knew.

Then something very interesting: interior shots of a maggie Hab. I was as familiar as anyone with their exteriors. The twisted, drooping silver loops were a design cliché. I had a pair of earrings shaped like that. But here were walkways, rising unevenly out of training pools, past racks of skins, golden, brown, auburn, and black. Here was a mat full of necklaces: light, titanium beads strung with bone fragments and flat, rough-textured air-vine seeds.

Smooth black fingers were frozen in the act of lifting a strand for the viewer to examine. I wondered if I could pirate the book these stills came from. Or maybe I could even just ask for it.

There were several more. One, which showed a small maggie, a toddler of perhaps two or three Years, had a caption in alpha below the image. I struggled to decipher it. Something about the skin growing on his scalp and neck, still attached, and how carefully it needed to be groomed to prevent painful over-stimulation. No mention, as far as I could see, of anyone doing so on purpose.

That made me wonder how old the book was. It had to have been written pretty soon after the rebellion, before the maggies decided to exclude us from their Habs. Or maybe it pre-dated that. The whole thing might be in alpha. That'd be a challenge to read. Anyway, it'd keep me busy till I got some more school.

I decided to find Dad and tell him it would be a truly enlarging experience for me to get a copy of this maggie book. I tried to home in on him by listening for voices, but there were none. The ventilators sighed. The glass glittered silently as I passed up and down the shining paths.

"I can't." That was my father, very quiet, very close. They must be just on the other side of this set of shelves, to my left. "I can't," he said again. I'd never heard him like this. He sounded small and helpless. "I can't."

"I know." Tata's voice. "I'll go tomorrow, as soon as my skin is ready. And I'll ask about this imbalance, about our paths, just to be sure, but—"

"I love you," he said, interrupting her, and he sounded more familiar now: bitter, and tired. "And I can feel it, I can tell what's going to happen next, and I mustn't do that with you, I *mustn't* hurt you the way I want to hurt you, *but I can't*—"

I realized that I was eavesdropping and jerked back, bumping two bowls together on a shelf. They chimed, a high, perfect hum that hung on the air after my father's voice choked to a stop.

"Kayley?" Tata called softly under the ringing glass.

"Coming." I turned a corner and there they were, facing each other and looking anywhere but in each other's faces. "Dad, can I borrow—"

"Why the hell not?" he said. "Sure." He brushed past me and I started to follow him.

"No," said Tata. She didn't sign. "This way. Where were you? I thought you were going to stay with me." She headed in the opposite direction, which turned out to be a shortcut to the door.

She took me to her room and pulled the curtain closed. I sat on her bed, waiting for her to ask me what I'd heard. But instead she turned to her skin, not brushing it but checking the ties that held it in place, loosening them to accommodate its growing fullness.

In dormancy, the skin's sluggish circulatory system accumulated an ever-swelling supply of hyper-oxygenated blood. Its nerve sheaths, worn by long contact, regenerated themselves. Tata held the back of one hand close to the skin's underside. I was too far from her to see it happen, but she had shown me before how the thin white funiculi erected themselves, anticipating connection with her wells. Like the curtains, they responded to pheromonal cues.

I couldn't tell from Tata's reaction if the response was satisfactory. Her face was smooth, her black body blank. When she spoke to me, she kept using words. "Kayley, in the Morning I will need to return to Quarters. For the balance of my highest head."

I tried not to sulk. She'd just gotten back, and she was going out again. "Why?"

"I must...consult."

"Oh." I felt stupid. Of course the work crews had to decide what to do about the new, more distant sites. That was what I'd overheard—wasn't it? I asked Tata if it was really bad to be out in a skin for Days. She looked at me blankly for a moment, then averted her eyes and answered.

"The elders say that it becomes a strain. We get 'tipsy'; our heads unbalance easily, going so long without enough oxygen, and we drop things. A tingling that grows painful, or numbness.... There is some compensation: danger pay, and the contract will be shortened if we take that path." When the contract ended Tata would leave. Unless my Dad or Penny purchased a permanent agreement.

"So is that what's going to happen?"

"Probably not. It would be cooler to move Quarters nearer to where the work is being done." This sounded depressingly likely. It was, after all, their module, at their command. It would take a couple of Days to shift and re-anchor, but they'd still save time in the long run.

I sighed and let my chin sink down into one cupped hand.

"Kayley?" said Tata.

"What?" I didn't bother to look up.

"Your sorrow equals?"

"You'll be gone so much, traveling back and forth..."

"Kayley, must you always try to reach so far in front of your arms? These troubles are unborn. Each path has many branchings." She came over to me and put her hands on my hunched-up shoulders.

"I'm here," Tata continued. "I don't have any work right now, and I'd really like to way with you. So ask your head to tell you what it's best for us to do."

My head was empty of suggestions. We wound up hacking my father's book codes. Despite what she'd said, Tata was not wholly there, and it took longer than it should have. We succeeded about supper time, fed her skin, then hurried to join Penny and Dad in the kitchen.

I watched them all carefully. Penny and Dad were already at the counter, sawing away at grilled swordfish steaks. "Something's wrong, Tata," he joked as we entered. "You forgot to program me the sword I need to cut this thing."

Penny winced. "Your wit, dear. Use your *wit.*"

"I am. Maybe yours is a little sharper. Mind if I borrow it a moment?" He reached over and started rummaging through her wild curls. "Looks like what you've got here is mostly hair."

All very jolly and fine, all throughout the meal. Except once I caught what Penny's book would have called a long, burning look. Dad to Tata. Tata to Dad. Then both of them were studying their empty plates.

Afterwards, Penny asked Dad to come cad with her. I stayed behind, pretending to help Tata clean up, wondering whether or not I was jealous. At last I decided I just wanted to know what was going on.

"You love him, don't you, Tata?"

Her hands stayed busily silent, smoothing creases from our crumpled paper napkins.

"Tata—"

"Yes. It hardly matters, but yes, I love your father very much." She tossed the napkins into the paper cycler and turned away to face the sink.

"What do you mean?" I asked. "It doesn't matter why?"

"Because." For a moment I thought that was all she was going to say. Then the words came flooding out.

"Because it is unlikely that this love will advance either of us on our path of light and destiny. Because your father knows this as well as I do, though we both wish we didn't. Because your father is strong for me, and I am weak for him. Because, because, because…" Tata stopped talking and turned on the water, flushing food scraps from the sink. "There are many, many reasons. Good ones."

"All right," I said. I kept quiet while she unloaded the washer and stacked our clean, dry plates in their hopper. When she was done, I followed her out into the corridor. "Do you still want to way with me?" I asked. "I could stay in your room tonight, if…if you'd like?"

She stood still, considering. "I might."

Tata's desk had such a tiny screen. "Or you could come spend the night with me." That way we could read.

"Perhaps that would be most cool." But when we came to her doorway, she stopped. "There are a few things it would be better for me to do tonight, before I leave for Quarters." I could see she was still trying not to sign, though her soft, dark shoulders curved in some awkward emotion: shame, embarrassment? I didn't know.

"Anything I can do, Tata?" I asked her.

"Wait. I'll come when I'm through." The glamp-light glimmered on her curtain's fur as it closed behind her.

I went on to my room. Leaving the curtain open, I activated my desk and took a look at this afternoon's discovery.

The book was called *Space-Apes in Eden: The Anti-Domestication of a New Racial Archetype*. It was a load of filth.

I was eleven Years old, up to my fortieth semester of school. I had heard of the antiquated notion that humanity is divided into races, special variations due to local inbreeding. But no one had ever discussed the inferences once commonly drawn based on this theory: that members of these racial subsets possessed differing abilities, qualitatively and quantitatively. That certain of these abilities made their possessors more fit to survive and reproduce than those possessed of other, and therefore inferior, abilities. That the inbreeding which had produced these races was a highly desirable occurrence, one to be cultivated and encouraged—"by any means consonant with the rapid colonization of space."

I struggled to comprehend these repulsive assumptions as they were presented to me. The murky mysteries of the written word forced me to formulate this nastiness within my own mind. There were a few useful pieces of information; the origin of the word "maggies," for instance. It had nothing to do with the works of Dylan, the Twentieth Century Welsh songwriter. "Maggie's Farm" may have been an anthem of the rebellion, but the name came first. It derived from magnesium, the only element the rebels couldn't mine or synthesize. With no access to planetary bases, it became their sole trade-link with Earth.

I also learned the names of the team that designed humanity's first (and only?) self-replicating artificial mutation. It *was* a team, though Harding gets the credit, for the maggies, the curtains, and all the other spin-offs.

The rest—I couldn't tell what was true, what contained a grain of truth, and what was pure, poisonous nonsense. The author implied, rather than stated, that maggies were animals, or anyway, less than human. Because they were made for us, to work for us. The more I read, the more

I felt like I was agreeing with things I absolutely knew were wrong. At one point I stared so long at the screen, too stupefied to scroll any further, that my default clicked on. The swimming clocks showed two sharp. Late. My circadians would be way off.

Where was Tata? She'd have to help me deal with this. I didn't care what she was doing. I needed her. I went down the tunnel to her room.

Her curtain was closed. I slapped it in frustration, and it opened slightly. Maybe it hadn't been drawn completely shut. Or if she had sensitized it to my touch, she did so without telling me. I swear I didn't know that it would open, that I would see them there like that.

Actually, I heard them first. A sound too soft to be a groan, followed by a low, desperate, sobbing. I was in the room, then, and I saw.

Tata lay on her bed, on her side, eyes closed. She was naked—no, without clothes, but not naked. Her long, beautiful breasts and her belly and thighs blazed black between the edges of her partially closed skin. With one gold-clad arm she lifted her leg, with the other she braced herself to thrust against him. Him. Dad.

Dad was behind her. I only saw his hairy knees, and his hands on her shoulders. But I recognized his voice.

"Tata, Tata, won't forget me Tata, won't forget who loves you, Tata—" Tension tore his words apart then, left ragged gasps fluttering in the air.

I should have gone away.

But I stayed.

It lasted a long while without changing, then slowed a little. Tata opened her eyes. I know she saw me.

It was my dad who spoke, though. "Sweet, sickin *God*, Tata, this will never be enough." And quite deliberately his hands sought out the edges of her open skin, touching her there, underneath.

She screamed. It was nothing like Penny's books. I wanted to die, I wanted to come, I wanted to run away and hide.

I was moving toward her, somehow, to help her. Spasming with pain, she signed me to stop.

My father's hands continued their torture, brushing and plucking at the skin's exposed funiculi. Tata's scream had subsided to a hoarse grunting, nearly drowned out by my father's moans. I hesitated, and she signed again: go. Her imbalance was extreme. I could not aid her. Go.

I went.

At the door I turned, still unsure. The hands went suddenly limp. Tata lay still beneath them. Then she showed me one more sign, simple, yet nuanced. Swimming through a virtual Nassea, she slipped into the contracting lock of Quarters, into the arms of healers, elders that would assist her in retrieving her coolness and alignment. She rested there, with them, depending on their love. And the memory of mine.

She was telling me goodbye.

I shut the curtain.

In the morning, Tata was gone, and next Day another maggie came to take her place. His name was Lebba. Dad didn't care how often he left the station, and he never tried to stop me from going out with him, either. I thought sometimes I'd ask him to tell Tata I was well, I was fine, I was growing, developing quite normally. I thought I'd ask him to convey to her my wishes that she continue to receive the blessings of her highest heavenly head. But I haven't done anything like that yet, and I still don't know if I'm going to.

It's been over six Years. With the last of the seeding done, my father has left New Bahama. I surprised him when I told him I wanted to stay here, with Penny, in what he called "this Surge-abandoned mud-hole." But I'm eighteen now, no longer in need of a guardian.

I have settled down here, sinking into the darkness and silence of the Nassea. Penny provides me with an easy, unassuming companionship, and I help her with her work. Which is about to move into construction. For soon, according to our maps, the carefully nurtured coral will break the surface of the Nassea.

When that happens, the maggies will be moving on, to another waterworld, or something rare, a world of ice or dust. Tata, too.

Does she realize how much I miss her, how the loneliness is always there, still curdled up inside?

I think she does.

Momi Watu

❊

I was just tired, that's all. That gritty feeling in my eyes, as if the lids were encrusted with sand; it would pass. Blinking helped, though not much. Maybe a really *long* blink.... No. Only two more braids to go. Then the laundry to bag and unbag. Then a bath for both of us. *Then* I could sleep.

I bent back to my work. Individual strands of hair feathered beneath my comb, and I examined them all closely. Too bad she was so fair. Took after her Dad. Too bad I spoiled her so. It really should all come off. But even with school coming up next week, I just couldn't. Every strand of heavy, golden brown was a link to Steve. Like dripping syrup, like the sweetness we had shared, making this child. Steve was gone, captured, disappeared. I just couldn't stand the thought of cutting these ties between us. That's probably why Lily threw a shit-fit every time I mentioned the idea.

Eleven p.m. and one braid left. Time for the news. I switched on the tv: just the picture, as accompaniment for the radio. That was where I got all my actual information. The pictures on the screen, when I glanced up at them, never exactly matched the stories I was listening to. But they acted as a sort of disjointed commentary, on the level of my lizard brain.

The Tigers were moving up into third place. They'd never make it past that, though, everybody knew. Not since they tore down the old stadium. The image of Tyree Guyton appeared on the tv as if in confirmation. He stood before one of his hoodoo houses, talking to an off-camera interviewer. Mannequin legs and bicycles sprouted from the veranda at his back. The spirit of Old Detroit lived.

Nina Totenberg did a thing on the "Cold Water Wars," part of a series. They weren't really wars, of course; no state had seceded from the union, no officials openly supported the "terrorist tactics" groups like Steve's engaged in, though they were only trying to enforce the law. But insurance rates had risen, security on dams and pumping stations soared sky high, underwritten by our taxes.

The tv showed beer commercials, several minutes of tanned, beefy men pouring glowing golden liquids for one another. The condensation on their glasses looked real good.

Back to local and the weather. Clear and in the 90s; no surprises there. But what was this? Adrenaline kicked in as I isolated a strand of Lily's hair. A small white fleck seemed to be attached to it, about an inch from the scalp.

With trembling hands I took up my scissors and severed the hair, carefully laying it on a scrap of black cloth. Dread burned like a fever, just below the surface of my skin. But when I rubbed the hair back and forth, the little speck of white detached itself from the strand. It lay there innocently, a mere flake of dandruff or dead scalp.

For a moment I let myself enjoy the cool ripples of relief spreading over me. It was always like this: the crisis, forcing me to focus all my senses on the narrow circle of immediate threat, then the resolution, and the corresponding sensation of floating, of release.

So far, anyway.

I finished the last braid without further incident, left Lily curled up on the floor and went to bring in the laundry.

Light from the kitchen window spilled yellow out into the yard and let me see enough to avoid the lopsided picnic table, the borrowed grill. The clothesline was a flapping shadow toward the back. I unpegged the clothes, mostly by feel. Into the wicker-creaking, plastic-rustling basket by layers: first underwear, then t-shirts, then socks, shorts, and scarves. The shaker pegs went into a separate bag. I carried the basket in, swung through the living room to check on Lily. Still sleeping. Her long braids swirled out in "esses" over the floorboards. Her lashes fluttered over her plump brown cheeks, then settled into stillness.

I hurried into the former study, sealed the laundry bag, and labeled it. Lifted it out of the basket, into the space awaiting it on my makeshift shelves. Pegs on top. I scanned the labels of the bags already in place. Some people say two weeks is long enough. They've studied the life cycle; they should know. I wait three, just to be sure. I found the bag labeled August 5, 2009, and carried it to our bedroom.

"Wake up, pumpkin, time to get ready for bed." I had the herbs all set out on the mat: sage, rosemary, lavender, artemisia. Lily scowled as I scrubbed her with them. I was as gentle as I could be, turning her with one hand while the other rubbed her up and down with the scratchy leaves. Poor pumpkin. She used to love it back when she was a baby and we used water. Bath night was tough on her now, but I insisted. Better a tired and grumpy little girl than a sick or dying one. We usually slept in Sunday mornings, waking just in time for her favorite cartoons.

The bruised herbs released their piercing scents into the air. They left trails of green on Lily's smooth, dry skin. I finished by massaging a little oil into her hair and brushing it through. "There. Now go dust yourself off and hop in bed."

I stripped off my house dress and grabbed another bundle of herbs for myself. "Got your pajamas on, amazon?"

A giggle floated through the bedroom door. "Ye-es." Good kid, I thought, beginning my rub-down. She's definitely worth it. Definitely worth the work.

❋

I had Saturday afternoons off so we could do laundry and go to the beach. A full day would have been more convenient, but that's retail. The clothing and bed linens we used during the week went into the dirty laundry right away. I kept it well-sealed, in triple-thick plastic bags. As the days passed, the black bags swelled threateningly. I stared at them and imagined I could *hear* eggs hatching inside. It was always a relief when Saturday rolled around again.

We waited for the bus for what seemed like an hour. Probably twenty minutes objective time; must have been several weeks for Lily. She squiggled around on the easement, scuffing her new green sandals in the gravel. People waiting with us mostly smiled, though a few of the careful ones looked a little bothered by the braids sticking out from under Lily's scarf. I'd have to get her a larger one;

maybe one of mine would do. I didn't really need a scarf, short as I kept my hair.

Lily balanced on the curb now and swung her white patent leather purse in big arcs, seeing how far she could go before she pissed someone off.

"Ow!" Not very far.

"Lily, come here." She obeyed reluctantly, dragging out each step into a long, stone-slithering slide. "Do you still have the tokens? Check and see." She dug into her purse, her expression cute and serious. The tokens were still there (I had back-ups, of course). So was a Garuda Guy finger-puppet, which she put on her thumb and waggled back and forth. Within seconds they were deep into a private conversation.

The man she'd whacked came up to complain. I pulled her closer and ignored him. He looked HIV to me. Suspicious spots sprinkled his neck and forehead.

"Did you know," I announced to the air, "that the common louse is capable of leaps up to 15 feet in length?" That shut him up for a moment. Long enough for the bus to round the corner. The HIVer got in first. I let him. I considered waiting for a later bus, but decided against it. I told myself that a few red spots do not an infestation make. Even if they did, who knew what'd be waiting for us on the next one that stopped? I spread white towels for Lily and me, and we sat in our seats.

Benton Harbor used to be practically a ghost town. It started turning around about the middle of the decade, with Mayor Todd's administration. Gil made a big dent in the drug gangs and muggers, the petty crime. Then he tackled the economy. He had a little help from the Feds there, no question. Three divisions of the National Guard stationed nearby perked things up a bit for most business-es. Homeland Security's response to the "Wars" reduced our back-and-forth with Chicago to almost nothing, fur-ther cutting back on crime. Smugglers switched to Mus-kegon and Grand Rapids, routes where things were under a little less scrupulous observation.

But Gil's dream of bringing back the big tourist trade that flourished here forty, fifty years ago? That was still a dream, and nothing more. True, the Lakes' shores lacked the sand fleas that infested ocean beaches and scared off those who couldn't tell them apart from lice. And water pirates sound romantic—but getting personally killed by one does not appeal to most. Rich resort-heads stuck to Traverse and the Upper Peninsula. Rents stayed low in Benton Harbor, and Lily and I stayed as close to the Lake as we liked. We got off after twelve roundabout blocks.

Silver Beach.

A giant rusting iron wheel, half-buried in pale sand. The time-eaten girders of the old roller-coaster. Further down, the Guard's gun emplacements, never used. The shell of Cook Nuclear facility in the distance, a dead-white mosque. No chance of contaminating leaks there; it was one of the first to be shut down.

Steve must be somewhere beyond that. He had to be. He had to be alive.

On clear days you could see the glittering towers of the greedy city that had swallowed him. Today there was a haze, melting at the horizon into the enormously blue water. "Momi Watu," he used to call the Lake, after some African goddess he studied in college. "Precious mother of us all; I would defend you with my life." That's what he said. So of course, that's what he did.

Filter House

There was a sign warning us off at the place where the crumbling asphalt ended. They could not be responsible for our safety from this point on. If there'd been any real chance of trouble today, the Guard would have been there to turn us away. The sign was a notice to liability lawyers and insurance companies. We ignored it and spilled along the beach.

"Race you!" I cried. I gave Lily a head start, then pretended to struggle to catch up. The soft sand sank beneath my feet, and I staggered playfully. She turned her head and whipped off her scarf, laughed gleefully at my clowning. "Wait! Wait!" She shook her head, being naughty. Her scarf and purse fell to the sand and she was off again, running harder, braids flying straight out over her back.

I dropped the beach bag next to her things, then really ran. I timed it so we hit the water together. *Smack! Splash! Slosh, slosh, slosh.* We kept trying to run, but a big wave knocked Lily on her bottom, and my wet skirts dragged me down next to her.

Lily stood up, defying the waves. I leaned back on my hands while she poured water on my hair, tiny little cupped palmfuls trickling down over my scalp.

Lovely, lovely, cool, cool water. We may not be able to pump much more of it into our homes than they do in Arizona. That's the law. But that's all right. It's better than an actual, true-to-life, all-out war. The water stays in the Lakes, where it belongs. And we stay near the Lakes, where we belong. A place for everything, and everything in its place, I've always liked to say.

Steve used to tease me about that—called me compulsive. Maybe I am, I told him one time, but you can't be too neurotic these days.

"Close your eyes, Mommy, I gotta do the front."

"Okay." It was easier with my eyes shut to imagine him there. The sun would glow golden through his fly-away halo of hair, finer than Lily's, but braided exactly the same. He probably wouldn't like my buzz-cut; he had always been envious of the dreadlocks I wore, always hated fear and compromise. Which is how he would see it. Which is why he left us, looking for a way to infiltrate Chicago's Water Authority, because he loved bravery and commitment. And I loved that he loved them. But...but it would have been better, especially for Lily, if he had not.

I opened my eyes. The little splashes of water had stopped. Lily was headed for the shore. I got up and waded after her. I tried to hold her hand and help her walk, but she was too busy tugging at her wet, clingy clothes. "You want to get rid of those, honey?"

She nodded, wrinkling up her nose. "Yeah, they won't stop *grabbin* at me. And they make me feel very cold." I stripped us both down to our suits, then rummaged through the beach bag for one of the plastic sacks I always carried. Probably at the bottom, underneath the lunch box. I sighed and started to unpack. There they were. I made a mental note never to organize things *that* way again.

I didn't want to put the lunch box back where it was before, so I held it out for Lily. "Hang on to this for me, would you pumpkin?" No answer.

I looked up. No Lily.

Back in the water? I ran quickly. She was just learning how to swim. No Lily. No pathetic, limp, bobbing remains, either. I spun around; fast, b-ball pivots. No golden brown braids, anywhere in sight. A gull whimpered.

I headed down the beach in a power walk, scanning, trying to look in all directions at once. Fighting back the tears; they wouldn't help me see her. How long had she been gone? Minutes. Endless minutes now, and where on Earth could she be?

The latrines? Yes! She'd probably had to pee since we left home, hence the squirm-dance routine while waiting for the bus. I'd always told her how rude it was to "go" in the Lake. I hot-footed it across the warming sand, lunch-box rattling. A little girl alone on a beach—anything could happen. My imagination busied itself with the details as I called her. "Lily? Lily Beatrice, you answer me! Don't you go talking to any strangers, Lily—"

Then I saw her. I saw it was too late for that particular warning. An older woman had her and was toweling her hair for her. *Toweling* it! Lily looked up from under the pink-striped terry-cloth with her "I-know-I've-done-something-wrong-again-but-would-you-please-tell-me-what-before-you-start-yelling-Mommy" face. I fell to my knees and hugged her fiercely, angrily. I pulled back to give her a piece of my mind.

Children are cute because otherwise they would die. It's a miracle of genetic engineering that any of us makes it to puberty. The dimples, the big eyes, the extra-long lashes—they worked. Once again. I thought—yes, she is worth it, the heartbreak, the trouble. And yes, she is the link, maybe the only link now, between me and her father. Her hair, however, is not. Not the connection. And not worth the trouble. Not worth the danger. Nothing is.

"Thank-you," I told the strange woman, fighting down the urge to pick like a baboon at her whitened head. "Most people wouldn't take a chance like that. Children are so prone, you know...." I let my voice trail off.

The woman blanched. "Oh, I...I never thought." No, she obviously never did. Probably went into Jake's and actually, physically tried on hats. Some people were never going to adjust, and it was useless pointing out their mistakes.

"That's all right." I stood and carefully folded up her towel.

"I'm sorry. It's so hard to get used to. And with all these diseases, too. When I was a girl, it was only a few people, the very poor."

I nodded, even though I knew that wasn't true. Head lice don't discriminate; they never did. They like children, but they don't care about rich or poor. Water discourages them a little. But you could be perfectly clean, even by pre-"Wars" standards, and still become infested. And these days that might mean infected. HIVed, or HEPed.

Like poor little Amy, who used to live next door. Her parents actually sent her to a salon to have her hair done. Regularly.

All it took was common sense.

I gave the woman her towel. "Come on, Lily. Let's go." I held out my hand.

"Do we gotta? I don't wanna go home yet." She pouted.

"Child, I could walk downtown on your lower lip." A twisted smile emerged from her sorrow. "We're not going home yet, anyway. Even though you've been a *very* bad girl. We'll talk about that later." Her little hand slipped into mine and we went back to retrieve the beach bag.

"Where we goin', Mommy?"

"We're going to Aunty Senta's."

"Yayy!" I lost the hand again as she spun around, clapping. I waited, then took it back.

"And you know why? Because we're gonna get you a brand new, big-girl hair-cut like Mommy's." There were no shrieks of protest; just a side-long, questioning glance. Lily knew she had pushed the envelope far enough for today, even if she didn't understand how, or why. She trusted me to tell her things like that. And I had to trust myself to figure them out. To figure out what was right.

We walked back up the dunes. We could save her hair, come to think of it. If it was all that precious. Tie it up in ribbons and silk and seal it away for safekeeping. Store it in the study, the attic. Anywhere at all was fine, so long as it wasn't on her head.

We got to the stop. A bus was coming down the street, about a block away. Say, ten, twenty minutes ride to Senta's house. If she was home, less than an hour till Lily's new "do" was done. A short time; nothing bad could happen before then. And afterwards, things would be easier. So much easier. I felt the waters of relief pool up and over me.

Deep End

❋

The pool was supposed to be like freespace. Enough like it, anyway, to help Wayna acclimate to her download. She went in first thing every "morning," as soon as Dr. Ops, the ship's mind, awakened her. Too bad it wasn't scheduled for later; all the slow, meat-based activities afterwards were a literal drag.

The voices of the pool's other occupants boomed back and forth in an odd, uncontrolled manner, steel-born echoes muffling and exposing what was said. The temperature varied irregularly, warm intake jets competing with cold currents and, Wayna suspected, illicitly released urine. Overhead lights speckled the wall, the ceiling, the water, with a shifting, uneven glare.

Psyche Moth was a prison ship. Like all those on board, Wayna was an upload of a criminal's mind. The process of uploading her mind had destroyed her physical body. Punishment. Then the ship, with Wayna and 248,961 other prisoners, set off on a long voyage to another star. During that voyage the prisoners' minds had been cycled through consciousness: one year on, four years off. Of the eighty-seven years en route, Wayna had only lived through seventeen. Now she spent most of her time as meat.

Wayna's jaw ached. She'd been clenching it, trying to amp up her sensory inputs. She paddled toward the deep end, consciously relaxing her useless facial muscles. When *Psyche Moth* had reached its goal and verified that the world it called Amends was colonizable, her group was the second downloaded into empty clones, right after the trustees. One of those had told her it was typical to translocate missing freespace controls to their meat analogs.

She swirled her arms back and forth, creating waves, making them run into one another.

Then the pain hit.

White! Heat! There then gone—the lash of a whip.

Wayna stopped moving. Her suit held her up. She floated, waiting. Nothing else happened. Tentatively, she kicked and stroked her way to the steps rising from the pool's shallows, nodding to those she passed. At the door to the showers, it hit her again: a shock of electricity slicing from right shoulder to left hip. She caught her breath and continued in.

The showers were empty. Wayna was the first one from her hour out of the pool, and it was too soon for the next hour to wake up. She turned on the water and stood in its welcome warmth. What was going on? She'd never felt anything like this, not that she could remember—and surely she wouldn't have forgotten something so intense.... She stripped off her suit and hung it to dry. Instead of dressing in her overall and reporting to the laundry, her next assignment, she retreated into her locker and linked with Dr. Ops.

In the sphere of freespace, his office always hovered in the northwest quadrant, about halfway up from the horizon. Doe, Wayna's honeywoman, disliked this placement. Why pretend he was anything other than central to the whole setup, she asked. Why not put himself smack dab in the middle where he belonged? Doe distrusted Dr. Ops and everything about *Psyche Moth*. Wayna understood why. But there was nothing else. Not for eight light-years in any direction. According to Dr. Ops.

She swam into his pink-walled waiting room and eased her icon into a chair. That registered as a request for the AI's attention. A couple of other prisoners were there ahead of her; one disappeared soon after she sat. A few more minutes by objective measure, and the other was gone as well. Then it was Wayna's turn.

Dr. Ops presented as a lean-faced Caucasian man with a shock of mixed brown and blond hair. He wore an anachronistic headlamp and stethoscope and a gentle, kindly persona. "I have your readouts, of course, but why don't you tell me what's going on in your own words?"

He looked like he was listening. When she finished, he sat silent for a few seconds—much more time than he needed to consider what she'd said. Making an ostentatious display of his concern.

"There's no sign of nerve damage," he told her. "Nothing wrong with your spine or any of your articulation or musculature."

"So then how come—"

"It's probably nothing," the AI said, interrupting her. "But just in case, let's give you the rest of the day off. Take it easy—outside your locker, of course. I'll clear your bunkroom for the next 25 hours. Lie down. Put in some face time with your friends."

"*Probably?*"

"I'll let you know for sure tomorrow morning. Right now, relax. Doctor's orders." He smiled and logged her out. He could do that. It was his system.

Wayna tongued open her locker; no use staying in there without access to freespace. She put on her overall and walked up the corridor to her bunkroom. Fellow prisoners passed her heading the other way to the pool: no one she'd known back on Earth, no one she had gotten to know that well in freespace or since the download. Plenty of time for that onplanet. The woman with the curly red hair was called Robeson, she was pretty sure. They smiled at each other. Robeson walked hand in hand with a slender man whose mischievous smile reminded Wayna of Thad. It wasn't him. Thad was scheduled for later download. Wayna was lucky to have Doe with her.

Another pain. Not so strong, this time. Strong enough, though. Sweat dampened her skin. She kept going, almost there.

There. Through the doorless opening she saw the mirror she hated, ordered up by one of the two women she timeshared with. It was only partly obscured by the genetics charts the other woman taped everywhere. Immersion learning. Even Wayna was absorbing something from it.

But not now. She lay on the bunk without looking at anything, eyes open. What was wrong with her?

Probably nothing.

Relax.

She did her body awareness exercises, tensing and loosening different muscle groups. She'd gotten as far as her knees when Doe walked in. Stood over her till Wayna focused on her honeywoman's new face. "Sweetheart," Doe said. Her pale fingers stroked Wayna's face. "Dr. Ops told a trustee you wanted me."

"No—I mean yes, but I didn't ask—" Doe's expression froze, flickered, froze again. "Don't be—it's so hard, can't you just—" Wayna reached for and found both of Doe's hands and held them. They felt cool and small and dry. She pressed them against her overall's open V-neck and slid them beneath the fabric, forcing them to stroke her shoulders.

Making love to Doe in her download seemed like cheating. Wayna wondered what Thad's clone would look like, and if they'd be able to travel to his group's settlement to see him.

Anticipating agony, Wayna found herself hung up, nowhere near ecstasy. Doe pulled back and looked down at her, expecting an explanation. So Wayna had to tell her what little she knew.

"You! You weren't going to say anything! Just let me hurt you—" Doe had zero tolerance for accidentally inflicting pain, the legacy of her marriage to a closeted masochist.

"It wouldn't be anything you *did!* And I don't know if—"

Doe tore aside the paper they had taped across the doorway for privacy. From her bunk, Wayna heard her raging along the corridor, slapping the walls.

Face time was over.

Taken off of her normal schedule, Wayna had no idea how to spend the rest of her day. Not lying down alone. Not after that. She tried, but she couldn't.

Relax.

Ordinarily when her laundry shift was over, she was supposed to show up in the cafeteria and eat. Never one of her favorite activities, even back on Earth. She went there early, though, surveying the occupied tables. The same glaring lights hung from the ceiling here as in the pool, glinting off plastic plates and water glasses. The same confused noise, the sound of overlapping conversations. No sign of Doe.

She stood in line. The trustee in charge started to give her a hard time about not waiting for her usual lunch hour. He shut up suddenly; Dr. Ops must have tipped him a clue. Trustees were in constant contact with the ship's mind—part of why Wayna hadn't volunteered to be one.

Mashed potatoes. Honey mustard nuggets. Slaw. All freshly factured, filled with nutrients and the proper amount of fiber for this stage of her digestive tract's maturation.

She sat at a table near the disposal dump. The redhead, Robeson, was there too, and a man—a different one than Wayna had seen her with before. Wayna introduced herself. She didn't feel like talking, but listening was fine. The topic was the latest virch from the settlement site. She hadn't done it yet.

This installment had been recorded by a botanist; lots of information on grass analogs and pollinating insects. "We know more about Jubilee than about *Psyche Moth*," Robeson said.

"Well, sure," said the man. His name was Jawann. "Jubilee is where we're going to live."

"*Psyche Moth* is where we live now, where we've lived for the last 87 years. We don't know jack about this ship. Because Dr. Ops doesn't want us to."

"We know enough to realize we'd look stupid trying to attack him," Wayna said. Even Doe admitted that. Dr.

Ops's hardware lay in *Psyche Moth's* central section, along with the drive engine. A tether almost two kilometers long separated their living quarters from the AI's physical components and any other mission-critical equipment. At the end of the tether, Wayna and the rest of the downloads swung, faster and faster. They were like sand in a bucket, centrifugal force mimicking gravity and gradually building up to the level they'd experience on Amend's surface, in Jubilee.

That was all they knew. All Dr. Ops thought they needed to know.

"Who said anything about an attack?" Robeson frowned.

"No one." Wayna was suddenly sorry she'd spoken. "All I mean is, his only motive in telling us anything was to prevent that from happening." She spooned some nuggets onto her mashed potatoes and shoved them into her mouth so she wouldn't say any more.

"You think he's lying?" Jawann asked. Wayna shook her head no.

"He could if he wanted. How would we find out?"

The slaw was too sweet; not enough contrast with the nuggets. Not peppery, like what Aunt Nono used to make.

"Why would we want to find out? We'll be on our own ground, in Jubilee, soon enough." Four weeks; twenty days by *Psyche Moth's* rationalized calendar.

"With trustees to watch us all the time, everywhere we go, and this ship hanging in orbit right over our heads." Robeson sounded as suspicious as Doe; Jawann as placatory as Wayna tried to be in their identical arguments. Thad usually came across as neutral, controlled, the way you could be out of your meat.

"So? They're not going to hurt us after they brought us all this way. At least, they won't want to hurt our bodies."

Because their bodies came from, were copies of, the people they'd rebelled against. The rich. The politically powerful.

But Wayna's body was *hers*. No one else owned it, no matter who her clone's cells started off with. Hers, no matter how different it looked from the one she was born with. How white.

Hers to take care of. Early on in her training she'd decided that. How else could she be serious about her exercises? Why else would she bother?

This was her body. She'd earned it.

Jawann and Robeson were done; they'd started eating before her and now they were leaving. She swallowed quickly. "Wait—I wanted to ask—" They stopped and she stood up to follow them, taking her half-full plate. "Either of you have any medical training?"

They knew someone, a man called Unique, a nurse when he'd lived on Earth. Here he worked in the factury, quality control. Wayna would have to go back to her bunkroom until he got off and could come see her. She left Doe a message on the board by the cafeteria's entrance, an apology. Face-up on her bed, Wayna concentrated fiercely on the muscle groups she'd skipped earlier. A trustee came by to check on her and seemed satisfied to find her lying down, everything in line with her remote readings. He acted as if she should be flattered by the extra attention. "Dr. Ops will be in touch first thing tomorrow," he promised as he left.

"Ooo baby," she said softly to herself, and went on with what she'd been doing.

A little later, for no reason she knew of, she looked up at her doorway. The man that had held Robeson's hand that morning stood there as if this was where he'd always been. "Hi. Do I have the right place? You're Wayna?"

"Unique?"

"Yeah."

"Come on in." She swung her feet to the floor and patted a place beside her on the bed. He sat closer than she'd expected, closer than she was used to. Maybe that meant he'd been born Hispanic or Middle Eastern. Or maybe not.

"Robeson said you had some sort of problem to ask me about. So—of course I don't have any equipment, but if I can help in any way, I will."

She told him what had happened, feeling foolish all of a sudden. There'd only been those three times, nothing more since seeing Dr. Ops.

"Lie on your stomach," he said. Through the fabric, firm fingers pressed on either side of her spine, from mid-back to her skull, then down again to her tailbone. "Turn over, please. Bend your knees. All right if I take off your shoes?" He stroked the soles of her feet, had her push them against his hands in different directions. His touch, his resistance to her pressure, reassured her. What she was going through was real. It mattered.

He asked her how she slept, what she massed, if she was always thirsty, other things. He finished his questions and walked back and forth in her room, glancing often in her direction. She sat again, hugging herself. If Doe came in now, she'd know Wayna wanted him.

Unique quit his pacing and faced her, his eyes steady. "I don't know what's wrong with you," he said. "You're not the only one, though. There's a hundred and fifty others that I've seen or heard of experiencing major problems—

circulatory, muscular, digestive. Some even have the same symptoms you do."

"What is it?" Wayna asked stupidly.

"Honestly, I don't know," he repeated. "If I had a lab—I'll set one up in Jubilee—call it neuropathy, but I don't know for sure what's causing it."

"Neuropathy?"

"Means nerve problems."

"But Dr. Ops told me my nerves were fine...." No response to that.

"If we were on Earth, what would you think?"

He compressed his already thin lips. "Most likely possibility, some kind of thyroid problem. Or—but what it would be elsewhere, that's irrelevant. You're here, and it's the numbers involved that concern me, though superficially the cases seem unrelated.

"One hundred and fifty of you out of the Jubilee group with what might be germ plasm disorders; one hundred fifty out of 20,000. At least one hundred fifty; take underreporting into account and there's probably more. Too many. They would have screened foetuses for irregularities before shipping them out."

"Well, what should I do then?"

"Get Dr. Ops to give you a new clone."

"But—"

"This one's damaged. If you train intensely, you'll make up the lost time and go down to Jubilee with the rest of us."

Or she might be able to delay and wind up part of Thad's settlement instead.

As if he'd heard her thought, Unique added "I wouldn't wait, if I were you. I'd ask for—no, demand another body—now. Soon as you can."

"Because?"

"Because your chances of a decent one will just get worse, if this is a radiation-induced mutation. Which I have absolutely no proof of. But if it is."

❁

"By the rivers of Babylon, there we sat down, and there we wept...." The pool reflected music, voices vaulting upward off the water, outward to the walls of white-painted steel. Unlike yesterday, the words were clear, because everyone was saying the same thing. Singing the same thing. "For the wicked carried us away...." Wayna wondered why the trustee in charge had chosen this song. Of course he was a prisoner, too.

The impromptu choir sounded more soulful than it looked. If the personalities of these clones' originals had been in charge, what would they be singing now? The "Doxology?" "Bringing in the Sheaves?" Did Episcopalians even have hymns?

Focusing on the physical, Wayna scanned her body for symptoms. So far this morning, she'd felt nothing unusual. Carefully, slowly, she swept the satiny surface with her arms, raising a tapering wave. She worked her legs, shooting backwards like a squid, away from the shallows and most of the other swimmers. Would sex underwater be as good as it was in freespace? No; you'd be constantly coming up for breath. Instead of constantly coming.... Last night, Doe had forgiven her, and they'd gone to Thad together. And everything was fine until they started fighting again. It hadn't been her fault. Or Doe's, either.

They told Thad about Wayna's pains, and how Unique thought she should ask for another clone. "Why do you want to download at all?" he asked. "Stay in here with me."

"Until you do? But if—"

"Until I don't. I wasn't sure I wanted to anyway. Now the idea sounds *so* much more inviting. 'Defective body?' 'Don't mind if I do.'" Thad's icon got up from their bed to mimic unctuous host and vivacious guest. "'And, oh, you're serving that on a totally unexplored and no doubt dangerous new planet? I just adore totally—'"

"Stop it!" Wayna hated it when he acted that way, faking that he was a flamer. She hooked him by one knee and pulled him down, putting her hand over his mouth. She meant it as a joke; they ought to have ended up wrestling, rolling around, having fun, having more sex. Thad didn't respond, though. Not even when Wayna tickled him under his arms. He had amped down his input.

"Look," he said. "I went through our 'voluntary agreement.' We did our part by letting them bring us here."

Doe propped herself up on both elbows. She had huge nipples, not like the ones on her clone's breasts. "You're really serious."

"Yes. I really am."

"Why?" asked Wayna. She answered herself: "Dr. Ops won't let you download into a woman. Will he."

"Probably not. I haven't even asked."

Doe said, "Then what is it? We were going to be together, at least on the same world. All we went through, and you're just throwing it away—"

"Together to do what? To bear our enemies' children, that's what, we nothing but a bunch of glorified mammies, girl, don't you get it? Remote-control units for their immortality investments, protection for their precious genetic material. Cheaper than your average AI, no benefits, no union, no personnel manager. *Mammies.*"

"Not mammies," Doe said slowly. "I see what you're saying, but we're more like incubators, if you think about it. Or petri dishes—inoculated with their DNA. Except they're back on Earth; they won't be around to see the results of their experiment."

"Don't need to be. They got Dr. Ops to report back."

"Once we're on Amends," Wayna said, "no one can make us have kids or do anything we don't want."

"You think. Besides, they won't *have* to make people reproduce. It's a basic drive."

"Of the meat." Doe nodded. "Okay. Point granted, Wayna?" She sank down again, resting her head on her crossed arms.

No one said anything for a while. The jazz Thad liked to listen to filled the silence: smooth horns, rough drums, discreet bass.

"Well, what'll you do if you stay in here?" Doe asked. "What'll Dr. Ops do? Turn you off? Log you out permanently? Put your processors on half power?"

"Don't think so. He's an AI. He'll stick to the rules."

"Whatever those are," said Wayna.

"I'll find out."

She had logged off then, withdrawn to sleep in her bunkroom, expecting Doe to join her. She'd wakened alone, a note from Dr. Ops on the mirror, which normally she would have missed. Normally she avoided the mirror, but not this morning. She'd studied her face, noting the narrow nose, the light, stubby lashes around eyes an indeterminate color she guessed could be called grey. Whose face had this been? A senator's? A favorite secretary's?

Hers, now. For how long?

Floating upright in the deep end, she glanced at her arms. They were covered with blond hairs that the water washed into rippled patterns. Her small breasts mounded high here in the pool, buoyant with fat.

Would the replacement be better-looking, or worse?

Wayna turned to see the clock on the wall behind her. Ten. Time to get out and get ready for her appointment.

"I'm afraid I can't do that, Wayna." Dr. Ops looked harassed and faintly ashamed. He hadn't been able to tell her anything about the pains. He acted like they weren't important; he'd even hinted she might be making them up just to get a different body. "You're not the first to ask, you know. One per person, that's all. That's it."

Thad's right, Wayna thought to herself. AIs stick to the rules. He could improvise, but he won't.

"Why?" Always a good question.

"We didn't bring a bunch of extra bodies, Wayna," Dr. Ops said.

"Well, why not?" Another excellent question. "You should have," she went on. "What if there was an emergency, an epidemic?"

"There's enough for that—"

"I know someone who's not going to use theirs. Give it to me."

"You must mean Thad." Dr. Ops frowned. "That would be a man's body. Our charter doesn't allow transgender downloads."

Wayna counted in twelves under her breath, closing her eyes so long she almost logged off.

"Who's to know?" Her voice was too loud, and her jaw hurt. She'd been clenching it tight, forgetting it would amp up her inputs. Download settings had apparently become her default overnight.

"Never mind. You're not going to give me a second body. I can't make you."

"I thought you'd understand." He smiled and hunched his shoulders. "I *am* sorry."

Swimming through freespace to her locker, she was sure Dr. Ops didn't know what sorry was. She wondered if he ever would.

Meanwhile.

❀

She never saw Doe again outside freespace. There'd still be two of them together—just not the two they'd assumed.

She had other attacks, some mild, some much stronger than the first. Massage helped, and keeping still, and moving. She met prisoners who had similar symptoms, and they traded tips and theories about what was wrong with them.

Doe kept telling her that if she wanted to be without pain, she should simply stay in freespace. After a while, Wayna did more and more virches and spent less and less time with her lovers.

Jubilee lay in Amends' Northern latitudes, high on a curving peninsula, in the rain shadow of old, gentle mountains. Bright-skinned tree-dwelling amphibians inhabited the mountain passes, their trilling cries rising and falling like loud orgasms whenever Wayna took her favorite tour.

And then there were the instructional virches, building on what they'd learned in their freespace classes. Her specialty, fiber tech, became suddenly fascinating: baskets, nets, ropes, cloth, paper—so much to learn, so little time.

The day before planetfall she went for one last swim in the pool. It was deserted, awaiting the next settlement group. It would never be as full of prisoners again; Thad and Doe weren't the only ones opting out of their downloads.

There was plenty of open freshwater on Amends: a large lake not far from Jubilee, and rivers even closer. She peered down past her dangling feet at the pool's white bottom. Nothing to see there. Never had been; never would be.

She had lunch with Robeson, Unique, and Jawann. As Dr. Ops recommended, they skipped dinner.

She didn't try to say goodbye. She didn't sleep alone.

And then it was morning, and they were walking into one of *Psyche Moth*'s landing units, underbuckets held to the pool's bottom, to its outside, by retractable bolts, and Dr. Ops unlocked them and they were free, flying, falling, down, down, down, out of the black and into the blue, the green, the thousand colors of their new home.

Good Boy

֍

"As out of several hundreds of thousands of the substrate programs comes an adaptable changing set of thousands of metaprograms, so out of the metaprograms as substrate comes something else.... In a well-organized biocomputer, there is at least one such critical control metaprogram labeled *I* for acting on other metaprograms and labeled *me* when acted upon by other metaprograms. I say *at least one* advisedly...."

Feels like floatin. Wrong smells come under the right ones, like the last few times. She got the table polished with lemon oil, or somethin similar, but what *is* that? Stronger than before, what is it, fish? Also stinks like Fourth a July, after all the firecrackers set off. I look around but only thing burnin is the candles, big circle of em, waverin on the table in front a me.

Her daughter sittin on the other side, lookin damn near white even with them African beads and robes she wear. Wonder she don't put a bone through her nose. I laugh at that picture, and the poor girl jump like I shot her. The music stops. It been playin soft in the background, but it cuts right off in the middle a Billy Strayhorn's solo.

I remember what she named her daughter. "Kressi," I say, "what you do to that record? Put it back on, girl, don't you know that's the Duke?"

"Sorry, ma'am." She sets back up this little white box she knocked over with her elbow when I laughed. "Chelsea Bridge" picks up where it left off, and I get outta my chair for a look around.

Room always seem to have way too many walls, twelve sides or maybe more, and they don't go straight up to a proper ceilin, but sorta curve themselves over. All plastic and glass and metal. I don't like it much. Cold. Black outside; night, with no sign a the moon.

On a bed in one a the too many corners is a man, the reason why she brought me. Face almost black as the sky, and shinin with sweat. He got the covers all ruched up off his legs and twisted around his arms. Fever *and* chills, it look like. His eyes clear, though.

"Hello there, young man," I say to him, bendin over. This body light, almost too easy to move. I like to throw myself on the bed with him. "What seems to be your problem?"

"Hey," he says back, smilin tired. "You must be Miz Ivorene's Great-Aunt Lona, yeah?" I nod. "Well, I hate to admit it, Miz Lona, but nobody seems to know exactly what the problem is. At first it was just tiredness, and they made sure I was getting a proper diet—"

I keep noddin while he talks, though a lotta the words he uses don't tell me a thing. Words very seldom do, even at they best. It's his cloud I'm interested in, his cloud a light. The light around his body, that should tell me what's wrong with him and what he needs to fix it.

But I stare and stare at this man's cloud, and I don't see not one thing wrong. He ain't sick.

But sweatin and in pain like that he ain't well, either.

By the time I figure this much out, I have stayed long enough. The young man stopped talkin, and he and Kressi lookin at me, waitin for golden truths. All I know is I got no work to do here. Place starts gettin dimmer and I turn back to the table, to the candles, I go back to the light. As I'm leavin I think of somethin I maybe *could* tell them; it's pretty obvious to me, but they so stuck in time, never know a thing until it's already done happen to them. "Good Boy," I say, on my partin breath. "Good Boy. Go deeper out. Get Good Boy." And wonder like always if they'll understand.

❦

"Some kinds of material evoked from storage seem to have the property of passing back in time beyond the beginning of this brain to previous brains…"

Ivorene McKenna slumped forward in her chair. Her head lowered slowly toward the tabletop, narrowly avoiding setting fire to her short locks. Her daughter Kressi slipped a bota into Ivorene's hand and cradled her shoulders as she sat back up, helping her guide the waterskin to her lips.

"What's wrong? What happened?" Edde Berkner had propped himself up on one wobbly arm. He peered anxiously through the gloom.

"Nothing. Lie down and rest. We have to play the session back and talk before we decide what to do." Kressi did her best to sound cool and professional. Like the rest of the colonists of Renaissance, she placed a high value on the rational and the scientific. They called themselves

"Neo-Negroes," and they didn't have much use for anything that couldn't be quantified and repeated.

As a child on their outbound ship, Kressi had enjoyed the lessons on Benjamin Banneker, George McCoy, and technology's other black pioneers. She'd wanted to *be* Ruth Fleurny, maverick member of the team that perfected the Bounce. It was because of Fleurny's stubborn insistence on cheap access for all descendants of enslaved Africans as a condition of the "star drive's" sale that the Neo-Negroes and a handful of similar expeditions had gotten off the ground.

In her daughter's opinion Ivorene was as intelligent as Fleurny, and just as stubborn. Maybe misguided, though. Ivorene's controversial theories, while couched in scientific terms, had a hard time finding acceptance among the Neo-Negroes. Sometimes Kressi wished she would just quit, right or wrong.

"That's enough, sweetheart." Kressi laid the bota on the table and picked up Ivorene's arm by the elbow, walking with her as she took her shaky body to bed. It was always this way, afterwards.

Kressi set her player on "sound curtain," and the rush of a waterfall filled the room. She aimed it towards Edde's bed and then stepped behind it into her mother's silence. The redbrown skin of Ivorene's face seemed slack and lusterless. Her long-boned hands were clammy. Her daughter chafed them briefly to warm them.

"Well, Kressi, what did Aunt Lona have to say?"

"Nothing. Nothing much." Kressi shrugged, trying not to show how much she hated having to act like anyone else besides her mom and Edde had been in the room. "I knocked the player over, and she scolded at me to put the music on again."

"What about Edde?"

"She looked at him, but he did most of the talking. I can show you the—"

"No, save the record for later. If she didn't say anything.... Who else can I ask?" Great-Aunt Lona, the New Orleans roots-woman, had been her only hope. Other *egun*, accessible ancestral spirits, were available. But none of them knew much on the subject of healing.

"When she was leaving—" Kressi broke off. "At first, you know, I thought it was just that weird way she talks."

"Southern."

"Right. So I wondered if maybe she meant 'Good-bye,' but what it sounded like was 'Good *boy*,' so it had to be a compliment to Edde, I guess...."

Ivorene pushed her lower lip out, brought her eyebrows together. "'Good Boy.'"

"She said it more than once."

"How many times?"

"Three."

"Aw, hell." Ivorene raised a hand from Kressi's clasp and flung one forearm across her eyes, fending off the inevitable. "I don't want to have to figure out how to bring *him* up."

"We have an ancestor named Good Boy?"

"No. Goddamit. Pardon my francais, sweetheart." Ivorene sighed and let her hand fall to the quilt-covered bed. "But goddamit. Good Boy."

❧

"We know something of the radiation limits in which we can survive. We know something of the oxygen concentrations in the air that we breathe, we know something of the light levels within which we can function…. We are beginning to see how the environment interlocks with our computer and changes its functioning."

Edde wanted to go home. Ivorene had told Dr. Thompson that they'd bring him back to the infirmary when they were through, though, so Kressi bundled him onto their flatbed cart with a stack of fresh sheets and extra blankets. He winced as she jolted the wheels over the ridge between the yurt's foundation and the ramp down to the colony's corridors.

"Sorry," Kressi muttered, embarrassed. The ramp hissed grittily under the cart's plastic wheels, and a fine white dust rose in their wake. Most of Renaissance City's surfaces had been sealed with plastic spray shortly after its excavation, but some private passages remained natural.

Kressi held the cart one-handed; only a negligible amount of control was needed despite the tunnel's 35° slope. With her other hand she fished in her robe's pocket for her remote. As she found and fingered it, the blind at the ramp's bottom rose.

At its bottom, the ramp leveled out. The wide cart made for a tight fit between the two bench-shaped blocks of likelime flanking the exit. Edde's berry-dark face shone with sweat. He closed his eyes as she turned into the corridor; vertigo was another symptom on his growing list.

Also, sensitivity to light. The tunnels of Renaissance City were just about shadowless, with frequent fluorescent fixtures on the walls. Kressi saw how his eyelids tightened and threw a pillowcase over Edde's face. He hadn't been this bad on the trip to the McKenna's from the infirmary. The pillowcase looked weird, but Edde thanked her, in a somewhat muffled voice. Another voice came from speakers set in the ceiling. Kressi listened for a moment.

"—Ship Seven concerns, Captain? As opposed to City-wide?"

Kressi withdrew her attention. She didn't care much for politics. She knew she was in Ship Four, a non-geographical ward named for one of the ten colonizing vessels. She knew that Ivorene had once been active, been elected as the Ship's Captain, and had lost her position due to her experiments in programming psychology. Renaissance Citizens studied and revered their ancestors but stopped short of desiring their actual presence. Ivorene's clinical practice had dwindled to nearly nothing; her status in the City's economy now rested solely on her position as an Investor.

Kressi headed into the main body of the ancient shallow sea from whose fossilized coral and sediment the city had been carved. As she wheeled her cart along, ramp openings and tunnel intersections became more common. Sometimes the ramps led upward, to storage areas and workshops. More often they led downward. Most Citizens preferred deeper dwellings. Though the atmosphere provided some protection from meteorites and radiation, it would be too thin to breathe comfortably for several generations.

As she approached the opening to one ramp in particular, Kressi's shoulders hunched in anticipation. They relaxed a little when she came close enough to see its lowered blind, then went back up as the blind began to retract. Kressi might have been able to clear the entrance before the blind rose high enough for Captain Yancey to hail her down. But the Captain would be offended to see

Kressi speeding away along the corridor in an obvious attempt to avoid conversation. Besides, she couldn't race off with poor Edde on the cart. She stopped and waited for her least favorite neighbor to appear.

Captain Yancey had a build like a gas tank. While not precisely cylindrical, she was tall, round-shouldered, and solid. Her floor-length robes, usually of dull silver, enhanced the illusion. She accepted Kressi's respectful greeting as her due, with a nod. Edde pulled off his pillow case, opened his eyes, groaned, and closed them again.

"Young man!"

"Edde's feeling real bad," Kressi explained. "I'm taking him over to the infirmary."

Captain Yancey's jaw relaxed a bit. "Dr. Thompson just told me how his beds were starting to fill up."

Kressi didn't wonder why the infirmary's Head should bother to inform Captain Yancey how things stood there. The infirmary wasn't her responsibility, or any other Captain's. But everyone told Captain Yancey everything.

"What are people getting sick from?" The planet Renaissance itself was supposed to be sterile, and the colonists had been well-screened and quarantined, then inoculated with benign "placeholder" microbes designed to discourage harmful ones that could cause diseases. Only 140 beds in the infirmary, and they'd never needed more than a fifth of them for the 3500-plus people. There was plenty of room for any who succumbed to illnesses caused by the placeholders' genetic drift.

"I'm not sure *what's* going on," Captain Yancey complained. "Dr. Thompson said he didn't have much time to talk. But as far as he could tell it wasn't anything catching, more like an allergy. Though how thirty people came to be all of a sudden afflicted with the same allergy he didn't bother to explain."

"Maybe I'd be better off at my place," Edde said in a worried voice.

"No, I'm bringing you back like we promised," said Kressi. With a polite smile she steered to Captain Yancey's right.

The Captain shifted so she still blocked Kressi's way. "Young lady, your mother hasn't been practicing any of her necromantic mumbo-jumbo on this poor boy, has she?"

Kressi's hands gripped the cart's handle tightly. Maybe she wasn't so sure how legitimate her mother's work was, but she didn't have to listen to other people put it down. Not even Captain Yancey. "That's not the way we prefer to think of it, Ma'am. Dr. Thompson referred Edde to us because he thought a psychological approach—"

"Call it what you want to, I say it's a disgraceful set of superstitions we ought to have left behind us in Africa. I always thought that your mother was a bright enough researcher, but I fail to understand why she has to clutter up our brand new paradigm with that sort—"

The conversation ended abruptly as Edde succumbed to a fit of coughing (yet *another* symptom). Captain Yancey retreated back down her ramp, saying over her shoulder that she was sure it couldn't be contagious, Dr. Thompson had sworn, but just to be on the safe side—

The ramp's descending blind cut her off.

In Renaissance City's core, the tunnel widened. Citizens sat in small, companionable groups on likelime benches outside ramp entrances.

Kressi greeted the people she knew by name, those from her Ship and several others. More knew her than vice versa. She'd been one of twenty kids on Ship Four.

Twenty of 350 passengers. And the other nine Ships had carried even fewer children. Kressi and the rest were celebrities by simple virtue of their age. A seven-year gap, the length of the voyage, separated them from the generation born here on Renaissance.

Of course Kressi knew all her peers, from whichever Ship. Edde was more popular than she was, and as she wheeled him through the City's center, they accumulated a small entourage.

Passela recognized him first. "Edde!" she crooned. "What's *wrong* with him?" she asked Kressi accusingly.

"He's sick." Kressi didn't like Passela much. She made too big a deal of her position as the oldest of the hundred-odd ship kids, and she had an irritating way of overemphasizing every other word.

But Fanfan, Passela's cousin, was cool. "Can I help you with that?" he asked. "You're headed for the infirmary, right?" Kressi let him put one hand on the cart's handle, though she could manage well enough on her own. They picked up speed. Passela and her sidekick Maryann stuck with them.

The infirmary lay on the far side of the core's white tunnels. Here the likelime took on a bluish tinge, legacy of the coral species that had burgeoned in this area of the slowly evaporating sea. The wall outside the infirmary's ramp housed the delicate remains of a huge, semi-shelled vertebrate. Kressi let Fanfan steer the cart down the ramp as she fondly stroked the fossil's curving, polished case and lightly brushed her fingertips along the arching trail of its skeletal extension. How had it felt, dying in the drying mud? Had it called upon its ancestors to save it from the sky's invading vacuum?

Kressi's lingering communion with the fossil lasted long enough that by the time she got inside the infirmary, Passela had taken over Edde's case. "He won't be *any* trouble, *really*, he won't; *I'll* nurse him with my *own two hands*," she told Ali, the staffer at the admitting console.

"Oh, good," said Ali. "I was afraid you'd ask to borrow a spare pair."

"What? Oh, you're putting me *on*, we don't grow limbs for *that* kind of stuff."

"I can go home," Edde offered. "I'm not so——" He interrupted his own protests with another painful-sounding coughing fit. That brought Dr. Thompson from behind the console's screen.

"Who's that? Edde Berkner? It's about time you checked yourself back in here, young man. Seems you've started some sort of psychosomatic epidemic. Half the symptoms showing up here this shift are the same as yours. I want you under observation."

"But, doctor, we don't have the staff——" Ali protested.

"I'm bringing in some contingents. And Anna Sloan's been malingering here long enough. Nothing much wrong with her." Dr. Thompson reached out one-handed and tapped at the console with barely a glance at its screen. "There. I'm releasing her. Pack up a couple of cold/hot compresses. I'll go break the news."

He turned to Passela and smiled. "You come help me get Miz Sloan out of Cot Twenty so you can strip and change it."

Passela gaped at Dr. Thompson as if she were a fish on an empty seabed and he were a hurtling black meteor headed her way. Kressi stepped between them. "Well, actually——"

"Kressi?" The doctor appeared to notice her for the first time. "Of course. You show her what to do," he said, dismissing both of them from his mind.

"And who are all these others? Patients? No? More volunteers? Train them or get them out of here, Ali." With an apologetic shrug, Kressi wheeled Edde around the side of the console in Dr. Thompson's wake. Passela made no move to follow them.

The infirmary was mostly one big, high-ceilinged ward, with honeycombed screens between the beds for a bit of privacy. Dr. Thompson had gone ahead of her to the cubicle containing Cot Twenty. A high, sharp voice cut through the honeycombing. "My feet, you haven't done nothin about my feet—"

Kressi hesitated at the doorway of the small space. There was barely room for her in there, let alone the cart with Edde. Miz Sloan was someone she'd never met before, but that didn't matter. "I know you," declared the woman on the bed. "You're that crazy Ivorene McKenna's daughter. You turnin me out for a mental case, doctor?"

"My mom's not crazy," said Kressi. She felt an angry flush creep up her pale cheeks, felt it deepen in her embarrassment at being able to flush so visibly. "Miz Sloan," she added, a tardy sign of respect for her elder.

Miz Sloan's feet stuck out from the near end of Cot Twenty. They seemed normal, neither swollen nor discolored, the soles a fairly even pink, but she winced as she swung them around off the side of the bed and lowered them into the see-through slippers sitting on the floor.

"Kressi's here to help you home, Anna," Dr. Thompson told Miz Sloan.

Miz Sloan lived close in; still, by the time Kressi had delivered her to the rooms she shared with two sisters, a niece and nephew, and the half-brother of her ex-husband, and listened to a rambling explanation of how Ivorene was crazy, but not pure-D crazy, and everyone knew she meant no harm with her attempts at talking to spirits, going home seemed pointless.

The lobby had held only one patient when she left. Now three more sat beside the closed door to Dr. Thompson's office, and another four leaned on the counter, talking earnestly to Ali.

Before she clocked in to help them, though, she had to call her mom. She squeezed past the waiting patients and scooted a wheeled stool in front of the screen. Her fingers drummed impatiently on the touchpad as her cursor swam through the city's directory. Dr. Thompson claimed voice rec caused problems with the infirmary's patient monitors. Finally, after what seemed like forever, she reached her home room.

Ivorene was logged on. Kressi got her to activate the live feed. Her mother sat in bed, propped up on pillows, working on a tray of food. She ate methodically, absentmindedly. Her dark eyes, so different from her daughter's hazel, shifted between the camera and two screens. Kressi could see text on one, but the resolution wouldn't quite let her read it.

"I'm starting my shift early, I guess," Kressi wrote.

"You guess?" Ivorene disliked sloppy statements.

"If it's all right with you. There are so many patients. Lots of them as bad as Edde…."

"Fine. Will you be home on time?"

Kressi glanced at the line of incomers, managing not to catch anyone's eye. "I'm not sure. Maybe."

The screen behind Ivorene showed what looked like an elongated brown bowling ball rotating in three dimensions.

With each pass, a new three- or four-armed cross appeared on its oblong surface. "Get home as quickly as you can, sweetheart. I have lots more work for us to do."

Kressi signed off, a little disturbed. It sounded like Ivorene wanted to go under again. If only she'd stick to more useful topics.... But Kressi had to put her personal concerns aside.

When her break came, Kressi did a few stretches and went right on working. Three days on, she'd had now, and the patient load heavier than ever. She wondered how she'd adjust to full adult status and the doubling of her hours requirement. One more year. She could hardly wait. She headed for the nearest blinking call light.

❀

"To hold and display the accepted view of reality in all its detail and at the same time to program another state of consciousness is difficult; there just isn't enough human brain circuitry to do both jobs in detail perfectly. Therefore special conditions give the best use of the whole computer for exploring, displaying, and fully experiencing new states of consciousness...."

Ivorene lowered herself slowly into her tank. Its refrigerator clicked on immediately. She'd been running a little hot lately—maybe coming down with Edde's mysterious ailment, like a major portion of the colony seemed bent on doing.

The tank was small, but held her without cramping. She hooded herself and checked the breathing apparatus. Like most of the colony's equipment, it was solidly put together, though based on dated technologies, "breakthroughs" discarded years before their departure.

She'd expected her daughter home almost an hour ago. The fail-safes were fine, but she wished Kressi had come back from her shift on schedule and helped her with this part.

Off with the hood for a moment so she could set the timer on the tank's lid. How many hours? Three. Good Boy had an affinity for that number.

About to re-hood, she remembered to check the water's salinity. A little on the low side. Shivering, she climbed out and grabbed a scoop of crystals from the bucket she kept beside the tank.

Salt was not a problem. Renaissance's seas had left behind plenty of pans and flats. Water was a little more expensive, dug up frozen from deep crevices, melted, and purified. Power was cheaper, about as easily available as salt. The cloudless skies of Renaissance did little to dim the light of its yellow-white star, Horus. The McKenna's unconventional surface dwelling gave them a great opportunity to convert that constant flood of photons to electricity.

She strapped on her hood again and let the blood-warm waters of the isolation tank lap over her, and the buoyant fluid lifted her and let her lose all connection with her physical surroundings. But her consciousness clung stubbornly to mundane concerns. Why was Kressi so late? Had she come down with this mysterious ailment, this Edde-Berkner-illness?

Ivorene's calls to the infirmary had all been answered by loops. Everyone was to remain calm. No contagious agents had been isolated. Infirmary beds were reserved for those in serious condition, and most complaints could be dealt with on an outpatient basis, no appointments necessary, first come, first served. The main thing, really, was to remain calm....

Which was what Ivorene would do if it killed her. She would not leap from the tank and rush to the infirmary, streaming salt water along the City's corridors. She would not embarrass her daughter with overprotectiveness, with the same overreactions her own parents had fallen ridiculous prey to. At fifteen, Kressi was as independent and self-sufficient as Ivorene had been able to make her.

And what if she was sick? She was at the infirmary, right? What better place? Dr. Thompson and his crew would do what they could for her. Ivorene would stay here and find out what else was possible.

Uselessly, she strove to still her thoughts. Then she stopped striving and let a million details wash over her mind, the way the waters of the tank covered her body. This had happened before, in the early stages of her research, the sessions where she'd made first contact with Aunt Lona and Uncle Hervey, the mechanic. She'd prepared for it. She'd stacked the deck, cramming for the last five hours, filling herself up with facts and speculations, clues for her wayward will to follow in the search for Good Boy, Exu, Papa Legba, Ellegua…his names strung themselves out before her in a mocking procession. Grasp one, gain none. The names grew brilliant feathers and flew off with raucous cries, but they went only a short distance. How to catch them? Salt their tails? But no, Good Boy preferred sweet things.

Candy. Visions of sugar plums danced in her head. Sticky and glistening, striped with pink and green. Ivorene concentrated on a hypnotic looking swirl of red and white, a gigantic lollypop with loads of projectability.

Sure enough, she was able to slow its swirling. The spinning disk resolved itself into a three-legged eye, then sped back up and streaked away.

Ivorene followed it. The disk's thin edge flickered as images imposed themselves over it at a rate too fast for her to perceive. She strove impatiently to focus beyond their interference. Suddenly, her perspective shifted and she was beside the disk—no, *above* it. The spinning spread, then slowed and stopped.

The disk's three legs were now composed of art-nouveau curves of thin red plastic. Its eye was gone, and its center pierced by a tall, silver pole. Legs and pole sat at the center of a papery circle of black and red, surrounded by a large, intricately grooved platter of thicker plastic, shiny black alternating with a duller, deep, dark grey.

She'd seen this sort of thing before. In an antique shop on Earth, during one of her expeditions to uncover portable cultural treasures. She'd decided against this particular one, then changed her mind in its favor, only to find it gone on her return to the shop.

It was a record. On a record player. She raised her gaze to the stone face before her. Shell eyes squeezed half shut, a shell mouth pursed in an amused smile.

"*Laroye, ago Elegba!*" Stay cool, trickster, the Yoruban greeting ran in translation. Coolness having a very high value in equatorial Africa. Ivorene launched into her prepared petition for Good Boy's assistance in healing her godson Edde of his strange affliction. She stopped abruptly as the image before her faded and threatened to break apart. Hard to hold abstractions in her current state. She tightened down on her desire. Squeezed. The enormous face before her brightened, though it remained amorphous. Encouraged, she produced for him the lump of her longing. It shone like a milky diamond, lustrous yet clear, then flew off toward him of its own accord. On impact, her prayer spread in ripples that seemed to sharpen and set the stone face, rather than disturbing it.

Shell eyes twinkled. The great head moved. A nod yes? Or instruction, a wish to be imitated? Ivorene looked down again, reading the label on the record. Atlantic. Chic. "Good Times."

So what did that mean? So Good Boy would help her if she played a record she knew she didn't have?

The spinning began again. Ivorene seemed now to stand on the record's surface, swinging around the silver pole as a scratchy song rose from below. Beyond the pole, white walls with gigantic murals pursued a stately rotation. Mushroom-haired women with impossibly long legs raised shapely brown hands against invisible enemies. Bald, athletic young men in flowing furs saluted crowds of admiring children with casual waves of large, lethal-looking side-arms.

Actually, there were a lot of weapons.

"Boys will be boys," a nasal voice advised her. "Better let them have their toys."

Well, there weren't any firearms on Renaissance. Explosives seemed like a pretty bad idea in a contained and pressurized atmosphere. Maybe the miners.... No. "No, sorry." She shook her head firmly. "No guns."

The world screeched backwards in its tracks, jerked violently forward with a wheezing shriek. Ivorene fell on her figurative ass as the process repeated itself. She clung to the record's ridges, shooting back and forth around its axis without warning. An eery choir wailed in time to the wild stops and starts.

The disturbance ended as suddenly as it had begun, and the world's smooth spin resumed. A new number played, a steady march. "On guard! Defend yourself!" its singers admonished her.

No doubt.

A flash of brilliance at the pole's tip drew her attention. It grew into a humming globe, an irregularly-rayed ball of slowly coruscating light. Flickering arms of color drew her closer—her prayer? So much bigger, now. So strong—it had to be more, more than she'd asked for. It had to be—

She resisted. But the pole loomed larger and larger. If she touched it—if she grasped it firmly, with both hands, she could call down that ball of lightning on her head. She could know Good Boy in her heart, as her personal savior. She could cure the colony of its mysterious non-epidemic and get the respect she deserved, the respect she'd already more than earned. She could fill herself with the power, the glory—

She could get herself possessed while she was alone, without anyone to help or protect her, or see to it that she ever came back to normal.

On guard. Defend yourself.

She made an effort. A step backward. It turned into a lunge forward. Off-balance, she caught herself on the silver pole and clung there as the light descended, swift and slow.

⚜

"…There may be other controls and controllers, which, for convenience, I call *supraself metaprograms.* These are many or one depending on current states of consciousness in the single self-metaprogrammer. These may be personified *as if entities*…."

Kressi walked slowly home, leaning heavily on the handle of the flatbed. Maybe she should just lie right down on it. She could have pushed herself along the walls if they weren't so far apart. She felt very, very tired. A shift and a half she'd worked. The infirmary was now completely out of pulp sheets, which was just as well. The plastic bed pads might be less comfortable, but they cleaned up efficiently.

She hoped her mother wouldn't be too mad. Ivorene hadn't said *not* to work late, not exactly.... And Dr. Thompson wanted her back early, too.

At the top of the ramp she hesitated. The yurt's familiar hollow was filled with darkness. The only light filtered in behind her, shining up the ramp. Power out? She shifted cautiously to her left. No. Two red tell-tales glowed in her field of vision like the mismatched eyes of some squat monster: Ivorene's isolation tank. Her mother had gone under. Alone. Guilt tweaked at her; she should have come home earlier.

But Ivorene *ought* to have called her.

The yurt's polarized glass panels showed blankness. No stars. Not for the next few hours. Horus was setting now, triggering the glass's reflective properties. Why was she standing there in the dark? "Light one. Light two," she commanded.

Her stomach grumbled at her loudly. Hungry and tired. Tired and hungry. And she had to talk to her mother about going back early.

She shoved the cart into place next to the ramp and went to the tank to see how much longer Ivorene would be inside. The timer was counting up, not down. Ivorene had been due out of isolation half an hour ago.

Anxiously, she activated the mike. "Ivorene, I'm home. Can you come out now? It's Kressi," she added. No telling what state her mother's mind was in. How could Ivorene have missed the alarm?

A long pause, then her mother's voice came through the speaker, a bit odd. "Right."

"Okay." Kressi eyed the tank suspiciously till Ivorene emerged dripping from its depths. "Rough session?" she asked her.

Ivorene stared around the yurt absently. Kressi assumed she was looking for a towel and brought one over. "Mom?" Ooops. Ivorene hated for Kressi to call her that. But she seemed not to notice the slip-up. Or the towel. Kressi laid it over Ivorene's shoulders. "I'll get you a robe."

When she turned back from the closet, Ivorene was walking around the yurt in great strides, toweling herself off vigorously. But shivering, Kressi saw as she draped her mother in soft red fabric. It must have been bad. Why hadn't Ivorene waited?

Why hadn't she come home on time?

She picked the damp towel up from the floor where Ivorene had dropped it. "Let me get your hair for you." A loud, hoarse cackle made her start.

"Ha! I have my hair already where it belongs, here upon my head!"

"But—I—but it's wet!" Kressi protested, confused.

Her mother frowned. A drop of water slid down her forehead and trickled along one slanted brow. "You are correct. Remedy this."

She let Kressi lead her to her chair at the kitchen table and towel dry her short locks, then got up and strolled restlessly around the yurt's perimeter. She picked up random objects and examined them, then lost interest. A loud crash sounded as Ivorene emptied a jar of trade beads onto the floor. After watching the tiny cylinders of colored glass roll away from her, she moved on, slipping and unconcernedly righting herself whenever she stepped on one.

Kressi was pretty sure by this time that she understood what had happened.

From her mother's perspective, Ivorene had become possessed. From the perspective of everyone else on the planet, she was insane.

Only temporarily, of course. All Kressi had to do was—

Was remember her instructions. What to do if things went wrong. And believe they'd work.

Her mother stood holding a cube of her ex-husband, Kressi's father, the white man she'd left behind when she became a Neo-Negro. Her face wore a remote, detached expression.

Kressi's first memories were of quarantine. She'd never really known her father. She wondered if he'd have been able to help her, if he were here.

Resolutely, she removed the cube from her mother's hands, held both of them in her own, and stepped firmly on Ivorene's right foot. Two sharp jerks down on both arms at once—like that—

Laughing, the face in front of her split wide into a most un-Ivoreneish grin. "What, you want for me to leave already? Is your mother's body, though, and she invited me to come, to solve your mystery. So I am going to stay!"

৵৪

"...one cannot know as a result of this kind of solitudinous experiment whether or not the phenomena are explicable only by non-biocomputer interventions or only by happenings within the computer itself, or both."

Light receded, poured out of her like water from a strainer, left her sitting in her own chair, dressed in her red robe. She knew how she'd gotten there, knew Kressi had come home and roused her from the tank. Nothing was lost. What happened while Good Boy rode her remained in her memory, only faded, thinned of all immediacy. And her body felt so heavy now that she had to lift it on her own. But she made her hand rise, reached out to touch her daughter's cheek.

"Don't worry, Kressi. I'm still here. This is right, what Good Boy's trying to do—"

"Ivorene? You're okay?" Tears filled her daughter's eyes and voice.

"Yes." She wanted to sound surer. "Listen, I'm going to let him come back again, I just didn't want—"

"'Him?' Ivorene, why won't you—Good Boy's not *real*! Admit it!" Kressi stood and stormed away from the table so Ivorene had to turn to see her. Now the tears were of anger.

"Define real," Ivorene said, then sagged in her seat. She was too tired to argue. "No, never mind. Don't. Whether Good Boy or Aunt Lona or any of them are 'real' doesn't matter in the end. Just act like they are and everything will work out fine."

"But—"

"For three days, that's all. That's how long I asked him to stay." Stubborn silence. At the edge of Ivorene's vision, whiteness flickered. With each pulse it grew, drawing in, a bright tunnel down which her daughter's once-more-worried face receded. Saying words she couldn't hear. Apologies? Ivorene overrode them with her own instructions: "Three days. Promise me that."

❧

"…each computer has a certain level of ability in metaprogramming others-not-self."

Posted on Citynet 01.18.2065, 08:18:14
FROM: goodboy@mckenna.home
TO: ALL USERS:
Subject: Be a Souldier in the Army of Uncle Jam!
Body:

PARTY UP!

You are hereby notified that in accordance with the
wishes of the Supreme Funkmeister,
you are required to bring your Waggity Asses on over to
McKenna's Mothership
for the
CELEBRATION!
of our Grand Ascension to the status of
Chocolate City, Capitol of the Known Negro Universe, said
CELEBRATION!
to commence on the evening of 01.21.2065, promptly at
21:00 hours.
IT'S THE BOMB!!
[link to mckennapage.home]

❧

Sent via Citynet 01.18.2065, 13:34:10
FROM: pearl@yancey.home
TO: ivorene@mckenna.home
CC: CAPTAINGROUP, samthompson@infirmary.city
Subject: Attached Posting
Body:

Allow me to bring the attached to your attention, Miz McKenna, as it may somehow have escaped your notice. It purports to issue from a "goodboy," currently unlisted as a Citizen. But the voice ID closely parallels your own, and reveal commands show your login.

Miz McKenna, aside from the highly questionable language of this "invitation," the obvious irresponsibility of organizing a frivolous assembly now, at the height of an epidemic, leads me to conclude that the posting is a clever but childish hoax on the part of your normally quite level-headed daughter. Please take immediate steps to disavow it as such.

Far be it from me to meddle in your personal affairs, Miz McKenna, but I'm sure you'll agree that her understandable longing for popularity does not excuse Kressi's participation in a prank of this magnitude.

❄

Sent via Citynet 01.18.2065, 18:42:33
FROM: maryann@gonder.home
TO: goodboy@mckenna.home
Re: Be a Souldier in the Army of Uncle Jam!
Body:

Passela told me to tell you this is such a swollen idea! Or I guess I should say it's The Bomb! Those fashions on your page were just wild, and I hope we can get our printers sufficiently togetha in time for the big partay!

Now for the important news—I heard Fanfan ask his daddy if he could borrow his record player! *And* some of his old jams! I bet he has lots of the songs your page listed, because I was over at their place one time, and in one closet they had this whole big rack of those black plastic circles! So it's only the guns you have to worry about getting.

Are you sure your mother won't mind?

Filter House

❄

Sent via Citynet 01.19.2065, 00:16:29
FROM: samthompson@infirmary.city
TO: pearl@yancey.home
CC: CAPTAINGROUP, ivorene@mckenna.home
Re: Attached Posting
Body:

Are you purposely TRYING to set off a City-wide panic? Of all the officious, unscientific nonsense I've heard on this expedition, yours, Pearl, takes the pound cake! This is not, repeat NOT an epidemic.

There is no, repeat NO single, underlying organism that I can discover at the root of this recent wave of disorders. On the other hand, whatever it is seems to be affecting just about everyone on Renaissance. To a greater or lesser extent.

I've attached several tables I've been working on in my copious free time.... I don't know what they mean yet, but there's an unprecedented variation in the degree to which symptoms manifest, in the number of symptoms any case exhibits, and in the comparative seriousness of symptoms. Fear of insanity, salt cravings, heart palpitations, fevers, hernias, sore feet, sprained backs, tonsillitis—what have they got in common? Nothing. Except that they all cropped up as problems at about the same time. But not in the same household or among workers on the same shift at the same plant.

So whatever this thing is, it's not contagious. There's no excuse for your killjoy attitude, Pearl. Let the kids have their party.

⚛

Sent via Citynet 01.19.2065, 12:12:12
FROM: ivorene@mckenna.home
TO: pearl@yancey.home
CC: CAPTAINGROUP, samthompson@infirmary.city
RE: Attached Posting

The invitation is entirely legitimate. Those who find the language in which it's couched to be odd should refer to the available historical data on mid-Twentieth Century black musicians, specifically *Sun Ra, Parliament, Funkadelic,* and *Earth, Wind & Fire.* A notable space-travel mystique developed around their work, and it is to honor its creative impetus that I've arranged for y'all to party up! Everybody party up! Come fly with me! I *am* the Mothership Connection. You *have* overcome, for I am here!

⚛

"At times the cross-model synesthetic projection may help…
excitation coming in the objective hearing mechanisms can be
converted to excite visual projection. The commonest excitation used
here is music…."

A good long ride on this one. She a strong horse, Ivorene. I even let her get some sleep, talk to her tickety-tap machine a little, calm her daughter down with some kinda explanations. No danger of losing my seat. She don't buck, don't rear. Three days.

All the partay people comin now. I made many preparations. Poor nervous daughter Kressi done helped, shown me how ta cook the candy and color over them too bright lights. But the pole, I erect that sucker all myself.

We sit in chairs by the door. "Raise up the blind," I say. She a good, obedient girl. And wearin the blue I said, most pleasin to the ocean. Her mother and I both told her time and again, till I do my business I ain't goin nowhere.

Fillin up the ramp, the peoples who been waitin come in. They laugh, but not too loud yet. One brought me some a my music. Kressi gets up to make it play. I watch while more people arrive. Everybody stop an stare when they see my big ole pole. It stuck up in the middle a everthing, hard to miss.

The expression on that there lady's face make me wonder how she ever gonna reach escape velocity. Don't she know this a partay?

Apparently not. "I couldn't believe you'd actually allow this to take place," she tells me.

I smile. "I allow all sort a things." I offer her Kressi's seat.

"Well, no, I can't really stay..."

"But how else you gonna know all the people wind up comin?"

She give me a narrow-eyed look. "Ivorene? What's gotten into you? Are you—you're not—you haven't been—"

She think my horse drunk. "Siddown and fine out," I say, and now she accept my invitation. I get her to take some candy, too. Lemondrop. Ain't no need to shock her system with too much sweetness.

All this time, guests keep arrivin. All dressed up, nice, bright colors, shiny fabrics, boots, big belts—not quite right, not exactly how they did it, back in the day, but— they lookin pretty good! I keep handin out the candy, hopin everyone get to enjoy themself.

Grooves start jumpin. I can't contain myself, never no good at that. Fore she know it, Miz Mealymouth holdin my candy bowl, and I am out on the dance floor actin like anybody's fool. "Put a glide in your stride and a dip in your hip!" I sing over the music. Why they all just watchin me?

Next song. Kressi come up behind me, stand still a minute. I turn so she see me smile. Take her hand, spin her round, dosi-do an play the clown. She lose some a her worry, gain some grace. Soon she swishin her robe like waves and dancin like light on the water. Very Yemaya, very Mother of Fishes. Good. That's who we got to bring down here tonight.

Boy over there wanna dance with her. I get out the way. In a minute a whole bunch of em cuttin loose. Flyin elbows, flashin feet. Funk start to rise.

Someone important at the door. I go see why they not comin in.

Cause the one told me she really can't stay tryin to keep him out, that's why! Big shinin man in a paper dress standin there while she tell him get on back in bed. She call him Edde. "Yes, Miz Yancey," he say, and nod. Too polite to push her out the doorway.

Not me. But I do it without touchin. All a sudden, she sittin down. I help her back up. Edde head for the pole.

"Call Dr. Thompson!" this Yancey tell me. *Tell* me. Tell *me*!

She won't leave, now I wish she would. I could make her, but I rather dance. Rather she did, too. Like everybody else *but* her. Funk steady risin, but this woman drag us down. And we close, so goddam *close*.

Gotta get over the hump. Gotta get over the hump.

Where my bopgun?

I look all around. Someone shoulda brought it to me before now. Ain't I already asked? Sure, when my horse first pray to me. Nobody better make me ask a second time.

Edde hoppin all around, jumpin so he see over people's shoulders, headed for my pole. He there. He grab it.

Swing down, sweet chariot, stop, and let me ride.

Two now. I on two horses. Much easier. Look at me across the room. Look at me back. These are the Good Times.

Homin in on Miz Yancey. All she wanna do is stan there. I bring me some dancers. Soft music, an they swirl like liquid, spillin over the floor. Swoosh, shoosh, they spin Miz Yancey round, rock her shoulders, sway her hips, draw her deep into that psychoalphadiscobetabioaquadoloop. Carry her like a cup a foam on they tide. Over to my pole. Twirl her round, turn her loose and let her grab on to stand steady. She ready. I watch the funk gettin up for the downstroke. Watch it fall upon that horse's head.

She come! Mother of Fishes, she come! Twistin, slidin, slippin, ridin—here among us! Yemaya has come!

⁂

"...control is based upon exploration of n-dimensional spaces and finding key spaces for transformations, first in decisive small local regions, which can result in large-scale transformations."

Kressi opened her eyes on chaos. How long had she been dancing? It had felt so good to forget, to let the music take her far away. But where was she?

Surging dancers squeezed her against a wall. Perpendicular. Smooth, unjointed. She was in a corridor, outside the yurt. But Good Boy's music still surrounded her. Someone had patched the yurt's sound system into the City's speakers.

Miz Sloan capered by in Ali's arms, transparent slippers kicking high. Then the flood of dancers ebbed, trailing a pair she recognized with a shock as Passela and Fanfan. They were—he was—from behind Passela had shoved her hands inside the front of his pants, *way* inside. As she watched, Fanfan squatted down slightly, allowing Passela to leap astride his hips. Without dropping a beat, they vanished into the crowd. Kressi caught her breath, then started slowly after them, thinking hard.

Either they had all gone crazy at the same time, or it was a very good thing she'd spit out that piece of candy her mother gave her.

No. Not her mother. Whatever it was Ivorene had called up to help them. A supraself metaprogram, to use her term. Three days ago, Kressi had agreed to go along with anything it wanted. To believe that her mother had known what she was doing and that this—entity—would somehow perform the task it had been set and leave. It had been hard to stick by her decision. It wasn't getting any easier.

The corridor emptied. Kressi spotted her favorite fossil embedded in a nearby stretch of likelime. She was outside the infirmary.

She went into the empty lobby. Over the music's steady throb, she heard Dr. Thompson's angry protests. She had to see what was happening in the cubicles, in the ward. Even if there was nothing she could do to stop it.

There was nothing she could do, or even see. Nothing but the brightly colored backs of her fellow Citizens, pulsing rhythmically, flaring and floating and— She closed her eyes. Tight. But shining patterns formed, even more dangerous to her focus.

She opened her eyes again and pounded on the back before her. The drug would wear off soon. John C. Lilly used LSD, but Ivorene had opted for a tailored version of Narby's Amazonian formula in her early experiments. Presumably this was what Good Boy had printed out and put into the candy. The dancers' ecstasy would last no more than half a shift, and the effects on Kressi would be slighter, and of a much shorter duration.

Long seconds passed till the man blocking her way moved. He backed up suddenly, kicking her in the shins. Others did the same, and the tight knot of dancers dissolved into a loose semi-circle around the door of Cubicle One. Kressi peered between shifting shoulders and saw Captain Yancey emerge. Her unblinking eyes seemed to protrude slightly from her head. She raised dusty, chalk-white hands and held them clasped in front of her, then began to move them slowly together, as if working up a lather.

Without warning, Captain Yancey whirled and stalked off to her left. Kressi scrambled to follow her. A high, burbling voice wailed through the speakers: "I can't swim! I never could swim! Let go mah laig!"

Six's occupant looked oddly serene, though his room was filled with partying strangers. Two men sat on opposite sides of his bed, propping him erect. Sweat glittered on his forehead as he swayed lightly to the music. Kressi glanced automatically at the headboard: Charles Tobin— temp 40/heart rate 120—

Captain Yancey leaned forward and placed both hands on Mr. Tobin's head. The patient slithered down onto his bed as if to avoid her. She stooped to maintain contact and began to shudder slowly, so deeply she shook the patient and his cot. Mr. Tobin's body straightened, then arched like a leafspring, vibrating faster and faster. Horrified, Kressi tried to call up the courage to step forward and touch him, somehow stop what was happening. But it ended on its own before she could manage that. Captain Yancey stood back and left him flat on the cot. His hair and face were white with whatever she'd rubbed on her hands. He seemed to be asleep. The headboard thought so, too.

The room emptied. Kressi hesitated, then hurried out.

She barely made it into Seven. Dancers screened the cot. A new voice sang to what sounded like the same song, assuring everyone that they could swim in the water and not get wet.

A child's frightened crying cut through the music. It came from the cot. Kressi struggled to reach it. By the time she got there, the child lay quiet and calm.

It was Junior Watt. Kressi recognized the normally feisty ten-year-old despite his mask of white. His eyelids fluttered briefly as she called his name, then he sighed and smiled. As she watched, the headboard's readouts flickered, changing to those of a healthy sleeping boy.

"What are you *doing?*" she asked Captain Yancey.

In response, the older woman grabbed Kressi by her braids and pulled her closer. Shutting her eyes reflexively, Kressi felt a hand scrub her face with a slightly gritty powder. The press of dancers suddenly stilled to hold her motionless. She twisted stubbornly in place, getting nowhere. The hand's scrubbing motions softened, becoming oddly gentle, reminding her of—of—

Of how her mother washed her face one morning, grooming her for an online interview, just weeks before the ascent to their ship. She'd fought Ivorene, flung away the washcloth, but her mother had picked it up and persisted in her work. Captain Yancey's touch felt as tender, and as determined.

No. Not Captain Yancey's. This supraself metaprogram's touch.

It was cleaning its children.

Kressi relaxed. And sensed a lightness, a lifting. As if old, nameless, chains had fallen from her, training weights she'd put on long ago and since forgotten.

She opened her eyes slowly. The room was empty. Then Dr. Thompson walked through the cubicle's doorway holding a gun. "Kressi?" he asked.

"I'm okay. It's just—"

"What's that stuff on your face?"

Good question. "I dunno."

"It's on the others, too. I'll get a sample container." He turned to leave.

"Wait—you're not going to shoot Captain Yancey, are you?"

"No. Where'd you get—" He looked at the gun he was tucking absentmindedly under his robe's sash. "Oh. This. It's only a water pistol." He pulled it free again and looked down at it as if it belonged to another person, someone immature and hopelessly embarrassing. "I had it in my office for some reason, and when they all came in at once it seemed…."

"Here. Take it." Dr. Thompson handed her the gun. It felt heavy and wet. "I'm not going to try to stop them. This laying on of hands, or whatever you want to call it, it's working."

Kressi had come to the same conclusion, but it startled her to hear him say so.

"I knew from the beginning an unconventional course of therapy was called for, but—" He shrugged his shoulders and waved an arm vaguely in the air. "Next time you talk to Ivorene, ask her to give me a call so we can discuss what she's done."

It was at this point that Kressi realized that her mother had been missing from among the dancers. That she'd been absent ever since Kressi roused herself from her trance. Ever since the party's migration to the infirmary. So Ivorene must still be back at home.

No, not Ivorene. Or maybe, yes. If the wave of symptoms had been conquered, the Good Boy metaprogram might have finally given up his hold. It would be Ivorene waiting for Kressi at the yurt, worn out from her long ordeal, not even sure of her own success.

With that in mind, Kressi called home. No answer. Maybe all it meant was that her mother felt too tired to open the feed. But when A Shift's crew showed up minutes later, unaffected by candy, she was happy to leave Captain Yancey and her entourage to them. By then the music's volume had dropped, and a lot of partiers had drifted off; perhaps half their number remained. Dr. Thompson followed them through the ward, smiling and recording notes, nodding at Kressi as she took her leave.

The blind was still raised at the bottom of the yurt's ramp. She plodded to the top without shutting it, expecting to find drugged or sleeping stragglers, but the place was empty. Everyone had gone. Everyone except one slim figure robed in black and red, sitting at the base of the pole Good Boy had erected. Her mother?

No. The figure popped to its feet like a button and lifted its chin to peer at her through half-lidded eyes, and Kressi knew there was one more guest to get rid of.

But how?

"Well?" asked Good Boy. "I kep all a my promises now. How bout yours?"

Promises? "I said I'd help you for three days. I did. You said you'd cure the mystery disease. Okay, that's pretty much taken care of. Which means it's time for you to go."

Good Boy tilted his head consideringly. "There was the partay, yes. Music, dancing. Sweetness we shared. But these wasn't all a my requirements."

"I *require* my mother back! Good Boy, you gave your word—" Kressi lowered her head and took a deep breath, trying to imagine life if Ivorene never recovered possession of her body. Her mother would be locked up, drugged helpless. Kressi would get handed off to someone to be fostered till she reached sixteen, probably Captain Yancey or worse, and of course nobody'd ever be able to make Ivorene any better because there was nothing really *wrong* with her—

"Come now." Good Boy's tone had turned suddenly cajoling. He stepped quickly toward her, almost running. "I am aware you got it. Hand it over. All gonna be well."

"Hand *what* over?" Unnerved by his proximity, she put her hands in her pockets to prove that they were empty and felt something hard and slick.

Dr. Thompson's water pistol. She pulled it out. "This?"

Ivorene's teeth gleamed against her wide-stretched lips in a glad smile. "At last!" Good Boy received the gun reverently, cradling it in upturned palms as he examined it. The smile faded. "This a toy?"

"Good Boy, it's all we *have*!"

He aimed it at her. "It loaded?" And shot her full in the face.

Kressi choked, coughed, swallowing salty water and wiping it from her eyes. She heard him laughing, heard him stop, heard the clatter of something hitting the yurt's floor. Felt shaking arms wrap around her damp head and haul it closer, pressing it up against cloth-covered flesh.

She fought free, but when she could see again there was something different—

"Mom?"

"How many times do I have to tell you not to call me outta my name like that! Just because I *happen* to be your—"

"Ivorene!" She nestled back into her mother's arms once more. For however long she could.

❀

"New areas of conscious awareness can be developed, beyond the current conscious comprehension of the self. With courage, fortitude, and perseverance the previously experienced boundaries can be crossed into new territories of subjective awareness and experience."

Stars shone through the yurt's many windows. Everything else was dark till Kressi held her lighter to the three candles in front of her. Three long flames leapt up, wavering golden fingers that quickly steadied and grew still. Two people sat at the table, two biocomputers containing at least that many control metaprograms. One of them happened to have given birth to the other.

Dr. Thompson, Captain Yancey, and a dozen others waited to watch the night's proceedings through the live feed. A sheet from the printer contained a list of their questions.

Ivorene reached around the candles to grasp her daughter by her wrist. "Who do you think we should get for them to talk to?" she asked. Her palm slid against her daughter's in an almost unconscious clasp.

You, Kressi wanted to say, but no, this was research. Talking to Ivorene wasn't an option right now. Wasn't always going to be one. Not with *her* mother. "You decide this time."

Sensitive instruments recorded and broadcast Ivorene's reply: "Good Boy."

Kressi sat up in her chair, planted her feet more firmly on the floor, and released her mother's hand.

※

"...the bodies of the network housing the minds, the ground on which they rest, the planet's surface, impose definite limits. These limits are to be found experientially and experimentally, agreed upon by special minds, and communicated to the network. The results are called consensus science."

(All quotes are from John C. Lilly's *Programming and Metaprogramming in the Human Biocomputer: Theory and Experiments*, second edition, 1974, Bantam Books, New York, NY.)

Little Horses

The white candle on top of her dresser had burned dirty that morning. When she stood up from her prayers she saw its glass sooting up black. Big Momma would say that meant danger of some kind. But what? To who? Not Carter. It was after Carter's funeral Big Momma had made her promise to burn it.

Uneasily, Leora turned her gaze away from the boy beside her on the car's back seat. Sometimes it was hard not to stare at him. And sometimes, for the same reasons, it hurt.

It was her job, though, keeping an eye on him. Leora did her duty. Especially today; might be he was who the candle had been warning her about. If Big Momma had a phone, she could have called her and found out.

If it was her own self in danger, that didn't matter. Not that she'd commit the sin of suicide, but it wasn't natural she should be living on after her child.

In case her suspicions were right, Leora had stayed close as she could by the door to the boy's rooms when his teacher came that morning. She'd cut his sandwich in extra tiny pieces, even lifting the bread to check the chicken salad surreptitiously with her finger for bones. Left the lunch dishes for the maid to clear while she fussed at nothing in the basement, keeping an eye on him building his boat models till his mother came and insisted they go outside.

"Take the car," she suggested, standing on the stairs in one of her floaty chiffon numbers, designed to hide her weight. Against Mr. McGinniss's wishes, his wife had hired a new chauffeur. Now she needed to prove he wasn't a waste of money.

Outside the car's windows, Belle Isle's spare spring beauty waltzed lazily around them as they followed the road's curves. The man seemed to understand his business. Not real friendly, but then he wasn't getting paid to talk to the nanny. The 1959 Cadillac was the McGinnisses' third best car, last year's model. He had it running smooth and fine; she could barely hear the engine.

He had known the best way to take to the park, too, staying on course as the street name changed from Lake Shore to Jefferson and passing up the thin charms of Waterworks Park without hesitating one second. And he had circled the stained white wedding cake of the Scott Fountain as many times as the boy asked him. Now he steered them past some people fishing, practicing for the Derby coming in June.

Without looking, Kevin's hand sought and found Leora's. He was all of six years old. Six-and-a-half, he would have said. His fingers stretched to curl over the edge of her pinkish palm, the tips extending between her knuckles. Not such a high contrast in color as it could have been. His daddy was what they called "Black Irish," which was only about his hair being dark and curly and his eyes brown and his skin liable to take a tan easier than some white folks.

A gentle turn, and the road ran between the waters of Lake Tacoma and the Detroit River. Kevin's hand nestled deeper into her own. She let her eyes sweep slowly away from the window, over the car's plush interior and the back of the driver's head, the pierced-glass barrier dividing him from the rear seat, to the boy's snub-nosed profile. A pause; then she slid her glance past him through the far window to the Canadian shore. So much the same. But different. A different country. Slaves had escaped to Ontario a hundred years ago. Some of them settled there and never came back.

The driver spoke unexpectedly. "Here's the boat museum site coming up, Mester McGinniss." A pile of bricks, low and flat, ugly even in the late afternoon sun, occupied the road's left side. Holes gaped for windows. The driver honked his horn at a man sitting hunched over on a sawhorse with his back to them and turned sharply onto Picnic Way, stopping right on the road. Two red trucks and a beat-up black-and-purple sedan squatted on the muddy lot around the half-finished museum. "You want to get out, Mester McGinniss, take a look around?" What was there to look at they couldn't see from where they were sitting? With Kevin's clean loafers in mind, Leora told the driver to keep driving. Time enough for them to visit when it was open; Kevin wasn't like most boys his age, excited by earthmovers and heavy machinery.

They headed for the island's center. The Peace Carillon loomed up, narrow and white like that black-burning candle. Usually Belle Isle's spacious vistas calmed Leora's spirit, but not today.

At Central they turned east again, toward the island's wilder end. "Will we see any deer?" Kevin asked.

"No tellin," Leora answered.

"I think we should get out when we get to the woods. They're never going to walk up close to a car." He took his hand back to hold himself up off the seat cushions with two stiff arms, a sure sign of determination. "We could hide ourselves behind some trees."

Leora was about to tell him about the one time she'd seen them there, a whole herd, eight or ten wild deer, crossing Oakway bold as you please. But the driver interrupted her thoughts. "A fine idea, Mester McGinniss," he said, as if he was the one to decide those sorts of things. "We'll do just that."

No one else on the road before them or behind them, and the driver took advantage of that to step on the gas again. What was the man's name? Farmer, she recalled, and was ready to speak up sharp to him, white or not, when he slowed down. Way down.

He grinned back over his shoulder at the boy, a nervous grin not coming anywhere near his pale eyes. "Like that?" he asked. Kevin nodded, grave as his uncle the judge. "You ever try driving?" Leora clamped her lips firmly shut to make sure she didn't call the man a fool to his face.

"Maybe when we get safe into the woods I'll take you up on my lap, let you to steer a bit afore we ambush them deer, Mester McGinniss." Farmer turned to the front. "If your mammy won't mind."

"I ain't his mammy."

"Beg pardon, but I thought that's what—"

"Mammies is Southern. I'm Kevin's nanny."

Farmer muttered something, his voice low, lost under the quiet engine's. She should have kept her own counsel. She should have, but there was only so much a body could take, and after nearly thirty years of passing up on pound cake and plucking her eyebrows and creaming her hardworking hands and pressing her hair and dyeing and altering her employers' worn out gowns so you wouldn't hardly recognize them, Leora was not about to sit silent while some ignorant peckerwood called her after a fat, ragheaded old Aunt Jemima. And her so light-skinned. Even at forty-two, she was better looking than that. Not long ago, she had been beautiful.

Mr. McGinniss had called her irresistible.

Shadows covered the car hood, the road ahead, the view out of either window. Thin shadows, thickening as she noticed them, leafless branches crowding together to warm their sap in the spring sun. They were in the woods, and suddenly that ignorant driver had swung onto an unpaved side road. The car slowed to a crawl, ruts and puddles rocking it along. Farmer stopped, for no reason Leora could see. "Is this where we hide to look for the deer? And I can learn to drive?" the boy asked.

"Yessir, Mester McGinniss. This here's the place. Just let me take you on my lap." The driver got out and went around the back to Kevin's side. As Farmer opened the door, the fear smell came off him in great stinking waves like a waterfall. Leora reached for Kevin. She got him by his waist and held him as Farmer grabbed his arm, lifting him half off the car seat.

The boy screamed. They were pulling him apart, hurting him. Leora loosened her grip, but only a moment. Then she had him again, by his wool-clad thighs this time and they were both out on the ground, Farmer yelling and yanking Kevin's arm, jerking him around so she rolled in the mud. Sharp pains, blows to her sides that made her sick. Someone was kicking her and she screamed too, held on tighter as if the boy could keep away the pain.

"Stop." It was a man's voice, sounding quiet above all the noise, like smoke above a flame. Leora held Kevin solidly in her arms, sat up on the muddy ground, and looked.

There were three of them. The driver Farmer, or whatever his real name was, and two more. The others wore masks, but she recognized one by his sweater, a thick, grey cardigan bunched up over his broad hips. He had sat on the sawhorse at the construction site. He had a gun. It was aimed at her. And beside him stood a thin man in a long coat with his hands in the pockets.

"What do you want?" Leora asked.

The thin man snorted. "Shut up, mammy." Farmer rolled his shoulder, wincing like she'd hurt him. Good.

"Bring the car closer," the thin man said. The driver went off out of sight down the dirt road, past the Caddy. That left two. Could she run away and lose them in the woods?

"Stay down," said the thin man. "And no more noise out of either of you." The one with the gun lifted it, like it was something she might have missed.

She didn't ask again what they wanted. They were kidnappers, had to be: the danger that dirty burning signified. That's what these men were up to, like in the papers; why else would they be doing this?

Kevin started crying and shivering, and she turned her attention back to him. "Shush now," she told him. "Ain't nobody gonna hurt you, baby. They just gonna ask your daddy to give them some money is all." She hummed the lullaby Big Momma taught her, soft, no words, so only he would hear, and stroked his hair back from his face. No words. She had never been able to bring herself to sing them.

It worked well enough; his sobbing wound itself down to where she could listen in on their captors.

"—shoulda waited to give the signal on a day she wasn't riding along."

"Farmer said he'd be able to separate them. Said he'd have no problems." A short pause. "Find a way to tie and gag her, too. Give me the gun. Somebody could come along any minute." Smart, that one in the long coat. In fact, she heard an engine now, getting louder, nearer. The police? They had a station on the island's other side.

"On your feet, mammy." She looked up from Kevin's dark-lashed eyes. The sweatered man held out one hand to help her up; a dingy-looking red bandana drooped from the other. She got her legs under her and stood up on her own, the boy a soft weight in her arms. She could see through the leafless trees now, and it was only the black-and-purple sedan from the construction site coming to-wards them. The man took her by the elbow. The sedan stopped, and he started to steer her to its back door.

"No." She planted her feet as firm as she could. Pre-pared to fight. The thin man had said it himself; stay here and someone would come along eventually. No telling where they'd take her once they got her in the car. Not anyplace she'd want to go.

"I'll shoot you," the thin man said. He stepped nearer and the gun's muzzle dug into her neck. She couldn't tell if it was hot or cold or both. "I will. Give me half a chance," he said, and she decided she'd better believe him. Maybe he wouldn't; maybe a gun would make too much noise. She wasn't going to find out.

Leora laid Kevin down on the car seat the way she would for a nap. He looked up at her accusingly, as if the kidnapping was her fault, and opened his mouth to say something, but she shook her head and put her finger to her lips. She tried to get in next to him, but the gun pressed harder. "Hold up," the thin man told her. She stood as still as she could.

The driver got out with a short piece of clothesline hanging from his arm and went into the back on the other side. "Farmer, my father's going to be *very* angry at you." Kevin's voice sounded firm and fragile at the same time, like pie crust. "You'd better bring us home right away."

"All in good time, Mester McGinniss. Give me your hands here and put em together at the wrists. Don't make us have to shoot nobody, now—yes—that's the way. I'll have that gag now." The sweatered man moved to the other door. They stuck the dirty red bandana over the boy's mouth.

When they were done with Kevin, it was her turn. The thin man stepped back but kept the gun aimed at her face. "Take your jacket off. Now put it on again, backwards. Leave your arms out." He had Farmer jerk it down level with her elbows and tie the sleeves behind her. He searched the pockets, confiscating her keys, wadding up her gloves and handkerchief and throwing them in the dirt. Then he picked them up again and crammed the gloves in her mouth with her handkerchief on top, smashing her lips flat when he tied it in back. Farmer put her silk neck scarf over her eyes, knotted it too tight, and that was the last she saw for a while.

They shoved her in next to the boy, laying his head in her lap, she was pretty sure. That was what it felt like. The thin man crowded in beside her; she knew it was him by the gun muzzle he dug in her neck. He pulled her towards himself and pushed her face against his coat's shoulder. He smelled like Old Spice and dry-cleaning fluid.

Somebody started the car and backed it up the dirt road to where the pavement began again. They turned left and kept driving.

She could feel when they came from under the trees. The sun was so low it struck through the sedan's windows, warming the back of her head. Almost ready to set.

"They'll be taking off soon." That was the sweatered man talking.

"All right, we'll circle around the island a few times." The thin man. They didn't use each others' names. As they talked more she figured out the discussion was about the boat museum's construction crew going home for the weekend. Farmer said something about ransom money. She had been right. Such a comfort.

Kevin began crying again. With his gag in she felt more than heard him: hot tears soaking her skirt, shoulders trembling. She tried humming the lullabye, but this time her voice wouldn't cooperate. It cracked, wanted to rise up and up, roll out of her loud and high. The gunmetal pressing into her neck muscles put an end to that before it got properly started.

Where were they going? She lost track of the turns: angles, curves, left, right, hummocks and dips that might lead anywhere. Nowhere. The boy's weeping went on and on. She did her best to shut it from her mind and think how to escape.

❁

The scarf was too tight. Her coat was untied and off; the wind blowing from the river cut through the thin material of her uniform. Her shoes, heavy with mud, slipped on the unseen ladder's rungs and she held herself on as best she could, arms half-numb from being pinned to her sides. Then she reached the floor. The wind died, and the smell of earth and concrete rose around her.

A shove on her shoulder sent Leora sprawling to the side, but she stayed upright. What was happening? She had to know. She tore at the scarf, her short, blunt fingernails useless. Muffled sobs and shrieks came closer and closer, lower and lower, accompanied by the scrape of leather on wooden rungs.

"Dump him in the corner over there." That was the thin man, the one who had forced her down the ladder by telling her he had a gun aimed at her head. He gave all the orders. He was the one she had to convince.

She needed to get calm, get ahold of herself. She had a plan. It had come to her in the car. She willed her hands away from the knotted silk blinding her weeping eyes. Worked instead on the gag, wet with her own drool. Quickly, while they were too busy with Kevin to notice. The handkerchief was cheap, a gift from Big Momma, flimsy cotton. It tore easily and hung in damp shreds around her neck.

"I got a confession," Leora announced. "About my boy." Swear words and fast steps filled the darkness. Air brushed her cheek; she flinched.

"Wait." The thin man again. No blow landed. "Let's hear her out. Yell for help and you die," he promised.

"You gone and took the wrong one. This here's my son."

More swearing. The thin man cut through it. "You're saying Farmer made a mistake?"

"I nivver did! That there's the McGinniss heir—on my life it is!"

"That's what you think." She spun them her whole sorry tale. Mr. McGinniss had got her in the family way, she said, and Big Momma sent her off to her sister Rutha's house in Ontario to have the baby boy and leave him there.

Then Mrs. McGinniss got pregnant, too. But her child never drew breath in Leora's version of events, so Mr. McGinniss called Carter back to raise him as his son. Which he was. Had been.

It was true enough, and better than what actually happened.

"Well," said the thin man after she finished. "That's a very compelling narrative."

"What?" Farmer protested. "You believe that bullshit? I wouldn't raise some half-nigger as my kid no matter—"

"There are precedents.... Of course, without proof—"

"We'll still collect us a ransom, won't we?" The least familiar voice, so it must be the sweatered man.

"Maybe," the thin man answered.

And that was when Leora realized what a bad mistake she had made.

❀

The kidnappers didn't let them go. If the ransom never came, they weren't about to. Ever. Her lies had nearly made Kevin and Leora worthless. Only the kidnappers' disbelief kept them alive.

It was so cold. They had tied her arms with her coat again, but that was no protection.

She and Kevin were together in the same corner. Her new understanding of the criminal mind helped her reject the notion this had anything to do with how she or the boy felt. For whatever reason, it was simply more convenient this way for the kidnappers. Probably they had just the one gun.

The floor was cement, rough and uneven. Leora lay on her side, Kevin curled up in front of her like a question mark. His wool britches smelled like pee. His silent sobs were weak and hopeless, old-seeming.

At least no one had tried putting her gag back on. "You wanna hear a story, Kevin?" She waited while his sobs slowed. No other response came. That figured; no call for the kidnappers to take his gag off. She started anyway, her voice low and soothing. "Once there was a little boy. Now I'm talkin about *real* little, not a big boy like you. He lived far away, in another country, far away from his momma and his daddy."

"Why?" Leora made believe the boy had asked her a question, then answered it. "On account of he was a prince in disguise, and bein off in another land was the best disguise his momma and daddy could come up with."

She stopped. Was this idea any better than her last one?

She had something else to try first, something maybe a little easier; it depended on which kidnappers had been left to watch them. And how many. What seemed like hours ago she'd heard feet climbing up the ladder. Now she struggled to remember: One pair? Two?

"I need to use the lavatory," Leora said, loud enough anyone nearby could hear her.

"That's a shame, since we got no such *facilities* on the *premises*." Farmer. Him she could handle. "Guess you'll have to wet yourself."

"It ain't that...." Leora let her sentence trail off, pretending embarrassment she wasn't far from feeling.

Farmer laughed, but the thin man interrupted. "Take her through to the other room." Him she was afraid of.

"What? She shits, I'm supposed to wipe her black ass?"

"Don't act any stupider than you are. Untie her, let her take care of it herself." A pause. "Do it."

A hand on her shoulder helped her clumsily up from the floor. "I'll be right back," she told the boy.

Her plan wouldn't work so well with two of them there. But maybe she could overpower Farmer when she was untied and alone with him in this other room, take away any weapon he had, or do something to get him on her side. She shuffled carefully through the darkness, grit crackling beneath her feet.

By the change in the echoes around her, Leora figured they had entered a smaller space. Farmer shoved her front against a cold, damp wall and freed her arms. He was out of reach by the time she turned around. She took a step forward, another, hands extended, without connecting.

"What's the hold up? Do your business!" He sounded like he was talking to a dog.

"It's—I think I'm gettin my monthlies—" Leora improvised. "I won't know just by touching myself. I'm gone hafta see—"

"Jesus *Christ*! I don't—you expect me to take off your blindfold too? That's a lot of nerve you got, nigger gal—"

"No!" He was closer now, she could tell by his voice, the noise of his breath. "No, only, how about you...reach in for me...and find out yourself." Lord knew what she looked like, lipstick smeared off, mascara and eyeliner and rouge running all down her face, mud caking her uniform. She smiled anyway, and when he said "Yeah," sounding half-strangled in spit, she opened her mouth in anticipation, as if this was something she had waited for her whole life, his callused hand hiking up her skirt and skinning down her nylon underwear, parting the tangled hair and inserting one finger where no one had been in years. She sighed and rode up and down on it a couple of times for good measure, and he said "Jesus Christ," again, but in an entirely different tone of voice.

He had his pants unbuttoned in seconds, and replaced his finger without even laying her on the floor.

She felt a jackknife in his pocket as he scrabbled against the concrete. The blade wouldn't be longer than two or three inches, she judged, but good to have all the same. He slumped to one side, done. Before she could retrieve the knife he recovered and pushed himself away from her.

"You two having a nice time in there?" The thin man's voice sounded maybe forty feet off.

"Yeah. I'll be out in a jiffy." He tied her arms again without saying another word, not a bit won over, and Leora had no choice but to let him.

Time to put her new plan in action.

"Well," the thin man said as they re-entered the first room. "I see you *did* have a nice time." Her face and neck went hot. "Unfortunately, you're not my type." He laughed at his own joke.

"Listen," Leora said. "I lied before. About the boy. I—"

"Sure you did. What happened—you had a chance to realize the consequences if it was true?"

"Well, some of it—"

"Sit down and shut up."

Farmer pushed her to her knees.

"I'll tell you the—"

"Shut up!" Farmer knocked her the rest of the way to the ground. "There must be something to—I'll stuff your drawers in your mouth, I don't care!" He rolled her back and forth, wrestling her skirt up again.

"The real one's still alive! I know where they hid him!"

"Will you—"

"Wait a minute! Why are you so determined to keep her from saying what she wants? Something you'd rather I didn't learn about?"

"But you told her shut up!"

"I changed my mind. A gentleman's prerogative." The thin man bent over her. "All right. Upsy daisy." He helped her sit with her back to the wall. "Now talk."

"It—he's my son, but you let us go I can tell you where they took the other to be raised."

"Let you go. That's rich. Yeah, that's exactly what we plan on doing, let you go and head off on some wild goose chase looking for a boy who died or don't even exist." Farmer slapped her hard. This time the thin man let him.

Half her face was numb. She made her mouth work. "I told you the truth! We swapped them two at birth, and only they daddy ever knew. He was thinkin ahead to when somethin like this would happen. You want the ransom or you want Mr. McGinniss to be laughin at you? You already sent him the note, right? He ain't answered you yet has he?" A guess. She hoped it was a good one. "And he ain't gonna. You know why? Cause he don't care!"

Silence. Then the unclear sounds of them moving around—doing what? If only she could see! Their voices came from more of a distance, muffled and senseless. All she could tell was that they were angry, till they returned and the thin man said, "Here's the deal.

"You tell us where the heir is. We release you, but we keep your kid till we find the real one's hideout."

Leora breathed huge gasps in and out. Oh, God, she wanted like hell to agree, to get out of that hole in the ground where they had her, she had done her duty and then some, and what was Kevin to her anyway? Just a job, and maybe even the reason her own boy Carter had died, lost in the woods when he wandered off from Great-Aunt Rutha's cabin because his momma hadn't been there to take care of him, gone and disappeared while Leora watched over this white child who she owed nothing, *nothing*! She was crying, crying hard, she couldn't do anything about that or what she heard herself saying, which was, "No! NO! You cain't take him! I won't letcha! No I won't!"

Farmer hit her again, but it was the thin man's unbelieving laughter that brought her back to her right mind.

The kidnappers were standing her on her feet. "So we believe you now about this one being your kid," the thin man said. "Otherwise you would have taken us up on our offer. So let's have the rest of it."

Their test, and she'd passed it without knowing. "You gonna—"

"Tell us where the McGinniss heir is or we'll shoot your son and throw him in the river."

"Canada," Leora said. "Ontario."

"Windsor?"

"In the country. I can give you directions—"

"You'll do better than that. Here you are, Farmer." The thin man's voice moved away. "Keep it trained on her. I'll be back fast as I can. Try not to have too much fun." The sound of his feet rising up the rungs. Then another noise: wood on wood, something dragging, scraping, then falling loudly on the ceiling, the floor above her head.

She was alone in the basement with a rapist and a helpless, tied up white boy.

Who she should have left to his fate. At least she should have tried to. When Farmer yanked him out of the car seat like that, she could have let him. And she would have, too, if only she'd been thinking instead of feeling. Using her brain, not her heart. If Kevin hadn't looked so much like his brother. Carter.

She wasn't going to cry. Leora had done enough of that already. Big Momma had taught her to be strong, to survive. Do whatever it took, even if it went against the Bible.

One more plan.

She struggled to remember the words to that lullabye. She had always known she'd need to use it someday, in the special way Big Momma had learned her. How did it go now?

"Hush-a-bye, don't you cry;

Go to sleepy, little baby;

When you wake, you shall have—"

"Okay, turn around so I can take this thing off," Farmer interrupted her thoughts, tugging at her blindfold. Which was when she realized her arms were untied again. Why? She hadn't sung a note, and anyway, it wasn't supposed to work like that.

Maybe she wouldn't have to, after all.

The knots in her good scarf proved too tough for Farmer, too, and he sliced them apart with his knife. She heard him open it, felt the silk give way.

Her eyes hurt. They were in a cellar, big metal buckets over in one corner with a fat flashlight standing on one on its end. In another corner lay a short, lumpy shadow, white patches showing where Kevin's skin contrasted with his clothes and the bandanas over his mouth and eyes.

No sign of the ladder they'd made her walk down.

She whirled quickly to find Farmer behind her but out of reach, and grinning like a natural-born idiot. He had the knife and the gun both, but the gun wasn't aimed. "You want another fuck?" he asked. "I think there's time before we head out."

With a one-minute man like him there'd always be time, Leora figured. She didn't say that, though, mindful of the weapons. She gave him her back and went to Kevin.

Farmer followed her, pushing her out of the way. He cut the line holding the boy's legs, then his hands. Leora took them up in her own, kneeling beside him. They were cold, and mottled looking in the dim light. She rubbed them to start the blood moving. Farmer got rid of the boy's blindfold; she saw when she looked up at his face. *Bees and butterflies, flutterin round his eyes....* Those same long lashes—

"Why you doin this?" she asked Farmer. "You lettin us out of here?" She might be wrong about the man, and he'd taken a fancy to her, after all.

"So I am, after a fashion." He brought the knife up against Kevin's neck. "We'll be taking a drive over the border, and you're less likely to stick in folks' memories without the ropes and things. Think you can convince your kid to keep his mouth shut when we cross the bridge?" Dark eyes darted to hers and away in every direction, taking in the room. Leora couldn't talk. She nodded yes. The knife moved up to the bandana's edge and ripped its way through the stained fabric. Not the bruised, white skin.

Kevin couldn't talk, either. He'd been gagged much longer than Leora. He needed water. When she had him sitting up she asked Farmer for something to drink and got a flask of what smelled like cheap whisky, the sort of thing the Purple Gang once smuggled in. She gave it to the poor child; better that than nothing. Then she made him walk a little. He stumbled like a baby. She held him by his arms, surreptitiously looking for the ladder or some other way out.

There were three rooms counting the main one, the one where Farmer took her earlier, and what amounted to a closet. Doorways opened between them without doors. None contained stairs or a ladder, and Leora suddenly recalled the sounds she'd heard as the thin man left, the scraping and bumping. Like a picture she saw it in her head: he had pulled the ladder up with him and put something over the hole he went out of to shut it.

No wonder the kidnappers weren't worried about letting loose their hands.

After helping Kevin go the bathroom she sat down with him in the corner the furthest they could get from the stink. "Now what?" he whispered, the first words he'd spoken since the gag came out.

A hopeful sign. "We wait, I guess."

"For what? What are they—"

"None of that, now! Speak so I can hear you, or else!" Farmer stood from the bucket where he sat and took a threatening step toward them, gun up.

"He just wants me to finish the story I was tellin," Leora lied.

"Go on then. So I can hear."

She hadn't gotten far past the beginning before, she was pretty sure. "So this prince was sent to a foreign land—"

"What was his name?"

"Foster."

"That's a dumb name." Sounding more like himself every second.

"Anyway, he was a prince, so you don't have to feel sorry for him. And he lived on a farm with a kindly old couple who always let him have whatever he wanted." Even if what he wanted killed him. "They had rules, but when he broke them, those old people would never raise not a hand against him."

"No spankings?"

"Not a swat. He was a prince; hittin him was against the law. Now one day, the little boy got up early, before anybody was awake. And he went down to the kitchen and fixed a bowl of cereal, and then he went outside and walked off into the forest all by himself, although he had been told not to." And told and told and told.

"Why wasn't he supposed to go in the forest?"

"Because he wasn't supposed to go anywheres. Remember, he was a prince in disguise. He couldn't be runnin around where folks would see and recognize him.

"Then, of course, he went and got lost." In the great Canadian wilderness, trees and rocks and marshes—miles and miles of loneliness— "Lost. And he was hungry and tired and miserable, and he wished he'd never, never left that kitchen table.

"But what he didn't know was his momma—"

"The queen?"

"Yeah, that's right, his momma the queen, she had lit a magic candle to proteck him." Like Big Momma said to do. If only she had done it instead of worrying was conjure the devil's work. Well, that wasn't going to stop her now.

"The sun went down. Night was fallin. All of a sudden he seen a light."

"The candle?"

"The candle! You such a smart boy!" Same as Carter. "That's right, the prince seen the flame of his momma's magic candle, and it led him straight home to the farm where he lived. The End."

Kevin stayed quiet, thinking the way he usually did when she finished a story. She always knew he was thinking by the questions he would ask later, long after she'd forgot the things she said.

The candle she lit after the funeral had been for Carter. Not to protect him. Too late for that. It was to commemorate his spirit, Big Momma had said. And to be what she called a *conduit*, a way they could speak with one another.

Of course Leora had never attempted such a blasphemous thing.

Banging and a blast of cold air from the ceiling told her the thin man was back. The ladder slid down to rest its foot on the floor's middle, and the thin man descended it, aiming his thin smile and a second gun through the rungs at them.

It took her till the sweatered man came down, too, to work out what was different. No masks.

It took her till they'd exchanged some talk she didn't follow and herded her and Kevin between them up out of the cellar and into the black-and-purple sedan to understand why this made her sick to her stomach.

No mask to prevent her from seeing the thin man's blonde moustache and the way his nose tipped up at the end and the squint lines radiating from the edges of his eyes. No mask to stop her noticing the sweatered man's freckled forehead and the crease in his chin he didn't look to bother shaving.

So what was to prevent her from describing them to the police when they set her and Kevin free?

But of course the kidnappers had never been going to do that, since there was nobody except Aunt Rutha and Uncle Donald at the cabin, no secret heir. No prince in disguise.

Only Leora knew that, though. She had thought.

She had thought she could wait till they got there, but no telling what these white men had in mind.

As soon as Farmer stopped driving, she'd have to sing.

The black-and-purple sedan's motor made more noise than the Cadillac. Of course it was older. The island looked empty for a Friday night. Then they reached the mainland, and she saw all the traffic lights flashing yellow. No reds. That late. Or early; early Saturday morning.

And when would the kidnappers stop the car? Where? Would she even have time to open her mouth before they shot her?

Kevin snuggled up against her on her right, both arms wrapped around hers at the elbow. In the regular flare of streetlamps Leora saw him staring up at her, worry and trust tugging him back and forth in nervous twitches. If she saved his life he was truly hers. That's what she'd heard the Hindoos would say.

The thin man had stuck a gun under her left ribs. On Kevin's far side the sweatered man crowded against the fogged-up window, flicking some switch on the gun he held. Tense or bored? Both, she decided. Wait for a change in that, then.

The lights came less often. Fewer of them; they must be near the rail yards now. Maybe here—Leora discovered she'd been holding her breath and let it go. The sweatered man stopped fiddling with his gun, but only to light himself a cigarette.

"Put that thing out," the thin man told him. "Filthy habit." He reached past her and snatched it away to stub it in the ashtray. A sudden sharp left. Lights ahead, low and steady. "Get the toll ready, Farmer," the thin man ordered. He jabbed the gun harder into Leora's side, a silent reminder to keep quiet.

They sailed through the toll booth and onto the Ambassador Bridge almost without a pause. Golden lights hanging on either side swooped their shadows across her eyes. They passed under its two signs, the red letters first facing forward, then backward.

Slaves had crossed all along here. In winter the water froze, and they walked to freedom. In the darkness, on the ice, they ran over the river to the land they'd been so long dreaming of…. Leora loved that freedom, the kind that came only in your sleep.

And then they were in Canada. The gun switch clicked so fast it sounded like a bent fan blade hitting its frame. A low roof lit from beneath by blue-white fluorescents chopped the horizon in half. Customs check. Farmer pulled up to a booth. The man inside raised his eyes from his magazine, frowned, and waved them toward the parking lot.

The clicking stopped. "Shit," swore the thin man.

"Should I go where he's pointing at—or maybe I oughta make a run for it—"

"See those cop cars waiting up ahead? Think you can outrace them?"

The kidnappers continued to quarrel as Farmer veered off the road into a parking place. He left the engine idling, but they weren't going anywhere for a while. Not before they got a thorough inspection.

She smiled down at the boy beside her. This would be her best bet. Big Momma had taught her, and it was not a sin—especially in self-defense. And if it worked she would light a second candle. She opened her mouth to sing the lullaby until they shut their eyes, every mother's son.

Filter House

Hush-a-bye, don't you cry,
Go to sleepy little baby;
When you wake, you shall have,
All the pretty little horses.

Blacks and bays, dapple grays,
All the pretty little horses.

Way down yonder, in the meadow,
Lies a poor little lamby;
Bees and butterflies, flutterin round his eyes,
Poor little thing is crying, "Mammy."

Go to sleep, don't you cry,
Rest your head upon the clover;
In your dreams, you shall ride,
While your mammy's watching over.

Blacks and bays, dapple grays,
All the pretty little horses;
All the pretty little horses.

Shiomah's Land

I guess I'll never really know for sure whether my mother meant to throw herself to her death beneath the wheels of a god's carriage. She certainly had something in mind, for she kissed my forehead before she left me, first brushing my dark, unruly locks aside. Then she told me to stay still, and ran off towards the road. It looked to me as though she slipped, though she was actress enough to do that on purpose.

Perhaps she only meant to be maimed, slightly. Stories were told of mortals who had been restored after such accidents and given handsome gifts as well: metals, or strange fabrics. She may have been aiming for these riches.

I didn't try to stop her, confident that she must know what she was doing. I was very proud of my mother; was she not the greatest glee-woman walking? She taught me all I knew.

Of course, anyone who has passed a Fertility Trial is exceptional, but the thrilling tale my mother told of hers convinced me that she was without match. Apparently she agreed with me, for when she was fit for travel we spent very little time with my father and his people.

I must have been about nine or so when we heard that my father's people had sent someone out to look for us. Or for me, to be more specific. They had been content to leave me in my mother's care at first, but I was now big enough to work strongly in the fields. Naturally, we decided to flee.

We took a raft a long way down a river, singing our way to Kimp Sinn, the city. It was said that the walls of Kimp Sinn were lined with foodholes, that one could see the gods on every corner. In a manner of speaking, these marvels were quite true.

Kimp Sinn is on an island in the sea. It is reached (unless you are a god) by a long, waltzing causeway. I still can remember the feeling of exhilaration we shared as my mother and I walked through the blue and white sky, gulls screaming around us.

In the city we found that many people had arrived there before us and were already well entrenched. The plenteous foodholes, which produced more than enough food for all, were controlled by certain individuals and groups. If no one could give them something of value in return for it, the food they could not eat was dumped into the sea. The gulls love Kimp Sinn. Their droppings whitewash the walls.

And as for seeing the gods on every corner, that was almost right, for everywhere there were glowing colored squares busy with flickering images of the gods. Some of them were said to reside upon the mountains of the island. Once in a great while one of their little silver carriages would roll down the hollow god road....

Not many considered our "songs, dances, plays, and fooleries" as worth watching above a moment, much less offering goods for the privilege. Not when they could watch the god shows for nothing. That first evening my mother traded her horn earrings for some dairy and ceery for us, some sweet for me, and a little smooth for herself. We had to trade again to get a roof space to sleep on.

The next day we learned to catch and kill rats. There were two foodholes in Kimp Sinn that operated only when a ratskin had been dropped in. The generous caretakers of these places inserted the ratskins for one, taking only part of the food for themselves. Thus we made our way in a place where our work meant nothing.

We were waiting for one of the ships that Kimp Sinn's natives boasted sometimes came calling to the port. None came for a long time. They told us it was because of storms, though the sea was calm as far as any could see. My mother believed them, she said, "for the sea is very big, Teekoige." At last a ship came, but it was going North, back toward my father's home.

As we waited for a Southern voyager, passing the days on the pier and the streets, hunting for rats and trading away our trinkets, I became aware of a secret interaction between my mother and a man named Obelk, one of those who took our ratskins. I got the feeling that he wished her to do something that she would rather not. It must have been something awful, or she would have told me about it, I am sure.

My mother cut off and traded her hair. I remember how heavy and dark it was, like sweet or sorghum.

One day Obelk refused to trade with us. The others did the same, at his foodhole and the other where ratskins were accepted. We could not even get fresh water.

So I know my mother was in a desperate state as we walked alongside the god road. But I do not know what was in her mind. I did not see her expression as she died.

She was thrown high into the air, then came thudding down in the road behind the slowing carriage. I ran screaming to her, but just as I reached her I was seized in a cold grip and lifted from her side. I stopped my screaming then, too frightened to breathe. I was carried to the carriage; up to a window in the wall, a window covered with glass.

Behind the glass I saw a beautiful round white face, appearing to me like a full moon in the night. The moon smiled and said something I couldn't hear through the glass. The cold grip deposited me in a sort of bin at the back of the carriage, shutting the lid on me and plunging me into total darkness. I felt the carriage move.

I finished crying for my mother. I knew that she must be dead. After the movement had stopped I was taken from the bin by the cold grip, which I saw belonged to a tall, shiny man, astonishingly costumed all in metal. For some reason I could not fathom, I fell instantly asleep.

When I awoke I was alone, and I felt far away from death, my mother, silver carriages, rats, Kimp Sinn, gulls, the moon, and myself. I know now this was the result of the chemicals with which I had been treated. I lay there then not knowing this and not caring. I finally got up because I had to pee. Hunkering over the slit, I noticed that my locks no longer fell over my shoulders. Feeling with my hand I found that an outrageously short fuzz was all I had covering my head. Also, I was naked (something that had not sunk in while I squatted peeing). I looked around for my clothes, but they were not in sight.

There was a mirror on one wall. At first I did not realize what it was, because I was unaccustomed to such large, clear mirrors. It showed me not only my bony face but my pitiful brown nakedness, the pale sea-colored walls behind me, the slit, the foodhole, and the bedmat from which I had just risen. It acted like a mirror, so I believed it was one. But suddenly it was no longer a mirror; it glowed like the god images on the walls of Kimp Sinn. Like a growing jewel, a picture of the moonface appeared, framed with lavender hair. I looked away.

"Teekoige!" called the picture's voice. My name, I thought, but I did not respond. "Teekoige? Teekoige!" The image faded.

I turned to the foodhole. It gave me some bean and veg and some nice flavored water. I did some stretches, automatically at first. As my body warmed up, my thoughts began to cohere. I went over recent events. My mother's death maintained its distance. It was like something I had been sad about a long time ago.

One heard of those who had been actually taken up by the gods. These rare individuals were never again seen by mortal eyes.

In a little while the square called me again. I ignored it. Then it threatened to shut off the foodhole and the sluice for the slit until I "learned to mind my manners." This provoked me into answering that I did not need to use my manners to deal with a talking picture square. After a brief silence the light dimmed out and the mirror returned again.

Shortly, it began to move, opening inward like a door. I snatched up the sheet from the bedmat to wrap myself in it. I need not have bothered, though; my visitor was also naked. Her skin and hair shining, the god who had killed my mother (but it must have been a *very* long time ago) said hello to me, half frowning, half smiling.

"Hello, Teekoige, then, if you will have no graven image," she addressed me.

"Hello——" I replied, with a heavy pause.

She took her cue. "Amma."

"Hello, Amma, midam," I said, happy that my mother had taught me something of the ways of the gods. Amma is worshipped for her effect upon moods, storms, accidents, and sudden changes. I curtsied deeply.

"I am sorry about your mother, Teekoige," she said, as if that took care of everything. For her it did. For me it only brought the realization that my mother may not have been entirely responsible for her own death.

Amma immediately wanted to know why I "would not speak with her over the vee," gesturing to the mirror. I could not answer her, so she continued. "Why did you manipulate me into coming here? Are you planning to kill me?" she asked with a friendly sneer. "No, of course not; we both know that that is impossible. Why?"

"I will do what you want me to do, midam," I replied slowly, "but I had no idea I should have treated that trick as though it were a real god. Such a thought never occurred in my head." I had a lot to learn.

Amma, however, seemed well pleased with my answer. My ignorance was exactly what she wished for, "for I shall not have to unteach you a lot of tiresome misconceptions, like those city-bred mortals.

"My dear girl," she went on, "you are absolutely perfect. Except for that horrible name." She clasped her hands together above her breasts, her nipples glowing like large rosy pearls. "You must have a stage name, something more mellifluous and resonant. Shiomah, that is it. Amma's Shiomah."

Amma was a merry god, though capricious. Her form was always that of a beautiful, slightly plump woman with hair and skin of varying colors. She used also to remove part of the weight of her hair so that it floated up shimmering behind her head as she walked or glided along. She never cheapened her elegance with so much as a ring. This was a marked divergence from universal custom; even bioservs wore shorts or tunics or *something*.

Amma created and recorded adventures and dramas that were highly popular among the gods. She had nothing to do with the pictures that moved on the corners of Kimp Sinn. Those, she told me, were Nyglu's idea, produced by machines.

Machines are the gods' power. Machines give them their lives and their beauty. Amma showed me large and small machines, simple and complicated ones. Some are inside the gods, some embedded deep within the world, some fly constantly around the sky. Carriages, vees, food-holes, and servs are all machines. Machines speak and listen and reproduce and repair. They are toys and tools and objects of desire.

Amma knew me inside out with the help of these machines. Silver circles embedded in her hand allowed her to instruct them as to her wishes. They gave her all my secrets as I slept. They whispered to me through my dreams, teaching me things I would not remember until I needed to know them. I wore a ring in my ear that spoke her commands to me when she herself was elsewhere.

She controlled me in many ways; at first through my awe and also, I later realized, by using the words and intonations of my mother. After a while I just wanted to please her, and for a very long time she did not even have to threaten me with the punishments she held in readiness.

I controlled nothing, directly. I could not even cause a door to open until Amma ordered a serv to accompany me everywhere, operating its fellow machines for me. Even over this I had less than absolute power. It did nothing that conflicted with its basic paradigms, and often, at first, I gave it impossible instructions.

"Go drown yourself," I told it one day, in a foul mood after my sixth failure at forming a difficult construction in the Creative Mode (the gods' most difficult language). I knew perfectly well that the serv was operable under water, but I thought that it would at least try to obey me. Instead it put itself on standby, locking in place and emitting a distressed, hiccuping click. Some device must have alerted Amma, for she came into my room almost immediately, with another serv that deactivated and removed my companion.

"You must not deliberately incapacitate my machines, Shiomah," she said, calm but stern. Her eyebrows lowered into a lovely frown. "This particular episode does not stem from ignorance, does it?" I shook my head, chagrined. "If this continues, you will be denied all service."

I glanced around my quarters. They were pleasant: sand-colored, papery-feeling walls, russet and amber appointments, wide windows from which to see the sea. Still, it was no place in which to be involuntarily confined. But I did manage to confound my serv on one other occasion, though not exactly intentionally. It was just that I couldn't understand why I didn't miss my mother more, and I thought perhaps if I had something tangible to mourn....

This time two units came; one to attend to the damaged serv, the other to accompany me to Amma's tower. I followed it up, a heavy lump of apprehension inside my chest refusing to respond to the lift of the glide-way.

A rain the color of peridots curtained the entrance to my mistress's apartment. I stepped through. As sometimes happened, the rain failed to cease falling, and I was drenched.

The sun was at its zenith, and the iris of the tower's ceiling had contracted to a slit. Below its short overhang, a long window curved continuously, circled by blue sky. Amma sat with her pale green legs curled beneath her, bent forward to look at a display board set in the floor. Raising her face to me, she seemed about to laugh at my wetness, but then a deliberate lack of expression smoothed away the beginnings of her dimples. I took a towel from a knob on the wall behind me and dried myself as I went to sit before her.

"You sent your serv to bring you your mother's remains," she half asked, half stated.

"Yes, midam."

"You knew the task would be difficult. Did you know how difficult?"

"I thought that it could ask for assistance; take a carriage; make inquiries."

"Inquiries of the gulls? Assistance from the herring? What do you suppose has become of your mother in all the time I have had you?" Her questions brought up that strange numbness in me, stronger than ever, a broad, flat humming that drowned out my answer as I formed it. I suppose I must have imagined the citizens of Kimp Sinn taking her away, burning her, urning her ashes. But the overwhelming nothing that I felt negated all possibilities. I hung my head in silence, ashamed of my speechlessness.

How could I know that she had suggested this, had planted in my mind this bland substitute for grief?

"I will tell you what happened, my dear," Amma said, perhaps moved to some sort of divine contrition by my dumbness. "She was removed and disintegrated by the road's maintenance mechanisms. By now she is scattered far and wide, and still dispersing."

She paused, her soft green fingers touching me under my chin, tilting my head upwards. "You were asking for all the birds of the air, all the fish in the sea, every blade of grass upon the dunes, every sandcrab on the beach." She stopped again, holding my eyes with hers. "Why did you not ask me?"

The spell of numbness had passed at her touch, but still I couldn't answer. It had come to me that Amma did not want me to have a mother, alive or dead. How could I tell a god she was jealous of a mortal?

"Why did you not take her up in your carriage, with me?" I asked, neglecting to use the honorific. Her eyes narrowed, measuring me closely.

"I thought you might be of use to me," she replied, dropping her arm, "but I saw no need to carry around a corpse. Would it have been pleasant for you, in that dark, unfamiliar place, crowded in with your mother's body? I wanted you in the best shape possible, confident, unbroken, trusting yourself against the unknown." She stood suddenly, and raised me delicately with her fingertips. "Even in shock, your face seemed so dazzlingly young, yearning to see me through my window.... I thought you might be of use to me," she repeated, "and it begins to look as though I was right." Affirming her own good judgment, she nodded, smiling a small but brilliant smile.

To please her, I learned. I learned the shape of the world and the depth of the skies and their ways. I learned the gods' habits and slow history. Sometimes I came upon obstacles in my search for knowledge: blank walls or steps built up into empty air. Amma approved of my frustration as a sign of my curiosity, helping me when she could and promising that in time I would know all.

Contrary to what my mother had taught me, I learned that individual gods do die. If they are not done in by one of their peers or by some accident during one of their frequent flirtations with death, they do themselves in. Five hundred years is the average lifespan. Many extend this several times, however, by being reborn.

But even this measure can only temporarily rescue a world-weary god. Sooner or later one particular copy will develop such a deeply ingrained disgust for the futile repetitions that the process is discontinued.

I discovered that the gods did not take such a deep interest in the affairs of mortals as was generally supposed. The interest was sporadic, shallow, a matter of fashion. During one of the periods when it was considered stylish to notice mortals, the causeway and the city of Kimp Sinn were built, the scattered foodholes installed about the land to supplement the crops, the Fertility Trials viewed avidly. But the divine population of the island had been steadily decreasing, the wonder of mortal ways having palled centuries ago for most.

The exception to this was the ancient river god, Nyglu, the aforementioned producer of the vee shows of Kimp Sinn. He was also the innovator of the ratskin-trading foodhole. Nyglu's all-consuming passion was the study of mortals, by means of any and all disciplines. Considered by most a boring eccentric, Nyglu was included in Amma's circle partly because of some obscure genetic relationship between the two and partly, I think, because of Amma's taste for the odd and sensational.

Throughout their friendship she had humored his harmless pastimes, learning mortal speech at his insistence. Hearing of my acquisition, he had made her promise that I would be introduced to him at the first opportunity.

Amma held back on this for some time. She relieved me of some of my awe and fed my own good opinion of myself until she felt I was ready. It was her plan that I should confront Nyglu with at least an elementary knowledge of the gods' languages and etiquettes, and with all my native audacity intact.

The meeting took place in my own quarters: familiar ground for me, new to my interviewer. He stared as though he would like to trap me on his sticky tongue. His eyes glittered beneath large, horny ridges. His skin was rough, wrinkled, and sprinkled with warts. He addressed me in First Speech, the one used with low-order mechanisms and bioservs. "Is it good that you are Amma's Shiomah?"

"Couldn't be cleaner," I replied, using the latest Juvenile Swerve. I switched to Obligatory Contract. "I understand that the information I represent carries some value to you, Mr. Nyglu?"

He actually blinked. Then we got down to negotiations, which went very much, I thought, in my favor. Credit goes to Amma for coaching me in being able to read the face of one so—different. But Nyglu had never needed to be shrewd, as I and my mother had. It was like bargaining with soft wax.

Amma was delighted with the outcome. She rewound the contract and played it through after Nyglu had gone, chuckling at the extent of my boldness. "So he actually paid you for the recordings I made when I found you, before you first woke up? He might have gotten those as a gift from me, had he asked."

"But I gave him no time to think of asking. And you said that I could offer them, midam."

"Yes, but it was your idea. And so was this performance you scheduled. I suppose you will need to use a bioserv for at least part of it."

"If I may."

She glanced at me from the corner of one mirthful eye. "Of course you may. I wouldn't miss it for an asteroid." She returned to scanning the contract. "Very good, especially this last part."

"The consultant clause?"

"Yes. Nyglu has never been able to get anyone to wade through his material before, so you flatter him, even at this price."

It bothered me for a while that I had not asked for a higher fee to review his work, but as my mother always said, it does no harm to have your customer feel he's gotten the best of the deal. And I certainly did well with what I had won.

The gods lived in weary anarchy, most having rubbed away the edges of their more troublesome desires by way of fulfillment, long ago. Aesthetic and social pressures exercised the only control. Any serious problems that developed (usually with the younger deities) were dealt with by somewhat interested parties, informal groups with as much license to punish the offenders as their own level of annoyance allowed.

Under Amma's protection I had just about any rights she chose to give me. She bestowed upon me all the privileges and powers she thought I could grasp. I set out to increase my earthly store with an earnest intensity that my protectress found amusing. To the gods, wealth is no more than a diversion. I was a bottomless coinpurse, an everladen tablecloth, for Amma.

She adored the havoc my childish temper and unconventional questions wreaked upon her circle of acquaintances. These occurrences were a little like my earlier effects upon the servs, but for some reason she found them much less irritating.

For instance, once she brought me with her to try out a new toy, a boat a lover had just given her. The lover, a minor god without physical affectations, was called Weyando. He was on board to demonstrate the boat's principles of operation, as he was the engineer of both the hull and the living sail. Also present was a certain young Lizore, related somehow to Weyando, and apparently to be my charge should Amma and Weyando find themselves too busy to attend to her.

Had she been a mortal I would have judged Lizore to be about four years of age. Actually she had just turned twenty-five, though she was still considered a child by divine standards. Although she appeared properly aloof in the presence of Weyando, her eyes took on a more interested expression the moment she was left in my care.

"Hurry, show me," she asked at once. "Are your genitals like mine?"

"Somewhat," I admitted. "Would you like to look at them, midam?"

"Yes, I just said so," she snapped. "I suppose you will want to see mine? All right, then." She reached for the hem of her shift.

"No," I said, "just tell me something, please. Answer a question."

"A question you shouldn't ask?" I nodded. "All right."

"What relation are you to Weyando?" Even I was astounded by my daring. Held distinct from sexual practices, the reproductive secrets of the gods are exactly that. Secrets. This was one of the topics upon which Amma had adamantly insisted that I remain uneducated. Any bioserv that became precocious enough to be coaxed into speculation upon the subject promptly disappeared.

Lizore's steely eyes glinted with new respect as she answered me. "His eggson is my spermfather." She looked up at me expectantly, and I nodded in a show of understanding, lifting my hem to her examination.

"We are very nearly identical," she reported, in a disappointed voice.

I was quite as dissatisfied with my end of the bargain, until Amma explained Lizore's terms and others just as confusing. But that was much later, when she asked me to have her child.

Weyando's gift was a success. The water foamed and hissed away below us, constantly changing into itself, showing all the colors of my mistress's moods. The sun warmed the sail, which turned itself constantly to the heat, a billowing net filled with a wind of light. At night soft breezes pushed against its unfurled membranes, sailing us through the phosphorescent dark.

Day or night, Amma and Weyando were together: guiding the ship, gazing into one another's eyes, satisfying themselves with one another's sight, or sound, or smell, or touch, or taste.

Lizore and I were much in each other's company. Five days after our first encounter, I posed a question with an impact that far outweighed that of the first one I had asked. As Lizore and I silvered ourselves with glittering scales from the hull, she laughed at some witless pun I made. "Really, Shiomah," she giggled, "you're not at all boring. I find it hard to believe you are a mortal." She said it to praise me, so I tried to hide my offended pride, but my reply came sharply.

"If we mortals are so boring, midam, why did you gods bother to create us? If we *are* inferior, we are your work." The paradox struck Lizore just as if I had slapped her baby-fat cheeks. Mortals, she had been taught, were tacky. Stupid, clumsy, disease-ridden—they were all this, and a great deal more that was anything but necessary.

"Come," she ordered, heading for the stern. At our approach, her spermfather's eggfather locked the controls and turned to her trouble-filled face. Amma lifted herself up from the deck on one elbow, watching with the expression of one about to be entertained. "Weyando," Lizore asked, "why do we need mortals? What did we make them for?" A short but devastated silence followed.

Amma rose from her languid pose. "I'll call the copter," she said.

"But why did..." Lizore started again querulously.

"Later," Weyando told her, with a quelling and emphatic glance in my direction.

After her guests left, Amma began to laugh aloud, tickling my ribs till I joined her. Her voice sounded like a wind-chime, the separate notes hanging in the air and striking one another like strung shells, soft yet clear.

When we had calmed down a bit, she made me sit with her on a little wooden bench. Then she took me by both hands and explained at length why my question had caused such discomfort.

"The gods do not *need* mortals at all. For *any* reason." At times, she said, there had even been crusades to have them wiped out. "But that's not at all fashionable now," Amma reassured me.

"And—" I coaxed her, knowing there must be more.

"Yes. Go ahead."

"And the gods did not make the mortals."

She nodded, pleased at my quickness. "The gods—*were* mortals, at one time."

"It is not general knowledge. Especially not among children. But, yes, our remote ancestors and yours are one, the same." Her cheeks dimpled; she was fond of the unorthodox, and I piqued her with my impertinence.

"No doubt these facts had a bearing on the defeat of the drive for our extermination, midam." She nodded, eyes and hands suddenly intent upon disentangling some snarl in my hair. I continued my conjectures silently for a moment as we skimmed over the still sea.

I myself could see the advantages of maintaining some sort of gene pool. I asked her whether there were any mortals who had been made into gods. I had in mind those who had been "taken up" before me, and of whom I had never heard or seen anything during my time with the gods.

She answered me with irritating equivocation. "Yes. Well, no, not really, although in a way, yes." I begged saucily for her to be more explicit.

"You know how we grow ourselves again, after we are dead?" I did. "Well, sometimes that is done with mortal flesh, and we turn them into a god that way." I thought it a rather crooked path to immortality, but I could not disapprove of it when I reflected upon the sort of god that Obelk the rat-trader would make.

I thought again of the foodholes and those who held command over them when I went for the first time to one of Nyglu's mudrooms. At all his homes he had these moist, dark retreats.

While reviewing here what he had written (more material was available for my scrutiny now that Amma had made the mortal origins of the gods explicit), I asked him his opinion of Kimp Sinn.

He seemed unsure at first of how to answer. "It works well enough, I think," he equivocated, paddling his webbed feet in a dark pond.

"Well enough at what?" I asked impatiently. I sat cross-legged atop a table of long stone slabs, the driest spot I could find. "What is this city of the gods supposed to *do?*"

"It—you see, it provides a goal for the ambitious, and even for the less motivated an example—" he broke off and glanced up at me shyly "—of the beauty of our relationship."

"*Our* relationship?" I asked incredulously. We spoke Modal Society, but business still formed the main basis of our intercourse, as far as I was concerned.

"I speak generally, of course," Nyglu hastened to assure me. "Of the relationship between mortals and the gods, the gentle mentoring, the poignant reminder of our slower yet always inevitable decline, experienced in miniature before our eyes by your own people."

"Oh." From the divine vantage, all our petty strivings, Obelk's and my mother's and those of me myself must look equally vain, foolish and pointless, and harmless on the whole. "How old are you, Nyglu?" Another of my tactless questions, with a wholly unexpected answer.

Nyglu flopped down on his knees before me. "What matters the difference in our years, charming child? My love for you is ageless."

I felt lost. Was this a scene from some play in my repertoire? My lines, what were they? Cautiously, I extended my hands. It took a moment for the god to look up from his submissive pose. Then he seized my palms in his slippery grip and touched them several times with his sticky tongue. I withdrew quickly, disguising my disgust.

"Amma," I managed to pant out in my fright and confusion. "She must not discover us." And I felt this to be true, no mere excuse for separating myself from him.

"Oh, sweetness, surely not," he said, his voice sad with longing at the loss of contact. "I can conceal our involvement from her. Trust me. Trust in my powers. Oh, Shiomah, we could make each other so happy." I didn't think so. But I let him touch me, just a little. Just a little more.

It was not too long after this that I progressed to the point where Amma felt I was of some use to her in her dramas. I played first for her the role of Juusli, a young god who rebels against the ennui of immortality by refusing to behave in a socially responsible manner. Among Juusli's foibles was a refusal to allow her body to age into puberty. The piece was years in the making, so Amma had my growth temporarily halted.

Weyando came back to play the part of Jez, a more conventionally minded contemporary of Juusli's. No mention was made of the way that I had provoked Lizore's speculative outburst, but he did not bring his eggson's eggwife's daughter to play with me again.

The part of Jez's spouse, whom Juusli spends much of the piece trying to seduce, was filled by a beautiful bioserv that Amma referred to as a dryad. Amma spent much time with this pale and lovely creature, giving it detailed instructions covering every nuance of its role. The dryad would try to follow her directions exactly, and if the results were not desirable, Amma would once more go over the entire action, changing it if necessary.

Sometimes I believed that the dryad performed poorly on purpose, simply to deprive me of my mistress's time. Professional pride kept me from following its example.

We spun around the globe, recording different parts of the story in different areas: ruins, deserts, the homes of friends, jungles, lakes, glaciers…. I saw that the sea *was* large, that mortals counted for nothing against the world's immensity. And that though outnumbered six-hundred-to-one, the divine five thousand leave more of a mark upon the earth than the mortal three million, because they are more able to work on the world's scale.

There was a valley along a dead, dry river. All soil had been stripped from the land by some bored deity, and the bedrock had then been chiseled into tunnels and spires, a maze for the wind. Low, shuddering groans and high sounds that yearned to become music played around us there. Haunting murmurs and keening whistles accompanied every scene. It was easy to portray Juusli's essential loneliness in this land that mourned for itself.

Once I looked up from the action of one of these scenes and saw to my surprise that tears fell from Amma's eyes. When she signalled an end to the session, I followed her to the other edge of the plateau we worked upon. As we walked she seemed oblivious to me, but reaching the drop-off she stopped and called me to her.

Her tears left starry trails on her indigo skin, shining like her hyalescent hair. "Your performance is quite moving, Shiomah," she told me in a low, steady voice. "I am proud." So was I, for the scene just completed had been rather difficult. Juusli was struggling with the ghosts of her dead selves as they urged her to fling herself to another death. The difficulty lay in creating the physical impression of resistance while wrestling with the air. Departing from her usual procedure, Amma had chosen to screen-animate these devils after the recording, rather than manufacture bioservs which would only be demolished during their plunge into the canyon below. I was glad to have met this challenge so well, but I didn't think Amma cried for joy in my competence. I waited and hoped for an explanation.

Instead she asked, "If I were to assure you, Shiomah, that you would be given immortality if only you jumped over the edge of this plateau, would you do it?"

I thought of my mother, tossed high into the air, dead, no doubt, before she hit the ground. "No." I paused, weighing my position. "Of course I would have to, if you commanded me to, wouldn't I?"

"But you have already answered my question," she stated, dismissing mine. "Here is another. If I asked you to throw me down there, would you?" I started to speak, but she continued. "If I did not tell you to, but asked, with no authority."

I could not picture autocratic, arbitrary Amma with no authority, though I tried. "What would become of me, if I did?" I inquired.

My mistress laughed, all melancholy suddenly gone from her manner. "You funny thing! So selfish, so practical. Never mind. I will not ask you to kill me, for you would surely find it an annoying task." Taking my hand, she returned with me to the others.

A later sequence was recorded on Nyglu's estate. Before his current obsession took hold of him, Nyglu had been fascinated with the order of amphibians, as his personal appearance showed. Perhaps this is why mortals associated him with rivers, and with fresh water in general. He certainly associated himself with it. Pools, bogs, swamps, and wet places of all sorts made up the bulk of his "grounds." When we visited he still took great pride in showing the estate to his visitors, pointing out the particular species he had reconstructed from his studies. Some were immense and ugly, others small and subtle, effacing themselves into the dark, decaying backdrop.

There were also experiments, whims come to life. My favorites were the triphibians, a sort of winged salamander. Mottled scarlet and sky blue, one came and perched briefly on my arm then skimmed away. Seeing my delight, Nyglu hatched three eggs for me, and I spent my free time feeding and observing the larvae. Soon I had tame triphibians of my own, but I had to leave them behind when we went to the moon. Nyglu promised that they would be mine again when we returned.

The dryad was packed away in her trunk, and we coptered off to meet Amma's sky shuttle. Weyando stayed behind; his character, Jez, didn't appear in the final scenes. As we floated away from the world, its immensity was belittled.

We spent a long time in orbit because of a hitch in the preparations for our landing. An ancient resort on the moon's surface was to have been restored to habitability without destroying the period flavor of the setting. Some too authentic material used in the repairs had ruptured and released most of the complex's air. The old oxygen machines below the surface had long since been dismantled, and regular flights to and from Earth had stopped decades ago, at the end of the last space craze. It was a couple of days before more air was brought up. Trouble arose, due, in part, to our long confinement on board the shuttle.

In preparing me for the profession she had chosen for me, that of acting roles in her creations, Amma had given me access to all sorts of old cubes and reels. After I used up all the sleep tapes, she even taught me to read; not pictos like mortal writing, but words composed of letters, like these. While examining some written antiquities during the delay, I learned with real shock that the Earth had once been almost literally covered with mortals.

I ran to Amma in her cabin, craved to see her, was quickly admitted. What atrocity, I demanded of my mistress, had reduced the mortal population fifty-thousand-fold? As I asked this, I actually clutched Amma's elbow to stop her from turning away from me. She froze.

I whipped my hand away, startled at what I had just done. I had tried to use force to press my will upon a divinity.

But when she again faced me, she was smiling. Sadly. As if she had expected this to happen, while at the same time hoping that it never would. As though I had pleased and pained her both, at once. "I will answer you, Shiomah," she said, "but first I am going to show you something. Something I ought to have shown you long ago." She extended her left hand.

Not for the first time I noticed that the sides of her fingers and the edges of her palm were lined with numerous shining dots. "Activation of one of these circuits," she told me, "will wipe out a selected memory in your brain. I have chosen your mother's name." She let this sink in, then went on.

"Activation of a second will deprive you of the use of the centers of conscious volition. And the third," she promised, "will prevent the operation of your autonomic systems. Do you understand me?"

I nodded. "Yes, midam."

"Now. There was no disaster, no epidemic, no mass murder of mortals. The current population, my dear, is a result of time and care and thoughtful planning." She made gestures with her hands like a prince in a story, dispensing coins to a crowd. "Birth-control, ample food, *lebensraum*—the ancient fifty billion never had it so good." I still had a lot to learn.

It was difficult after the revelation of these threats to reassume the role of Juusli, a character whose last motivation is fear. With relief I removed my pressure suit in the simulated vacuum of the closing act, the heroine succumbing to the hallucinatory call of dust sirens. It was an ambiguous ending, with Juusli unharmed, drifting away with the sirens (specially made bioservs, of course), leaving a sparkling trail of palpable looking dust.

When we returned to Earth, Amma let me age again, though more slowly than mortals are accustomed to do. She used me in other, smaller works, or in the social games she played with the other gods. Sometimes she devoted her enormous energies to my training, sometimes she seemed merely to relax and enjoy my company. Her attentions were far from constant. I would be ignored for months, a year at a time, then taken up again without, apparently, a beat skipped.

One afternoon, when I had been with her nearly fifteen years, she fancied she would make love with me. My body was that of a fourteen-year-old, an awkward, pudgy beauty, but she was attracted. How can the gods ever tire of such pleasure?

In time our desire was heightened by a burgeoning love. My adoration was natural, inevitable even. I think I had only been waiting to release it until I received some sign from her.

As to why she loved me I can only say that not even mortal passions are easily subjected to analysis. Amma's love was fierce—and ridiculous, on the face of it. I still had pimples, at times. My nose was too long. I thought perhaps she confused me with Juusli, the first character she had created for me.

No deity questioned Amma's absorption with me. Such fascinations were not unheard of. Sometimes the infatuated god went as far as actually regrowing the mortal undeified, merely in faithful reduplication of the beloved original.

Those foolish gods. They should have known that this would not be enough for Amma.

She contrived to have me conditioned into partial godhood while growing and then secretly disposing of the expected replacement. Immortality was given to me for as long as I can stand it, and the powers of the god machines were made mine.

The sins of my "mortal counterpart" were not visited upon the new Shiomah. Weyando's eggson's spermdaughter was again allowed into the circle of my influence. Others that I had alienated upon Amma's instructions made me welcome in my new guise, with calls of congratulation and invitations to their estates. With all this obligatory gaiety, it was almost a year before we settled in again back on the island.

Amma became more and more attentive. She involved me in the details of her creations, seeking advice on costume and dialog for her daring depiction of a god in mortal disguise. I decided to have my rooms dismantled, as I spent nearly all my time in hers. Everything was packed away except the terminal when she came to me with her offer of marriage.

I stared at her across the wide, bare floor. She was colored all turquoise, with hair like ethereal jade. She clashed horribly with what was left of the decor.

"Well?" she asked, a little sharply. "Don't you want to be my wife?"

"Oh yes, yes Amma," I managed to reply. Since being deified I no longer referred to my mistress as "midam." "I do, I'll be so happy, I'll make you so happy, only I am very much surprised...." I trailed off. I came towards her, one eye on the terminal's screen. I did love her, and it meant so much to me to please her. She kissed the top of my head and clasped me to her.

"You should be used to receiving surprises from me by now," she said as she released me, smiling. "In time, you will grow accustomed to my ways, and come to find me quite boring, no doubt."

I shook my locks in vigorous dissent. "Never, no, never, Amma." I took her hands in mine and kissed each sea-colored fingertip, saying "You are so sweet, so generous, so full of precious secrets—" I came to one of the little silver circles with which she controlled her underlings.

"Oh, yes, that reminds me," she said when I did not continue. "I almost forgot to tell you. I'm going to have those signals removed, those ones I told you about on the moon." I met her eyes. They were dark, gravely serious in her expressive face.

"The ones you said could erase my memory or destroy my nervous system?"

She nodded. "So. Now that you've consented to engage yourself to me, there's no danger of those circuits ever being engaged." She grinned, suddenly in an impish mood, and I perceived the pun (no pun at all in mortal speech) almost at the same time as I saw the call light blink on the com screen. Pretending to be disgusted with the lowness of her humor, I managed to shove her playfully through the door before she noticed the flashing signal.

As I had expected, it was Nyglu. His warty face showed satisfaction to my trained eyes. "I have the body," he reported, "and the other arrangements are under way."

"Very good," I told him. With the passage of time I had grown used to my deepening contact with Nyglu and the leverage it gave me. "Then you may count on my presence in your mudroom——" I hesitated. Amma had planned to leave for Nyglu's estate this evening, but there was no telling when I'd be left alone there, now that we were betrothed. "Whenever I can come without Amma knowing," I hastily amended. Nyglu looked like he wanted to protest, but to whom? Not to me. I switched off the screen and went looking for my mistress.

We were wed in a short but impressive ceremony aboard the ship Amma had been given by Weyando. I begged her to wear some form of clothing, and at last she compromised by causing her hair to cling to her nakedness, covering almost all the right places. By contrast, I was draped in fluttering, dune-colored fabrics designed to hide the tiny scars and other imperfections my body carried. True, we might have said that Amma had caused my replacement to be grown bearing these marks, but I desired to avoid explanations.

The wind sang in the rigging, our only choir. The sky, as ever in those latitudes, was a vaulted dome of blue. The child Lizore joined our hands as we pledged our love, "as long as its life continues." After kissing one another's eyelids, we turned to bestow our wedding gifts upon our guests, all of whom, at Amma's insistence, were present.

As we passed among her friends and relatives, Amma made sketchy introductions to those I had not yet met. "Hayvre, Lizore's eggmother," she named one black, black woman who reached out to clasp my hand in one sporting two thumbs. "Elleefaw" was a tiny, shaggy, sexless looking god in spiked heels. I recognized the name as belonging to the deity of unpleasant truths.

"He makes the best monuments. We used the Hill of Glass in my last piece, Elleefaw," she said to the short, red-furred god. "It was perfect, especially the way it opens and closes like an eye." Elleefaw nodded his approval of this tribute, running his own sharp eye up and down my pudgy awkwardness. I felt uneasy in his presence, and I wasn't made more comfortable by the remark he made as he walked way. "Now you'll each find out what the other is really like," he announced over his shoulder, clip-clopping off across the deck. But surely we had learned all that in over twenty years?

I was glad to see Nyglu, preferring his familiar strangeness to these upsetting new acquaintances. Our encounters had been curtailed since the betrothal, and he was glad to stay by my side when I asked him to, as a sort of buffer.

"I don't know why you couldn't broadcast the ceremony like everyone else does," he complained to us in a mildly fretful tone. "But I must admit that I am enjoying myself," he added politely (and perhaps also to prevent Amma from detecting his morose jealousy).

My mistress hadn't explained to me her reasons for an in-person celebration, but now she said, "This one isn't for show. *This* one is going to last." With a fond look she walked away from me, taking our glasses to be filled with the bright, frothy drink that was being served.

Still disturbed by Elleefaw's pronouncement, I was silent until Nyglu wondered out loud if anything was wrong. "Do you think everything will change now?" I asked him. I expected denial. His precarious happiness, his treasured times with me, would work to keep him from accepting the possibility of a different course in our lives.

Instead, he shrugged, resigned. "Change," Nyglu answered, "is Amma's only constant."

For several months after our marriage, all remained the same. I continued to work for Amma as before, to make furious or languid love with her, to study and transact my own business. I acquired islands, asteroids, and watersheds entirely my own, as well as other, less common commodities. Nyglu took care of this for me, with all the discretion I relied upon him for.

Then Amma decided that we were going to have a child. The new Shiomah might have asked upon deification how gods were born. Perhaps Amma attributed my lack of curiosity on the subject to habits formed in earlier days. I could hardly tell her of my source. Instead, I massaged her hands, pulling and stroking her pale violet fingers as she recited the possibilities to the tower's open ceiling, full of stars.

"We can mate as mortals do," she whispered, "or we can let machines do it for us. Two males can join genetic material, or two females. We can mate with ourselves or with those long dead. Just as soon as you're ready," she said, "we'll start taking the enzymes that neutralize the sterilizing compounds." She sighed as I dug into the fleshy mound beneath her thumb.

"And then?" I asked. But in answer Amma held her hand to my mouth and brought mine in turn to her delicately nipping teeth. Her excitement at the thought of conception made further details impossible to come by until dawn.

What Amma offered me was the opportunity to impose my genetic message over that of a microscopic animal. The animal would then be injected into a donated sperm cell, and the sperm cell would join with an egg of hers. This was fine with me; I leapt at the chance for another sort of immortality. Amma and I disagreed on only one important point; I wanted her to carry the baby in her own body. Even for just a short while. She would not; not even her innate love of the curious made pregnancy appealing to her.

I offered to bear the child within my own body. She pointed out that to do so would endanger the lie we lived. "Only a mortal would allow itself to be invaded in such a manner," she declared hotly. Anyway, what did it matter that our wombs were empty; we would still be mothers as the gods saw things.

It mattered to me.

Weeks passed. I took to sulking in my old refuge, the brown and russet rooms I had occupied before our marriage. Gradually I brought the furnishings out of storage, determined to be comfortable in the midst of my self-imposed exile. I avoided Amma, keeping to my own apartments as much as possible.

Finally she came to me, persuasive and proud. I slouched on my couch seat, not looking up as she lowered herself beside me.

"Don't pout, Shiomah," she said, putting an arm around me. She laughed. "I could walk to Kimp Sinn on your lower lip." That made me smile, but I quickly pretended that I never had.

"Our ways are better, you will see," she continued, coaxingly. Pale blue, she rested like a piece of sky on the brown slopes of my shoulders.

I shook her arm off, standing up and walking away angrily. "Your ways? You have no ways. You do nothing except let things be done for you." In the silence that followed I felt the presence of Elleefaw, happy that we did no better than he had expected.

"Oh, Amma," I said remorsefully, turning back to her again.

"Why do you oppose my will?" She was displeased that I had a will, rather than a mere collection of childish whims, that I had walked away from her, that I stood and she sat. Seeing this, I knelt, thus allowing her to continue to be gracious.

"Have I not treated you well, my dear?" she asked. Her fingers sought my hair, toyed with my tangles. "Have I not given you everything you ever desired, and more?" No, I thought, for my mother is gone, and you refuse to take her place. Deaf to my inner voice, Amma continued to talk of how she had spoiled me, ignorant of my deepening resolve.

"So you must understand," she concluded, "that it will be best for both of us if you yield to me in this."

"No," I said, and her hand ceased fondling my locks. "If you make a child this way, it will be without my consent. You will have to kill me then, to keep me from confessing our crime."

She stood, pushing me away from her. Her celestial face paled, a touch of cirrus in the sky. "You can't mean it," she said, quietly appalled. Bestowing immortality directly upon a mortal, as she had done, was inconceivable; the punishment for our deception would be of a kind with it. The gods are jealous.

"But I do mean it," I said, rising and meeting her eyes without wavering. "No machine or half-animal is going to carry our child, Amma, not while I live."

She stared until she saw that I was in earnest. Then, for the first time in my life I experienced divine wrath. She stamped the floor with one lovely foot and clenched her fists in front of her angrily heaving breast. "You fool!" she shouted, purple smudging her pale blue cheeks. She laughed harshly, metallically, an untuned gamelon. "You funny, funny fool." Then she activated the first of the three circuits she had shown me years ago as we orbited the moon and had, of course, never disabled.

My mother's name is gone, removed from my mind and all my records. And the erasure is permanent and self-reinforcing. Even if someone told me what my mother was called, I would forget the sounds as soon as they were said. Even if I wrote her name here as it was spoken, I would forget it as soon as it was read.

Amma is a capricious god, but thorough.

But shrewd as I am, I had made my preparations. Even as she was proving her remorse by destroying her other controls, I left and fled here.

I do not know if she was fooled by the death of my double. Nyglu was careful, but perhaps she will discover that he hid it for me when she thought she'd had it destroyed.

Perhaps she will not be deceived. Perhaps she will come and test my defenses. For all I can tell, though, she is even now working on another Shiomah, perhaps one just a little less hard-headed. I left her plenty of tissue samples.

It was foresight that made me search out this corner of the world, rich in plant life and rare minerals. It is mine through my efforts, and I have stocked it with my treasures. My horses and cattle and machines and Fertility Manna. My plunder and purchases.

And the men and women, my mortals. I will take very tender care of my little mortals. And they will bless the land in my name.

The Water Museum

When I saw the hitchhiker standing by the sign for the Water Museum, I knew he had been sent to assassinate me. First off, that's what the dogs were saying as I slowed to pick him up. Girlfriend, with her sharp, little, agitated bark, was quite explicit. Buddy was silently trying to dig a hole under the back seat, seeking refuge in the trunk. I stopped anyway.

Second off, the man as much as told me so his own self. He opened up the passenger door of my midnight-blue '62 Mercury and piled in with his duffel bag, and his jeans and white tee, and his curly brown hair tucked under a baseball cap. "Where you going?" I asked, as soon as he was all settled and the door shut.

"Water Museum," he said. "Got an interview for a job there." That was confirmation, cause I wasn't hiring just then. Way too early in the year for that; things don't pick up here till much later in the spring. Even then, my girls and me handle most of whatever work comes up. Even after Albinia, my oldest, took herself off ten years ago, I never hired no more than a couple locals to tide us over the weekends. And this guy wasn't no local. So he was headed where he had no business to be going, and I could think of only the one reason why.

But I played right along. "What part?" I asked him, pulling back out on the smooth one-lane blacktop.

It took him a second to hear my question. "What do you mean, what part? They got different entrances or something?"

"I mean the Water Museum is three, four miles long," I told him. Three point two miles, if you want to be exact, but I didn't. "You tell me where you want to go there, and I'll get you as close as I can."

I twisted around to get a good look at the dogs. Buddy had given up on his tunnel to the trunk. He was lying on the floor, panting like a giant, asthmatic weight-lifter. His harness jingled softly with every whuffling breath. Girl-friend was nowhere in sight.

The hitchhiker twisted in his seat, too. "Nice animal," he said uneasily, taking in Buddy's shiny, tusky-looking teeth. "Sheepdog?"

"Nope. Otterhound. Lotta people make that mistake, though. They do look alike, but otterhound's got a finer bone structure, little different coloring."

"Oh."

We started the long curve down to the shore. I put her in neutral and let us glide, enjoying the early morning light. It dappled my face through the baby beech leaves like butter and honey on a warm biscuit.

On this kind of bright, sunshiny spring morning, I found it hard to credit that a bunch of men I didn't even know were bent on my destruction. Despite the evidence to the contrary sitting right there next to me on the plaid, woven vinyl seat cushion, it just did not make sense. What were they so het up about? Their lawns? Browned-off golf courses, which shouldn'ta oughta been there in the first place? Ranches dried to dust and blowing away.... Yeah, I could see how it would disturb folks to find the land they thought they owned up and left without em. I just did not agree with their particular manner of settling the matter.

I drove quietly with these thoughts of mine awhile, and my killer sat there just as quiet with his. Then we came to that sweet little dip, and the turn under the old viaduct, and we were almost there. "You figured out yet where you're headed?" I asked.

"Uhh, no, ma'am. Just drop me off by the offices, I guess...."

"Offices ain't gonna be open this early," I told him. "Not till noon, between Labor Day and Memorial Weekend. C'mon, I got nothing better to do, I'll give you a tour."

"Well, uhh, that's nice, ma'am, but I, uh, but don't go out of your way or anything...."

I looked at him, cocked my chin, and grinned my best country-girl grin, the one that makes my cheeks dimple up and my eyelashes flutter. "Why, it'd be a pleasure to show you around the place!" By this time we were to the parking lot. I pulled in and cut the ignition, and before he could speak another word I had opened my door. "Let's go."

The hitchhiker hesitated. Buddy whined and lumbered to his feet, and that must have decided him. With what I would call alacrity he sprang out on his side of the car onto the gravel. Ahh, youth.

I let Buddy out the back. Instead of his usual sniff and pee routine, he stuck close to me. Girlfriend was still nowhere in sight. The hitchhiker was looking confusedly around the clearing. At first glance the steps are hard to pick out, and the trail up into the dunes is faint and overgrown.

I grabbed my wool ruana and flung it on over my shoulders, rearranging my neckerchiefs and headscarves. "You got a jacket, young man?" I asked him. "Shirtsleeves're all right here, but we're gonna catch us a nice breeze down by the Lake."

"Um, yeah, in my—" He bent over the front seat and tugged at something on the floor. "In my duffel, but I guess it's stuck under here or something."

Came a low, unmistakable growl, and he jumped back. I went around to his side. "Don't worry, I'll get it out for you," I said. "Girlfriend!" I bent over and grabbed one green canvas corner of my assassin's duffel bag and pulled. This is Girlfriend's favorite game. We tussled away for a few minutes. "She's small, but she's fierce," I commented as I took a quick break. "You got any food in there, a sandwich or something?"

"No. Why?"

"I just noticed she had the zipper open some."

The hitchhiker got a little pale and wispy-looking when he heard that. He stayed that way till I retrieved his duffel and gave it to him to rummage through. He took a while finding his jean jacket, and by the time he'd dug it out and put it on he looked more solid and reassured.

So now I knew where his gun was. Should I let him keep it? He'd be a lot easier to handle without a pistol in his fist. Then again, the thing might not even be loaded, depending on how soon he'd been planning on meeting up with me; simpler for him to explain an empty gun to any cops stopped him hitching rides. And I'd be able to get him relaxed faster if he was armed.

He threw the bag over his shoulder, and I locked the car. Girlfriend had already started up the trail. Of course he wanted me to walk ahead of him, but Buddy just looked at him with his dark, suspicious eyes and Mr. Man decided it would be okay if this time he was the one to go first.

I love the dance I chose when I made this path, the wending and winding of the way. As we climbed, we left the beech trees behind and ascended into the realm of grass and cherries, of white-backed poplar leaves, soft as angel fuzz. Poison ivy shone waxily, warningly, colored like rich, red wine.

We walked right past my offices. They look like part of the dune crest, coming at em from this side. I cast em that way, wound em round with roots, bound em with stems and sprinkled pebbles lightly over the top. The windows are disguised as burrows, with overhangs and grass growing down like shaggy eyebrows.

My assassin's Nikes made soft little drumming sounds on the boardwalk, following the click of Girlfriend's nails round to the blow-out and the observation deck. The promised breeze sprang up, ruffling our fur and hair. I watched my killer's reaction to his first sight of the Museum.

His shoulders straightened and relaxed, though I hadn't noticed they were crooked before that. He walked up and leaned against the wooden rail. "All that water..." he said.

I came up and joined him. "Yes," I said. "All that water." From the deck you can see it, as much as can be seen from down here on the Earth. Shadows still hung beneath us, but further out the Great Lake sparkled splendidly. Waves were dancing playfully, like little girls practicing ballet. They whirled and leapt and tumbled to rest just beyond the short terminal dunes five hundred feet below where we stood. "All that water. And all of it is sweet."

I took my killer gently by the arm and led him to the river side. That's where the work I've done is easiest to take in: the floating bridges over Smallbird Marsh, the tanks and dioramas and such. "Where you from, kid?" We started down the steps.

"Colorado."

"Pretty?"

"It used to be. When I was little, back before the drought got bad."

I stopped at a landing and waited for Buddy to catch up. He's all right on a hillside, but this set of stairs is steep and made out of slats. They give under his weight a bit, and that makes him take them slow and cautious, ears flapping solemnly with every step.

I smiled at my assassin and he smiled shyly back. It occurred to me then that he might not know who I am. I mean, I do present a pretty imposing figure, being a six-six strawberry blonde and not exactly overweight, but on the fluffy side. I'd say I'm fairly easy to spot from a description. But maybe they hadn't bothered to give him one.

I dropped his arm and motioned him on ahead. "By the bye," I called out, once he was well on his way. "I don't believe I caught your name. Mine's Granita. Granita Bone."

He sorta stopped there for a sec and put his hand out, grabbing for a railing I'd never had installed. Well, I thought, at least they told the poor boy that much.

"Jasper Smith," he said, then turned around to see how I took it.

I nodded down at him approvingly. Jasper rang a nice change on Granita, and the Smith part kinda balanced out its oddness. "Pleased to meet you, Jasper." Girlfriend barked up at us from the foot of the stairs. "All right," I shouted down at her, "I'm a-coming, I'm a-coming."

"Sheltie," I explained to my killer. "Herding animal. Makes her nervous to see us spread out like this." By that time Buddy had caught up and passed me. He knew this walk. I followed him down.

At the bottom, I chose the inland path, past pools of iridescent black blooming with bright marsh marigold. Stabilizing cedars gave way to somber hemlock, still adrip with the morning's dew.

"Water Music," I told Jasper, just before our first stop.

"I don't—"

"Hush up, then, and you will." Even the dogs knew to keep quiet here. It fell constantly, a bit more hesitant than rain. Notes in a spatter, a gentle jingle, a high and solitary ping! ping! ping! Liquid runs and hollow drums grew louder and louder until we reached the clearing and stood still, surrounded.

It was the tank and windmill that drew him first, though there's nothing so special about them. I went over with him and undid the lock so the blades could catch the morning's breeze. The tank's got a capacity of about four hundred gallons; small, but it usually lasts me a day or two.

With the pump going, the pipe up from the river started in to sing. It's baffled and pierced; totally inefficient, but gorgeous to my ears. From the other pipes and the web of hose overhead, drops of water continued to gather and fall—on glass and shells, in bowls and bottles, overflowing or always empty, on tin and through bamboo, falling, always falling.

Adding to the symphony, Girlfriend lapped up a drink from a tray of lotuses.

"Wow, Granita, this is really, uh, elaborate," said Jasper when he'd pretty much done looking around.

"Do you like it?" I asked.

"Yeah, but isn't it kinda, umm, kinda wasteful?"

I shrugged. "Maybe. But like my mama always said, 'You don't never know the usefulness of a useless thing.'" Right then I just about washed my hands of good ole Jasper. But he hadn't even seen any of the other exhibits, so I decided I'd better postpone judgment. My assassins did tend to have a wide stripe of utilitarianism to em. At least at first. Couldn't seem to help it.

Buddy stood where the trail began again, panting and whining and wagging his whole hind end. He was looking forward to the next stop, hoping to catch him a crawdad. The fish factory's never been one of my favorite features of the place, but Buddy loved it, and it turned out to be a big hit with Jasper, too. He took a long, long look at the half-glazed ponds that terraced down the dune. Me and some of the girls had fixed up burnt wood signs by the path, explaining the contents of each one, but Jasper had to climb up all the ladders and see for himself. He disappointed me by flashing right past all my pretty koi. Can you believe it was the catfish that caught his fresh little fancy? He must have spent twenty minutes to check out those mean, ugly suckers. Though, to give him his credit, he dallied a fair while with Yertle and that clan, too.

Meanwhile, me and the dogs kept waiting on my killer to make his move.

We looped under the deserted highway and came back by Summer Spring Falls and the Seven Cauldrons, then started across the marsh over the floating bridges, which Buddy doesn't like anymore than the stairs. Maybe it's the way the wicker that I wove em from sorta sags, or the dark breezes stirring up between the chinks, or the gaps you have to hop over going from one section to the next.

The breeze picked up again as we headed towards the beach. Small clouds, light on their feet, flickered past the sun.

I let him get behind me. Wicker creaks. I could hear his footsteps hesitate, sinking lower as he stood trying to decide was this the time and place. We were alone, he had a good clean line of sight, nothing but the wind between his aim and my broad back. But when he stilled and I turned, his hand wasn't doing nothing but resting on the zipper of his duffel bag, and that wasn't even open yet. His eyes were focused over my head, far off in space or time. He was listening.

Red-winged blackbirds. Sweet and pure, their songs piped up, trilling away into silence, rising again from that pool of quiet, sure and silver, pouring over and over into my ears. "When I was a boy..." said Jasper. I waited. In a moment he started again. "When I was a boy, there was a creek and a swamp, where the river used to be. I didn't know, I thought it was just a fun place to play. Some birds there, they sang just like this."

Well, making allowance for a few inaccuracies (swamp for marsh, and the bird songs had to vary a *little*), this sounded pretty much like his truth. And it made actual sense to me, not like them pipeline dreams of those cowboys sent him here. Now we were getting somewhere. Closer. He'd be making his attack real soon.

I turned back around and trudged a little more slowly along the baskety surface of the bridge. The back of my neck crawled and itched, like itty bitty Jaspers and Granitas were walking all over it. I kept myself in hand, though, breathing deep and regular, balanced on the bubbling well of power beneath my feet, telling myself soon—soon—

He didn't stop, he just slowed down a hair. I didn't hear any zipper, either, but when I turned again he had finally pulled his goddamn gun out and it was pointed straight at me. Was it loaded, then? He seemed to think so.

My chest cramped up and my temperature dropped like I'd been dumped head first into Superior. I could wind up contributing my vital nitrogen and phosphorus content to the cycle like right *now*. I let my fright sag me down and grabbed the rails as his eyes hardened and his gun hand tensed. He was a lefty.

With a sudden lurch I threw myself against the side of the bridge and tipped us all into the cool, ripe waters of Smallbird Marsh. The gun cracked off one shot, just before we all made a nice big splash. I shrugged out of my ruana and kicked off my clogs and I knew I'd be okay. Fluff floats. Buddy woofed and Girlfriend yapped, all happy and accounted for.

Girlfriend and I pulled ourselves right up onto the next basket, but the menfolks stayed in a while longer. Buddy loves to swim, and he's good at it, too. Jasper was floundering, though, wrapped up in weeds and trying to breathe mud. By the time I got him hauled out he wasn't more than half conscious. Still had a grip on that gun, though. I pried it loose and tossed it back.

Now how to get him up to the offices? I thought about it while I whipped a few of my scarves around his wrists and elbows and ankles and knees. My sash in a slip knot 'round his throat for good measure. I shoved him till he sat mostly upright. "Ain't this a fucking mess?" I asked him, tilting his head so he could see the tipped over basket, then back around to me. "I *just* had my hair done, got the dogs back from the groomer's *yesterday*, now you pull this stunt! What in the name of every holy thing were you trying to do?"

"Kill you." His voice was rough, sort of a wheeze now from coughing up marsh water.

"Well, duh. Yeah. Question is what you thought that was supposed to accomplish?" He just stuck out his bottom lip. Put me in mind of Albinia, age eight.

"Ain't I done told your bosses, time and again, getting rid of me is gonna do em not one whit of good? Ain't I told em how it's the oracle decides whether or not the Water Museum's ever gonna open up a pipeline and exercise its rights to sell? And if I hadn't told em, ain't it right there in our charter, a matter of public record for every passing pissant to read it if he remembers his A-B-Cs? Well, ain't it?"

My killer kinda shrunk his shoulders in. Breeze picked up some, rustling the reeds. I'm pretty well insulated, but Jasper couldn't help a little shiver. That was all I got out of him that while, though.

I left him and walked a couple of baskets to the boathouse for a life jacket. Had to untie his arms to get it on, and he wanted to wrestle then, having dried out enough to get his dander up. I got a hold on his nice new necktie and pulled. Finished bundling him up while he was trying to recall if he still knew how to breathe. I gave us both a chance to calm down, then dumped him back in the marsh.

Good thing I had Buddy's harness on him. I whistled him over, hooked up Jasper's life jacket and we were on our way once more.

"You're in luck," I told my assassin. "Usually we skip this part of the tour, but I noticed you gronking all the technical dingle-dangles. So I figure you'll get a large charge out of our sewage treatment facilities."

The jacket worked fine. Buddy paddled joyfully along next to the bridges. He likes to make himself useful.

It wasn't far to the settling ponds. I gave Jasper plenty of chances to tell me about Colorado wildlife and the dying riparian ecosystem, but he didn't seem to be in the mood. He was mostly silent, excepting the odd snort when Buddy kicked up too big a wake.

Really, the ponds weren't that bad. Joy, my youngest daughter, got the Museum a contract with a local trailer park, but they're pretty much dormant till early May. Right then, the park was mostly empty, just a few old retirees, so the effluent came mainly from my offices and the tanks of a couple friends.

I glossed over that, though, in my lecture. I concentrated instead on wind-driven aeration paddles, ultra-sound and tank resonance, and oh, yes, our patented, prize-winning, bacteriophagic eels. As the ponds got murkier and murkier, Jasper's gills got greener and greener, so to speak. He held up well. I had dragged him over two locks, and had him belly down on the third when he broke.

"Nonononono!" he gibbered at me. "What is it, what *is* it, don't let it touch me, please!" I bent over and looked where he was looking. Something was floating in the water. I fished it out. One end of a cucumber had my killer sobbing out his heart and wriggling like a worm with eyes to see the hook.

People are funny.

Girlfriend came up and sniffed the piece of cucumber. It was kind of rotten, and after all, she is a dog. I threw it back to the eels, unhitched Buddy's harness and rolled

Jasper over on his back. "You ready to come clean?" I asked him. He nodded desperately.

I wasted quite a few minutes trying to untie the wet silk knotted around his ankles. Then I got disgusted and sawed it through with my car keys. Still left him hobbled at the knees as I marched him off to the laundry room.

We came in through the "Secret Tunnel," what the girls like to call it. Really, it's just a old storm sewer from under the highway. But when I excavated the place and found how close it passed, I annexed the pipe onto my basement there. Handy, sometimes. Grate keeps out most of the possum and nutrias. The big ones, anyways. I locked that into place and set Jasper down on a bench next to the washer, under the skylight.

I nabbed a towel off the steam rack and wrecked it rubbing Buddy down. Took off his poor harness while carefully considering my killer.

He looked a sorrowful mess. His tee shirt was gonna need some enzyme action before you could come anywheres close to calling it white again, and his jeans and jacket weren't never gonna smell clothesline fresh no more, no matter what. His hat was gone, his hair matted down with algae and such. His eyes were red from crying, his upper lip glistened unbecomingly, and the rest of him steamed in the cool laundry room air.

I prayed for a washday miracle.

"Jasper," I told him, "you are in a terrible spot right now." He nodded a couple times, agreeable as any schoolchild. "Sometimes, the only way outta danger is in. You gotta go through it to get to the other side. You gotta sink to swim.

"I'm telling you honest and true that in spite of what went on out there I bear you absolutely no grudges. You believe me?" Again the nod. "Good. Try to bear it in mind over the next few days."

I reached my shears down from the shelf above his head and cut away the rest of where I'd tied him up: hands first, elbows next, then knees. Those were some nice scarves, too. One my favorite. I was sure hoping he'd be worth it.

"Strip," I told him. He only hung back a second, then he put off his modesty or pride or whatever, and the rest of his wet, useless things right after. Girlfriend tried to run off with a sock but I made her bring it back. "Dump that shit in the washer." I had him set it to low, hot wash, cold rinse, add my powder, and switch on. He didn't seem to know his way around the control panel, and I wondered who'd been taking care of him back home.

Pale goose pimples ain't exactly my cup of vodka, but Jasper was a nice enough looking young man. Given the circumstances. I admired his bumptious little backside as I scooted him on ahead of me over to the Sunshower. Light shafted down through the glass, glittering off the walls of black sand that lined its path for all of two hundred and fifty feet. It was midday by then, and the water pretty warm. He stayed under there a good, long while. I could tell he was finished when he started to look for a way to turn it off. Weren't none, of course. It ain't my job to tell the water when to stop, only to help it through the flow. And naturally, any little deviations I do participate in ain't nothing like what them so called "Water Interest" cowboys got in mind.

"Leave it, Jasper," I told him, motioning him on with my shears. Girlfriend gruffed a little bit to underline the suggestion. We took him along the hall past the Glowing Pool and the steps down to the Well. Later, on his way out,

I planned on stopping to offer him a sweet, cold dipperful. Like drinking a cup of stars.

Gradually, the way we walked kept getting darker, the skylights scarcer and more spaced out. Joy and Gerrietta's mosaics running up and down the walls barely glittered by the time we hit the Slipstream, and I heard Jasper gasp as he stepped into swiftly moving water. "Keep going," I told him, and he sloshed obediently on ahead. The dogs were between us, now.

Somewhere close by came the sound of icebergs calving, the underwater songs of whales. I barely heard them as I fumed to myself, wondering if I loaded up a fleet of helicopters to drop off leaflets and trained a flock of condors to fly across the whole United States with a banner in their beaks, if I could make them idiots realize they were not gonna get their Great Lakes pipeline open by killing me off.

Maybe the first few assassins were just to put a touch of fear on me. Maybe they thought the oracle wasn't nothing but a sham, and I could be bullied into letting them use the Museum's exclusive access.

For a while there, looked like they really did want to kill me. With my oldest girl, Albinia, off in the wild blue yonder, there'd be a bit of a legal tussle over the Directorship. Guess they might of planned to take advantage of the confusion ensuing upon my untimely demise.

Lately, most of their moves they seemed to make just purely to annoy me. Sending out an amateur like this here Jasper—

Up ahead, the sloshing stopped. My killer stood waiting for us on the ledge, in the dark.

"Here's where you'll be staying." I opened the door to the Dressing Room. He didn't seem much taken with the place. Sure, the ceiling's kind of low, 'cept for that two-hundred-foot skylight. And you got to sleep on the floor or in the sandpit. But that sand is soft, and nice and warm on account of the solar heat-exchanger underneath. "I'll give you a little while in here by yourself to figure out what you're gonna be when you come out. Say, a week maybe. Then I'll come back and you can tell me what you'll be needing."

"But—food, water!"

"They're here." He looked around at the bare driftwood walls. "You doubting my word? You're a bright boy, Jasper, I'm sure you'll find where they're at in plenty time."

"I don't understand. You're not trying to torture me are you? I mean, if you want a confession I've already—"

"You don't understand? Then let me explain. I don't need a confession. I got that the first time them cowboys sent someone up here to murder me, fourteen years agone. That's right, Jasper, you are by no means the first hired killer I met up with, though you have got to be the most naive by a crane's holler. *Hitchhiking* to the *hit*? Talk about your sore thumbs!"

Jasper turned red from the collarbone up. "My van broke down in Bliss."

"Yeah, well, guess you couldn't afford a rental, and probably just as conspicuous to get one of them, anyways. But you coulda just given up. Couldn't you?"

That's when my killer started in again about the black-birds, and added a sheep farm and I don't know what all else. It wasn't the sense of his words I paid attention to: none of them ever had much worth listening to to say at this point. The Earth owed them a living, and a silver teat to suck. And it better be a mighty long dug, cause it wasn't supposed to dry up, no matter how hard them cowboys chewed.

They all seemed to need to give their little speeches, though, so I had got used to sitting politely and listening to the kinds of sounds they made. Rattles and grates and angry, poisonous buzzings was what they usually come up with.

Jasper surprised me with an awful good imitation of a red-winged blackbird. Lower register, of course. But his voice trilled up and spilled over the same way, throbbing sweet and pure, straight from his poor little heart. A pretty song, but he was singing it to the wrong audience.

Once, I was one of the richest women on this continent. Powerball winnings. I took and built the Water Museum, then finessed an old congressman of a lover of mine into pushing through our charter. He secured us the sole, exclusive rights to be selling off the Great Lakes' water to irrigate them thirsty Western states.

Or not.

Didn't them cowboys kick up a dust storm! Kept us real busy for a while there, in the courts and on the talkiest of the talk shows.

I'm not rich no more. What I didn't use building the Museum or fighting to protect our charter, I wound up giving us as a donation. Not so famous no more, neither. And important? Not in the least.

During the season, I sell tickets and polish windows, hand out sea-weed candy to unsuspecting kids. Nothing but that would stop because I died, much less if I changed my feeble mind.

I sighed. Jasper had finished his aria, and I prepared to shut the door. Then, shears still held tight, and Buddy close and attentive at hand, I did the funniest thing. I kissed him, right on his damp, still-kinda-smelly forehead. He looked up at me, and he done something funny, too. He smiled. I smiled again, but neither of us said a thing. I backed out, still careful, and locked him in. I have a sneaky suspicion this one *might* turn out to be interesting. When he's good and ready.

But She's
Only a Dream

✴

An old man named Roscoe reminisces, tilting his chair back as the sun sets. "She musta been from somewhere 'round here. Kansas City ain't that big a town. But no one ever seen her 'cept at jam sessions and gigs. Sittin by, listenin in. Never liftin her voice above what was ladylike to speak let alone tryin to sing. She was always pretty much a mystery to everyone."

✴ ✴ ✴

Darktown pops and sizzles like a bonfire, but daytimes the flame's invisible. Charcoal and ash flicker to the strobe, faces grimace and turn to it, scarves snap to it, newspapers crackle to the nameless music of the streets.

This is a frantic song, a sixty-cycle-a-second scuffle. Not till evening does the light mellow. Then, golden horns fill certain cellars with a smooth hush, a yellow melody rising from below linked shadows. The soft sounds spill upwards, pooling at the feet of passers-by.

Laura seems a little nervous, standing there on the sidewalk, tugging at her hat, her clothes, her hair. Yet she is perfect: lipstick even, stocking seams straight, beige- and brown-dotted hem swirling just so, brown pumps clicking just right down the cement steps.

She opens the door on a room full of men and instruments; already the dampness is warming with body heat. They have traded axes, goofing themselves loose. Winks and nods greet her entry, and she smiles in return, working her way to the sofa at the far end of the room. A skinny, coal-colored youth sits there restlessly, waiting for the games to end.

It isn't long. First a slow blues. Then "Just You, Just Me," and they're really cooking. Smells good. Laura weaves her head in time to the fumes, delicate nostrils wide with pleasure. The next tune, a rhythm-and-blues, starts out at a medium tempo, but the drummer winds it up midway to a fast burn. At different times different musicians glance at Laura to see the music made visible. Her black eyes are afire with secrets.

During their break, the cellar darkens with smoke and brightens with talk, most of it about the foregoing jams. Laura doesn't say too much; once in a while, "Yes, I liked that," or "Uh-huh, it was real nice." Her voice is quiet, her words proper. Occasionally a man throws his arm over her shoulders, gives her a friendly squeeze, and her slight smile slightens.

Everyone knows when it's time to go back to work and play. Springs sigh, sheet music shuffles, places are resumed. Laura listens feverishly, her small, pointed chin cupped in one hand, elbow balanced on one knee. She can only stay for two more songs. Her mouth looks unsatisfied as she leaves. "Later, boys."

"In a minute, Laura."

She doesn't walk far. Scared of the dark, even the brilliant darkness of the black folks' wide-grinning night. She hails the first cab she sees, gives a fancy uptown address. The cabbie drives her right to the servants' entrance. She shorts him fifty cents on the fare. "Iffen you wants to wait, I'll get de res' fum Miss Anne," she says. He snorts, but what can he do, drive her back?

She goes upstairs to the empty boudoir next to the master bedroom. The decor is severely pink, scented, and stiffly starched. She sits at a marble-topped vanity, its surface a mirrored intricacy of shiny vials and pots. She opens a large alabaster box, smoothes a transparent cream on her already creamy skin. A man calls through the door without opening it. "Hey, honey, that you?"

"Yes, it's me." She pulls a pink tissue from a shell-covered box.

"You've been at that meeting this entire time?"

She wipes quickly, cleaning half her face. "Yes, I have." She looks long at her reflection. She is half full. She takes another tissue to her face. She is waxing. "We had a lot of work to do. Bazaar's coming up. You know those poor people depend on us organizing it."

"How you women can talk all night about a miserable bunch of niggers is beyond me."

She was always pretty much a mystery to everyone.

✵ ✵ ✵

"Okey-doke, Smoke." The cabbie slipped the worn dollar bill into his shirt pocket. He had his full fare now and a fifty cent tip.

"That ain't my name." The skinny, coal-colored youth turned away from the cab he had followed all the way from Darktown.

"Who said it was?" Backing down the drive, the cabbie kept his eyes on the street end. He missed seeing how the coal-colored youth melted into the shadows. Went around the corner of the house. Walked up the steps. Seeking something that he sometimes got a taste of at jam sessions. A pause, while he did something to the lock without using a key. Then through the door.

Inside, the large kitchen lay mostly dark. Light from a far-off street lamp filtered through white net curtains over a counter on one side. Straight ahead a glow silhouetted a door and leaked out over blue and green linoleum tiles. The skinny youth pushed the door, and it swung open on a passageway with oyster white walls, tastefully carpeted in beige.

The same carpet ran up the staircase. So did he, quietly. The stairs doubled back on themselves and left him on the landing where they ended, facing the front of the house. Two doors. He closed his eyes and followed his nose through the one on his left.

She was in there, seated at the vanity. She swiveled on the pink bench as he entered, giving him the look of a wild thing surprised in its natural habitat but still sure of escape. A silk robe embroidered with rose and coral chrysanthemums clung to the new ivory of her shoulders.

"Laura," he whispered.

"That ain't my name."

He shook his head. Didn't matter what she called herself here, or how much paler her face. Whatever tricks she played, he would know her anywhere. She was it—inspiration. The breath of air that fed the fire. He took a step closer, drawn by her scent, a mixture of fine cologne and fresh, faint sweat.

"My husband's in the next room. I can call him."

"But you won't."

"Be a shame if anybody found you in a white woman's boudoir."

"Who said you was white?"

She swung her legs around and planted them firmly before her, placed one hand between her knees and pressed them tight together. Touched the other to her loose, lustrous hair, silken as the robe she wore. "I did."

He shook his head once more. "I ain't come to cause no trouble."

The bare skin above her breasts rose and fell sharply as she let out a silent, humorless laugh. "Why, then? You followed me home from that jam session, somehow. You broke in—"

"No, I didn't. Didn't have to. Door was left open."

"I locked it."

"Musta been someone else come in after you. Maid."

"Annie would never neglect a thing like that."

"And your husband wouldn't never enter this here room less you asked him in. I know. You tooken care a him good as your servants. Wouldn't never believe he married no colored gal, neither, less you told him so.

"Or would he?"

She rose slowly, her hands swinging naturally at her sides. The right one held a gun now, but not as if she planned on doing anything immediate with it. "Why don't you stop making these threatening remarks and tell me what it is you want?"

"Honey? Are you coming to bed now?"

"I'll be in soon, Chester," she called back, her voice loose and flowing as her hair.

"Who's that I hear talking to you?" The man on the other side of the open door sounded nearer now.

"It's only Annie. She's helping me practice my part for the church play." She used the gun like a traffic cop's baton, waving the youth toward another door opposite the one her husband stood behind. It was shut. He opened it on a tiny bathroom, obeyed her gestures, and went inside.

"I thought you gave her the evening off."

"I guess she didn't have anywhere to go. We're as good as done, so I'll be right in, after I use the necessary." She stepped into the small room and closed the door behind her with a soft click. An overhead light came on as her hand fell from a wall switch.

The gun's muzzle pointed at him, almost, it seemed, of its own will. The opening glittered like an animal's eye. "I asked you before," she said. "What——?"

"What I want?" The stories he had heard agreed on one thing: this was no one to trifle with. He hesitated before the truth surged out of him, a wave desperate to reach an unknown shore: "I want to play."

"Play what?"

All the music, the sweetness, sharpness, rolls and riffs and changes he'd ever heard swept through his mind. All the instruments. Choose one. She was waiting. "Piano."

She looked at the mirror over the white washstand, smiled at a joke shared with her reflection. "And what present did you bring me?" The gun still pointed in his direction.

"It—in my coat pocket—I'll—" He moved to ease open the satin-hemmed slit above his breast, and her eyes were on him again.

"Hands," she said. Reluctantly, he started to raise them. "No!" The gun waved impatiently. "Hold them out here, where I can see them!" Barely a tremor showed as he stretched his forearms level with the floor: his fingers, long and thin, black as twigs burnt bare by autumn, nails ridged and trimmed to neat ovals.

"Turn em over."

His palms, rose creased with brown, oblongs seeming small in contrast to the fingers' spidery length.

"All right. In the tub. Take your shoes off."

He hesitated.

"Take them off first, then get in."

He wore black lace-up Oxfords, ancient but well-polished. He left them on the white tiles, climbed over the tub's curled porcelain lip, slipping awkwardly in his socks.

"Now strip."

He did nothing, as if unsure he'd heard her right.

"Off with your clothes. Unless you brought a spare set."

He shrugged out of his jacket. A good jacket, dark grey with a faint crosshatching of light blue. Folded it carefully, then looked around to see what to do with it. Balanced it on the tub's edge, at one tightly curving end. Loosened his tie and slipped it off from under the collar of his pale grey shirt. Unbuttoned that. Stopped. The thin cotton tee he wore beneath it barely veiled the darkness of his chest. "What—"

"Lie down." She swept the gun's muzzle sideways, describing a horizontal line for him to imitate. "You want to keep your clothes on, that's fine by me. I don't care about them if you don't.

"Me, I like what I'm wearing." As she said this, she unbelted the kimono and let it slide off her shoulders. Beneath, she was naked. She held herself the way she now held the gun: purposefully. The parchment of her skin glowed like a lampshade, color breaking out where the candle's flame came too close to it, burning it pink and red and brown and black. Her fingernails, the taut tips of her breasts, her hair—

"Lie down."

Limbs weak, he did as she said. It was easiest that way. He curled up on his right side, the drain gaping at the upper edge of his peripheral vision. He heard a cool, ceramic whisper as she stepped into the tub and slid down beside him. Facing him, lying on her left, looking directly into his eyes. It was a tight fit.

He regretted every stitch he wore.

Laughing, she lifted the gun above both their heads, rotating it as if displaying a rare device for his edification. Nickel glinted in the fixture's light. It seemed to be a perfectly ordinary gun.

"Where do you want me to put them?" she asked.

At first he could only gape at her, head empty as the tub's drain. "You gonna put— Put what?"

"The bullets. The magic." She frowned as if trying to remember the answer to a tough question. "You want me to shoot you, right?"

"No! No! I ain't said nothin like that—" Sweat slicked his skin, robbing him of traction as he scrabbled at the tub's sides, trying to get out. He opened his mouth wide, wider, sucking in air for a scream. She filled it with the gun's muzzle.

"You want to sing? All right." The knuckles stood out sharply on her gun hand. The frown deepened, cutting two deep verticals in her low forehead.

"Wait—"

The world did as she commanded.

"My present. I haven't even seen it, yet; maybe it's not enough. Not worth what you want. A hero's death. A musician's life. Let me have a look first."

He lay motionless.

"Go on, get it out for me." She pulled the gun's barrel from his mouth and swung it in a short arc, indicating the youth's jacket resting on the bathtub's rim. Then aimed it back at him.

Cold with drying perspiration, the youth raised one arm and dragged the coat down on top of him. From its inner pocket he removed a posy of pink and yellow rosebuds, their stems arranged in a crystal vial capped with a gold screen. The flowers were in not-quite-pristine condition, a few barely-opened petals crushed and darkened.

"Oh," she said. "Well, it *is* the thought that counts... under these circumstances... And at least you brought something...." She took the posy with her left hand, inhaling deeply.

"You—you mean you ain't gonna shoot me?" He levered himself up on one elbow, shivering slightly.

"Shhh! Hold still now. I don't know if I should. Let me think. Lie back down." Through all this she'd kept the gun trained on him, unwavering.

He lowered himself to the tub's floor.

"I like you," she said, smiling. "Even if you did lie to me about the door being open—"

"Might as wella been—"

"All right. Tell you what." She cocked the pistol's hammer, pointed it at the ceiling. The light. "Best I can do—"

An explosion. Brightness. Blackness.

Combustion combines opposites: Earth and air. Chemi-
cal secrets release the energies held inside dull matter.

Some fires are fast. Some slow as rust. Consumption.
Greed. Fever. Lust.

As if he can look through himself. As if the flame has
licked away what no longer matters. Left only that loud
sound, blowing through him. Lines of incandescence
leading to and from his heart.

He's still in the tub. With her. She still holds the gun.
A whiff of powder, the curled question mark of smoke
static in the air above them. And how can he tell that? In
the dark?

The radiant dark. Emptiness shining. The shot's echoes
dying down, the light fixture's glass tinkling into silence.
Then the sound of the door opening. The darkness van-
ishes and everything he imagined seeing in it: Smoking
gun. Naked woman. Tub. Walls, ceiling—he's in another
place. A bed, in another room, illuminated from outside
by whatever lies beyond. Only the door remains, and the
shadow standing just inside it. A woman's silhouette.

"Laura?"

"That ain't my name. You feelin any better, Chester?"

"Yeah. What happened—" He tries to raise his head.
Like hoisting a steamroller on pulleys made from putty.
Gives it up.

"Guess you must not be all the way recovered yet, you
don't remember what your wife called."

"My—what?" The woman walks toward him and
switches on a lamp sitting on a table beside the bed—his

bed? His *wife?* The lamp's bulb seems too dim, but it glares in his eyes anyway, obscuring her face.

The mattress tilts, slopping his stomach to one side. She's sitting on its edge. Now he can see. Her face is— not exactly, no, but a lot like Laura's. Same skin tone as when she showed up at jam sessions, same general shape. So what's different? He can't put his finger on it—brows thicker? Hairline higher? Faint imprints around the mouth and eyes…

"At least you talkin English again." The woman presses her lips together. Are they fuller? Thinner? "You shammin? Can't a forgot. I'm your Annie, and—" with the firmness of a doe licking a newborn fawn into shape "—we married in the eyes of God and the law. Five years now."

Five years. He would have been, what, twelve years old? Eleven? Frantically he tries to get up, get out of bed. He has to find a mirror. Hoarse, hacking coughs convulse him, and the woman—Annie—shoves pillows under his back, props him up, holds him like a baby against her rose and coral housecoat. At last he quiets down a bit and she offers him a drink—water, he assumes, and swallows a mouthful of vodka. That sets him off again, though not so bad as before. This time, Annie only watches.

And when she most likely thinks he isn't looking, slips something from her pocket, something small and shiny, with a nickel glint to it, and slides it inside the drawer of the table by their bed.

He gets his voice back. "How long—"

"You been out two days, Chester. I was all set to take you in the hospital." She strokes one pajama-clad shoulder in a gesture meant to soothe him. Which is when he realizes his shirt and pants are gone, and the things he'd carried in their pockets. Wallet, keys, money. Gone. Where?

His wife will know. With an effort he refocuses on what she's trying to tell him.

"—ain't missed one *gig*, that's what you so concerned about. Rehearsals, sure, but you gonna be fine for that agent tomorrow afternoon. He ain't interested in no one else in the band, anyway, even *I* figured out *that* much."

The agent from New York. Tomorrow afternoon. How can he have forgotten? He knocks the covers off clumsily, attempts to swing his feet to the carpet. The sheets cling to his nightclothes, charged with electricity from rubbing up against them in the dry air of a Chicago winter. "Help me, Annie."

"Chester, you can't get up now! You a sick man!"

The wallpaper wobbles, its printed flowers waving in an invisible breeze. "I need to practice. Help me. Gotta get me to the piano. Then I be all right."

Slowly, leaning on Annie's arm, he makes his way to the living room, where the slick, black, baby grand waits. It had cost a lot of money, and it takes up too much space in their little mortgaged-to-the-hilt South Side bungalow.

In its polished surface he sees himself. Hair dark, chin like a chisel. He is young yet. Yes. Still young, only twenty-five. Why has he been worried?

Sick, that's why. Annie uncovers the keys and he lets his hands fall where they want to be. A song based on a nursery rhyme. The music rises up, baking the ache from his bones. "Lavender Blue." A Latin beat, a rumba, banishing the chill pouring in off the big front window, and his fingers sparkle; they're laughing, they're living sunbeams, and all the colors of the spectrum break through him like he was a prism, all the music, the sweetness, sharpness, rolls and riffs and changes, coming out of him. He is the king.

Filter House

She leans on the piano's shining lid, relaxing slowly, melting like wax against her own reflection, arms stretching out softly, head resting on one side, ear to the sounding board, eyes closed, absorbing it. Now she is queen.

When the song is over, he looks up at her, at the way her lashes flutter open on black depths too profound ever to be filled, and allows, himself, for the last time, to remember the way things were before. And just for that final moment, to wonder why she has struck such an uneven bargain with him.

She was always pretty much a mystery to everyone.

The Beads of Ku

There was a woman named Dosi, and she gave birth to twins. At first both were weak and sickly, but the boy died, and then the girl prospered and grew strong. She was a good girl, willing to work hard, and with good sense.

When she was still very young, Fulla Fulla helped her mother in the market, running messages for her and bringing her the news. "Mother," she would say, "the women of Dit-ao-lane are over by the baobab, looking for cloth to make beautiful robes. Quick, give me that basket of feathers, that I may tempt them with bright colors." And Fulla Fulla would run to the river and sell all the feathers very dear. Or she would return from an errand leading a row of porters bearing salt. "Mother," she would say, "I have traded all our leather for this salt, and I got it very cheap. The merchant did not want to take it on with him and pay another duty. He did not know that in two days the taxes will be lowered because the King himself will be trading his salt for a new shipment of gold from the South...." And this was when Fulla Fulla was just a little girl.

Filter House

As the woman Dosi grew older, she began more and more to stay at home and to leave all the business to Fulla Fulla. At last she became ill, and though Fulla Fulla nursed her mother diligently, she died. Fulla Fulla grieved for her mother, but she did not let grief make her weak or stupid. Those who tried to take advantage of her state soon found that this was so. It was harder than ever to read her face beneath the grey ashes of mourning. And though her eyes were red and filled with tears, they missed nothing. So Fulla Fulla kept her place in the market and did well.

One day as she walked in the market she passed by the stall of a hunter selling cooked meat. "If I buy all your meat," she asked him, "will you give it to me for such-and-such a price?" The price she named was very low.

The hunter was a simple man, not a trader, and he sold the meat to her at the price that she had named. Then she took all that she had bought to the other side of the market and sold it for many times the price she had paid.

The next market day the hunter was there again, and she did the same thing. But the time after that he was not there. When he came again she asked him why he had not come to the last market. He said, "I hate to come to the city, where there are so many people, and noises, and ugly smells. I knew it was the market day, but I could not bear to leave the savannah. Besides, I was sure that you would buy all my meat, whenever I brought it." And he shrugged his big strong shoulders.

This gave Fulla Fulla an idea. "Come to my house," she said, "and I will fix you a fine meal from your own meat." The hunter was happy to hear this. He had lost his first wife many years ago, and he had not had a really fine meal since. He ate up everything Fulla Fulla cooked. When they were alone, he made her his wife.

For a while, the hunter and Fulla Fulla were very happy together. He stayed out on the savannah, hunting as long as he liked. When he wanted to, he came into the city and had a fine meal. He brought her all his meat, and she sold it in the market for a good price, and they prospered and grew very rich. But one market day, the hunter came to the city and Fulla Fulla was not there. He sent messengers all through the market. None found her. Angry and worried, the hunter stayed in the house. He did not know what to do. He felt helpless, and also he did not like to spend so much time cramped up in town. But just as he was getting ready to give up, his wife walked in the door. "Where have you been?" he started to ask her. Then he noticed that she was wearing at her ears a certain kind of bead, called "the Beads of Ku." Then he knew that she had been to the Marketplace of Death.

When she heard that she had missed the market day, Fulla Fulla was upset. "Time has cheated me!" she said. "I spent only a little while there, but you say I have been gone for days. This must not be so." She frowned in heavy thought. "I will ask my mother what to do."

At these words the hunter's stomach grew cold with fear, and he tried to dissuade his wife from going again to Ku.

But Fulla Fulla looked at him fondly. "You are a fine, great, man," she said. "But you have no understanding of business at all. Of course I will go there again." And she set about planning her next trip.

The hunter returned to the savannah. He killed an antelope and two duikers. He saw many beautiful and restful sights, but he was ill at ease.

When he returned to the house he found Fulla Fulla there. Again she had missed a market day, but this time she did not seem so concerned. "It's easy what we must do," she said. She handed him a little whistle. "You must always return to town a day before market and blow upon this whistle. Then I will be called back." Good.

So the hunter did as Fulla Fulla told him to do, and they were happy. But not so happy as before. Now he could not spend as much time hunting as he wished. He had to come back to the city every three days, to blow the whistle and call his wife from the Market of Death.

Also, it seemed as if his wife was becoming a little strange. She had strange ideas, and she knew things one should not know, from talking to dead people. Whenever there was no one else around to see, she wore the Beads of Ku.

She boasted to her husband of her dealings with the dead. "Those of Ku want very simple things," she said. "For yams and cassava, they will trade ornaments of ivory! If I were a camel, I could carry enough goods to make us richer than the King himself."

"Why would a camel want to be rich?" he asked. Fulla Fulla laughed.

She spoke much of her mother and her doings, and of her twin brother, Kinsu. The hunter felt she spoke too much of these dead people. "I am her husband," he said to himself. "Her thoughts should be of me." When he spoke like this to himself, he remembered his first wife, Agbanli.

Agbanli had thought only of him and how to make him happy. She had never laughed at him or known strange things one should not know. She had never gone to Ku until properly dead.

Thinking like this made the hunter think more. He wondered what it was like in Ku and if Agbanli was happy there, or if she missed him. He wondered how Fulla

Fulla went there and came back again. He wondered if he would be able to go and return, and if he might see Agbanli there and comfort her.

One day the hunter told Fulla Fulla that he was going out on the savannah. But he went only to the edge of the city and waited until it was dark. Then he went back to his house and hid himself nearby. Toward morning, his wife emerged from the house. The hunter followed her. She walked out of the city to the west. She walked for a long way, till she came to a cave in a hillside. A river flowed out of the cave and down the hill. Without stopping a moment, Fulla Fulla threw herself into the river. You would think that she would drown, but instead she was carried away quickly by the water. In an instant she was gone from his sight.

The hunter stood on the bank. He tossed a stick into the water. The water carried it away, but in the way a river normally carries away a stick. It did not just disappear, like Fulla Fulla.

"Something is very strange here," said the hunter. "But I already knew that." And he flung himself into the river, after his wife.

It seemed as though no time at all passed before he found himself in Ku. The river, which before had been like a strong wind blowing him on, became suddenly wet. He pulled himself from the water and up onto the bank. Fulla Fulla had already left for the Market, and he was surrounded by dead people he did not know. They looked sad and tired. He asked for Agbanli, his first wife, but when they saw he had no Beads, they would not speak to him. They only glanced at him and walked away.

He found his way to the Marketplace of Death. Wonderful goods were displayed there: lengths of cloth spun from gold, ivory carved into chairs and canopies, and many other marvelous things. But everyone was crowded at one end of the Market, trying to buy the goods at one little stall. "That must be Fulla Fulla's stall," thought the hunter. He was curious to see what she had brought, so he went closer.

Just then, the King of Ku came into the Marketplace. The hunter knew this was the King from the magnificence of his progress. Two giants went before him, beating on copper drums. Two dwarves came after them and swept the dust from the King's path. The King walked in splendid robes covered in strange jewels that shone with their own light. Everyone bowed respectfully to the ground and made a path for him. The hunter watched fearfully as the King of Death began trading with his wife. He hoped he would not be noticed.

The King offered a string of rubies for a package of Arabian raisins. Fulla Fulla was not satisfied. She wanted more. The King offered her a delicate chain carved from a single piece of ebony, but he demanded that she include a jar of honey and three figs. The hunter began to sweat. Fulla Fulla asked the King if he had any diamonds. She was agreeable as to the honey, but she positively had to have a large diamond for each and every fig. The King looked offended. He turned away as if to leave. The hunter could stand no more.

"Stop!" he shouted. "Fulla Fulla, what are you thinking of? He is the *King of Death! Sell* him all your goods, take whatever he will give, and *leave!*"

Fulla Fulla looked at him and screamed. "You, here? Oh, fool, you have ruined us. Truly, you have no understanding of business at all."

The King, too, was very angry. "Fulla Fulla," he said, "you have broken our agreement. You were forbidden to bring anyone, or even to speak of our transactions. Yet here is this living man, here where no man living should be. He calls you by name. You call him a fool. Can you deny that he is here because of you?"

The King of Ku was really most upset. He could keep Fulla Fulla here with him, and her raisins, and the honey and figs now, as well. But these would be the last.

Fulla Fulla was looking at her husband, and her heart softened as her eyes took in his beauty. She thought fondly of the many warm nights that they had spent together and how well he had provided her with meat. Also she thought how fearless he was and how much he must love her to come after her to Ku. She did not know about Agbanli. She only knew that though he was a fool, he was a brave one, and for that she loved him. But she did not let love make her weak or stupid. She thought quickly and made up her mind how to deal with the King of Death.

"Yes, King, what you say is all too true," admitted Fulla Fulla. "He is my husband, and an excellent provider of meat. He would have been most happy to hunt for you, and to bring you fresh antelope, and smoked duiker. But now you must keep us here and punish us both, and so you will get nothing."

"It is not for *you* to decide these things," flared the King. "*I* am the one who decrees how justice will best be served. I will retire and consider what must be done." And he withdrew to the far side of the Market, to think of fat pumpkins and savory stews.

Fulla Fulla knew what was in his mind. She took aside the hunter and spoke with him alone. "The King will give you two Beads," she said. "Accept them, and thank him.

But you must never use them. As he sends you back, let the Beads fall from your hands. You must never come here again in your life. I am afraid that if *you* tried to trade with the King of Ku, you would die long before your time."

Then the King beckoned to them, and they came before him. "This is how it will be," said the King. "Fulla Fulla must stay here. She gave her word, and her word was no good. But you, hunter, may come and go as she has done. Whenever you come you must be sure to bring me your own weight in meat, and any other good things I ask you to get for me." He smiled and held out his open hand. "Take these. They will allow you to return to the living when you wish. They are proof that I am no longer angry with you."

As the hunter took the Beads, he felt as if many things were just beginning to come clear to him. The faces of all the dead people became familiar. He thought he saw Agbanli in the crowd, though she looked different than he remembered. She looked as though she were about to speak. But the King made a sign with his hand, and then the hunter flung the Beads away, as he had been told to do.

Suddenly, he found himself at home. The sun was rising. It was morning, the same morning on which he had left.

At first he thought he had fallen asleep and dreamt his visit to Ku. He wandered through the house looking for Fulla Fulla. He wanted to tell her about his strange dream. But she was not there. And she never came back again, though he blew and blew upon the little whistle.

Volume 8 of the Conversation Pieces

Writing the Other

Bridging Cultural Differences for Successful Fiction

by Nisi Shawl and Cynthia Ward

During the 1992 Clarion West Writers Workshop attended by Nisi Shawl and Cynthia Ward, one of the students expressed the opinion that it is a mistake to write about people of ethnic backgrounds different from your own because you might get it wrong, horribly, offensively wrong, and so it is better not even to try. This opinion, commonplace among published as well as aspiring writers, struck Nisi as taking the easy way out and spurred her to write an essay addressing the problem of how to write about characters marked by racial and ethnic differences. In the course of writing the essay, however, she realized that similar problems arise when writers try to create characters whose gender, sexual preference, and age differ significantly from their own. Nisi and Cynthia collaborated to develop a workshop that addresses these problems with the aim of both increasing writers' skill and sensitivity in portraying difference in their fiction as well as allaying their anxieties about "getting it wrong." *Writing the Other: A Practical Approach* is the manual that grew out of their workshop. It discusses basic aspects of characterization and offers elementary techniques, practical exercises, and examples for helping writers create richer and more accurate characters with "differences."

For info about the Writing the Other workshop:
www.writingtheother.com

Aqueduct Press Conversation Pieces available at
www.aqueductpress.com

Praise for *Writing the Other*

The book is passionate, insightful, systematic and clear, and it is a good tool for writers and sociologists....

I highly recommend it. It should be read by every "dominant paradigm" writer for that is its true audience. Recommended also for schools, colleges, and creativity workshops, and sociology classes.

—Carole McDonnell, *The Compulsive Reader*,
http://www.compulsivereader.com

This portable volume tackles a tough, politically sensitive question: How to write, and write well, about people who bear no resemblance to yourself?

...Just raising awareness about this writing challenge is a literary service; many a writer (journalists included) fears a misstep when depicting someone outside their own orbit.

—*Seattle Times*, Feb 3, 2006

Author Biography

Nisi Shawl's stories of speculative fiction, which have appeared in *The Year's Best Fantasy and Horror* (edited by Ellen Datlow, Kelly Link, and Gavin Grant), *Asimov's SF Magazine*, and the *Dark Matter* anthologies, have been nominated for the Theodore Sturgeon, Gaylactic Spectrum, and Parallax awards. Her reviews and essays have appeared regularly in the *Seattle Times* since the turn of the millennium. She is the co-editor of *Strange Matings: Octavia Butler, Science Fiction and Feminism* (forthcoming from Wesleyan University Press) and the co-author of *Writing the Other*, a guide to developing characters of varying racial, ethnic, and sexual backgrounds.

She serves on the boards of the Clarion West Writers Workshop and the Carl Brandon Society and lives in Seattle.